Harbor of
the Heart

The Angel Island Titles

THE INN AT ANGEL ISLAND

THE WEDDING PROMISE

A WANDERING HEART

THE WAY HOME

HARBOR OF THE HEART

The Cape Light Titles

CAPE LIGHT

HOME SONG

A GATHERING PLACE

A NEW LEAF

A CHRISTMAS PROMISE

THE CHRISTMAS ANGEL

A CHRISTMAS TO REMEMBER

A CHRISTMAS VISITOR

A CHRISTMAS STAR

A WISH FOR CHRISTMAS

ON CHRISTMAS EVE

CHRISTMAS TREASURES

A SEASON OF ANGELS

SONGS OF CHRISTMAS

ALL IS BRIGHT

Thomas Kinkade's Angel Island

Harbor of
the Heart

KATHERINE SPENCER

BERKLEY BOOKS, NEW YORK

THE BERKLEY PUBLISHING GROUP
Published by the Penguin Group
Penguin Group (USA) LLC
375 Hudson Street, New York, New York 10014

USA • Canada • UK • Ireland • Australia • New Zealand • India • South Africa • China

penguin.com

A Penguin Random House Company

Berkley trade paperback ISBN: 978-0-425-26429-4

The Library of Congress has catalogued the Berkley Books hardcover edition of this title as follows:

Spencer, Katherine, (date –)
Thomas Kinkade's Angel Island : harbor of the heart / Katherine Spencer.—First edition.
pages cm
ISBN 978-0-425-26428-7 (hardback)
1. Physicians—Fiction. 2. Man-woman relationships—Fiction. I. Title.
II. Title: Angel Island. III. Title: Harbor of the heart.
PS3553.A489115T57 2014
813'.54—dc23

PUBLISHING HISTORY
Berkley hardcover edition / April 2014
Berkley trade paperback edition / April 2015

PRINTED IN THE UNITED STATES OF AMERICA

10 9 8 7 6 5 4 3 2 1

Cover image: *Morro Bay at Sunset* by Thomas Kinkade; copyright © 2005 Thomas Kinkade.
Cover design by Lesley Worrell.
Interior text design by Kristin del Rosario.

This book is dedicated to Abby, our beautiful chocolate Lab mix who was the inspiration for Edison, the canine character in this story. Just like Edison, Abby spent her life as the dedicated assistant to a somewhat harried, distracted inventor . . . me. If I was in my office, Abby was there, too, no matter how late the hour. Her silent, steadfast presence was a constant source of reassurance and encouragement. We wrote more than thirty books together, and this was the last one we worked on. She stuck with it until the story was done. I will miss our talks and her good advice, the way she shadowed my steps and brightened the day with her smile. (Yes, dogs can smile. Never doubt it.) But the most amazing thing about Abby was that she made each member of our family feel that they were her "favorite." We will always be grateful for loving and being loved by such an extraordinary dog.

—K. S.

Chapter One

"THAT's the last of the laundry. We can make the rooms up later. Or even tomorrow. There aren't any guests due until Friday." Liza set a basket of clean towels on a chair, then sat at the kitchen table to check her laptop.

"Oh, you never know," Claire said. "If the rooms are ready, an unexpected guest or two might arrive to fill them." She stood at the sink, cleaning up the breakfast dishes, and glanced at Liza over her shoulder.

As usual, Liza couldn't quite tell if her dear friend and right hand was serious or gently teasing. As usual, it seemed a mixture of both.

It was a Tuesday morning at the very end of June. The last of their weekend guests had just departed, and the inn was quiet again. It was always like this at the start of the summer, an ebb and flow of visitors and activity, with most of the action crowded into long weekends. Until the Fourth of July, when every room was filled. It would stay that way until the end of August. Labor Day weekend marked the last of the big rushes that swept in and out like the ocean tide. The inn grew quiet in September and quieter still in the cold, snowy months, though Liza and Claire entertained hardy winter weekenders and families gathering for the holidays. At least, this was the way the years had played out since Liza had inherited the Inn at Angel Island three years ago. It was hard to believe this was the third summer she would be running the inn. Time had passed so quickly, and every season brought surprises, and challenges, too.

"If you make the beds, guests will come—interesting theory." Liza looked up and smiled. "I never noticed that tip in my innkeeper's survival guide. I'm just happy to have a day off. I might take a walk on the beach or drive up to Newburyport. And I have a ton of e-mail to answer," she added, staring at the full inbox on her screen.

"I vote for the beach," Claire replied quickly. "You rarely set foot on the shore. And living only steps away from it, you should make time for a walk on the beach every day. Starting this morning," Claire advised decisively.

Liza doubted she would have time for a walk every day once the inn grew busier, though it was a lovely goal. "Good idea. But I'll feel better doing a little work first and saving the beach for my reward."

"I think you ought to go down now. The air feels heavy to me. There's rain on the way." Claire nodded to herself as she dried a heavy skillet with a dish towel.

Liza hadn't heard any official predictions for wet weather, but Claire's forecasts were practically infallible. If Claire said the air "felt heavy," Liza had no doubt a drop or two would fall before the day was over.

"Okay, you've convinced me." Liza shut down the computer and grabbed a sweatshirt off the chair. Even if it didn't rain, it was a chilly, breezy morning, and the beach would be even cooler. "I won't be long. If Daniel comes, tell him to check the bottom step on the side porch. A board is loose. And I finished that list of repairs he wanted. Please tell him not to leave until I get back?"

"I doubt he'd do that," Claire said with a knowing smile. "But I will get him started on the step."

Liza waved briefly and left the inn through the back door. She knew this information would be relayed without fail, but not until Daniel had been served coffee and some home-baked treat. Claire had made banana nut muffins that morning for the guests and had doubtless saved a few for her favorite handyman.

Daniel was the inn's go-to Mr. Fix-It for just about any ill or crisis that struck the old building. Though even from the first, he had been so much more. Liza often joked that she inherited him along with the property, since he had worked for her aunt as well. They met the morning after she arrived from Boston, armed with a plan to clean up the inn and turn a quick sale. Daniel helped her see the potential in the magnificent old building . . . and the possibilities of life on this remote but beautiful island. Liza had not stayed on Angel Island because of Daniel but, looking back, she knew their attraction and budding romance had definitely swayed her.

As they grew closer and the first spark grew into a true and steady love, Liza realized there were really no words to describe her feelings for him. Their relationship was an unexpected gift and a glorious blessing—a precious part of life she had never expected to find and now couldn't imagine living without.

Claire had known Daniel even longer; they were good friends. He dropped by nearly every day, whether there were repairs to attend to or not. His visits were a cheerful break in Liza's routine, especially in the thick of tourist season, and often the only time the couple could spend together for days at a stretch.

Liza walked down the gravel drive then strolled across the wide lawn in front of the inn, heading toward the wide, open view of the ocean. The salty sea breeze was bracing, but she found the air heavy, as Claire had said.

She crossed the road in front of the inn, heading for the steps that led down to the beach. She stood at the top a moment, taking in the spectacular view of the wide sky and ocean. The water was a deep blue-green color that also foretold a storm brewing. A stiff breeze rushed banks of clouds across the horizon and stirred up whitecaps on the waves.

She came down the long flight of wooden steps, feeling the wind push against her body. It was hardly ideal weather for a walk, and she wondered if she should turn back and take up Plan B: answer e-mail and drive to Newburyport. But the last few steps were in sight. She soon reached the bottom and kicked off her shoes to walk the shoreline barefoot.

The sweatshirt had been a good idea. Liza pulled it on and zipped it up to her chin as she began walking. This outing would not last very long, she quickly realized. But it felt good to get some air and feel the wind whip through her long hair.

The sea was so changeable; it had so many moods and personalities. Sometimes it was smooth as glass, with waves that rolled in as gently as a mother rocking a baby's cradle. Other days, like today, the waves were fierce and wild, crashing to the shore like miniature explosions, foam and spray flying in all directions.

Liza followed the lacy edge of white foam on the shoreline, feeling a cold sting on her bare skin. She loved the sound of the ocean's hollow roar and the feeling of the tide sucking the sand beneath her feet.

The shoreline stretched ahead; the gentle curve that ended at a rocky jetty was completely empty this morning. Not even a loyal jogger or surf caster in sight. The ocean was empty, too, except for a bold white sailboat.

A sleek boat, white with blue trim. Liza guessed it was over thirty feet long. Still, the water was so rough, it bounced out on the waves. Did the mainsail come down . . . or had it fallen down? It was hanging slack, the lines tangled, and she guessed the sailor had hastily decided to motor in to shore. That would be the wise choice. Even in the few minutes since she had come down the steps, the sky had grown darker, clouds massing low and gray over the water. Thick, slate-colored clouds now covered the sun, and the air grew much cooler.

Liza marched on, hands dug into her sweatshirt pockets. She rarely had a chance to spend any time on the beach and was determined to stick it out. It didn't have to be a perfectly clear sunny day for a person to have a good walk along the shore . . . even if most of her guests thought it did.

As if responding to her thoughts, a rumble of thunder sounded in the distance. A fat, cold drop of rain struck her cheek. Then another.

Liza stopped in her tracks and laughed. "Okay, I get the point," she said out loud to the ocean. "I give up . . . I'm going back."

Maybe I'll come back later, around sunset. It should clear off by then. Maybe Daniel will come with me, Liza consoled herself as she turned back toward the inn.

She brushed some damp strands of hair away from her face and looked out at the horizon, wondering if she would see lightning. The wind had picked up more; the ocean was rocking, dark and angry.

She watched waves peak to breathless heights, then curl and crash, like walls of water crumbling before her eyes. Liza was mesmerized by the sight. She suddenly noticed the white boat again. Her heartbeat quickened. The vessel had made little progress toward the shore. It seemed stuck out in the choppy, wild water, and now it seemed the mainmast had cracked, hanging like a broken toothpick, canvas and lines crumpled on the deck.

With her hands cupped around her eyes, Liza could just make out the figure of a man clinging to one side of the deck as the boat was tossed up and down, and tilted dangerously to one side and then the other, as if it had lost all direction and balance. Perhaps the motor had failed or the rudder had broken off?

The man was in big trouble, no question. Liza ran down the beach and waved. She wanted him to know someone had spotted the boat and would get help. But she didn't know what to do . . .

There was a skiff at the bottom of the wooden steps, but even if she could move it into the water on her own, she could never row out through the waves and rescue him. She pulled out her phone and dialed the inn. Claire answered on the second ring, and Liza took a deep breath.

"There's a boat on the water that's in terrible trouble. A sailboat. I can see a man on board. I think it might capsize any second—"

"Good heavens. Keep your eye on him," Claire said quickly. "I'll get Daniel. We'll be right there."

Claire hung up and Liza stashed the phone in her pocket. It was raining steadily now, and the drops got in her eyes as she stared out at the sea. She pulled up her hood without taking her eyes off the white boat.

Sucked into the curl of a huge wave, the boat was suddenly hidden from view. Liza held her breath, trying desperately to spot it again as the wave rose and fell. She squinted, looking for the man's orange life jacket and praying he hadn't been washed overboard.

Please God . . . where did it go? He hasn't sunk completely, has he?

Then she saw it, a flash of orange balanced on another rising peak and then tossed down again, like a toy in a bathtub.

That poor man. He was still close to the boat, she realized. He must have been clinging on for dear life. Or maybe he had tied himself to the boat, as some sailors did in rough weather, though that practice could be just as dangerous as falling overboard.

It seemed an eternity as she waited for help. Finally, she heard footsteps running down the stairs. Daniel came first, racing toward her across the wet sand. He wore a yellow slicker and carried binoculars.

"Where is he? Can you still see him?"

Liza pointed, shouting into the wind. "He's still afloat. Or at least the boat is. About eleven o'clock from where I'm standing. I saw him in the water a little while ago, but I think he may have pulled himself back on board. He's wearing an orange life jacket."

Daniel was already checking the waves through the binoculars. "I see it. I see the man and . . . someone else. Or maybe that's just another life jacket? No . . . there's someone with him—a child, maybe?"

"A child? Oh no, that's awful!" Liza's heart sank. A child out in that boat? She sent up a desperate plea for God's help.

"Help me get the skiff in the water," Daniel shouted. "Claire called the Coast Guard, but they won't get here in time."

Liza ran to the boat rack right behind Daniel. He already had the skiff off the rack and was dragging it toward the shore. Claire came down the steps and met them. She helped Liza pick up the far end of the boat, and they stumbled over the sand to the shore and then into the water, until they were almost hip deep.

"Hold the boat steady while I get in." Daniel had already tugged on an orange life jacket and grabbed one of the oars. He handed Liza the binoculars before jumping in.

Claire and Liza held on to the back of the light boat while the surf swirled around them, trying to claim the vessel before Daniel could settle himself.

"Give him a good push," Claire shouted as Daniel started rowing. The women turned the boat toward the waves and bore down, pushing him forward. Daniel rowed with swift, strong strokes, miraculously cutting through the water. The skiff rose up and over the crashing surf and headed out to the flailing sailboat, straight as an arrow sent toward its mark.

Liza gripped Claire's arm as they made their way out of the rushing waters and onto the sand again. She suddenly needed both the physical and emotional support.

"Don't worry. Daniel knows what he's doing. He'll be okay," Claire said quietly, as if in answer to Liza's unspoken worries.

Liza had felt relieved at the sight of Daniel rushing to the rescue of the sailor, but now feared for his safety, too. How many stories had she heard about people who tried to help drowning victims, only to be pulled under and lost as well?

Don't think about that now, Liza told herself. *We have to help that man . . . and the child.* There was no question about it.

"Look, Daniel has almost reached the boat." Claire's soft voice drew her attention, and Liza looked out at the sea again. She held her hand over her eyes, blocking the raindrops.

"Yes . . . he's nearly there. I hope the sailor can see him. He might be lying flat on the deck. Or he might be washed overboard by now," Liza added in an even smaller voice.

Liza looked out at the boat again, just in time to see a horrifying sight. A huge wave curled above the sailboat and the skiff, building and building until it couldn't grow any higher. The massive curve of water hovered for a moment, pulling both boats up in its smooth glassy shell . . . before toppling forward in a foamy flood.

Liza gasped and grabbed Claire's hand. "They're getting swamped! They're both going to drown!"

Claire closed her eyes. "Dear God in heaven, please protect Daniel and everyone in that sailboat. Please let them return to shore safe and sound . . ."

Liza had her eyes closed, too, and silently echoed Claire's humble, desperate plea. She couldn't look at the water again, afraid of what she would see. But Claire's clear voice broke through her dark visions.

"Liza, look! Daniel's okay! He rowed right through it. The sailboat turned over, and the man was tossed in the water . . . and Daniel's spotted him! He's got him on that hook thing they use to pull people in . . . I think they're going to be okay."

Liza grabbed for the binoculars that were tucked into her sweatshirt. She stared through them and tried to focus.

"What about the child . . . or whoever else was aboard? Daniel said he saw another figure, another life jacket . . ."

Raindrops clouded the lenses, but she could still see Daniel, kneeling now in the skiff, balanced precariously as he pulled in a long pole, hand over hand. All she could see on the other end was a body in a bright orange life jacket. Not too far from the skiff, a smaller form, also in an orange jacket, bobbed about. The sailor's arms were flailing, and it seemed he was trying to grab at the other, smaller body before he would get into Daniel's boat.

"What's that next to the skiff? Is it a child?" Claire asked with a gasp.

"I can't tell . . . It's definitely something . . . Oh, it's a dog! A big brown dog . . . wearing a life jacket."

The sailor had a hold on the other orange life jacket now, and Liza could make out the head and shoulders of the man and the sleek wet head and muzzle of a dog beside him.

"It looks like the man won't get in the boat without his dog," Liza said.

"Let me see . . ." Claire turned, and Liza handed her the binoculars. "Yes, it's a very big dog. The sailor's holding on to the edge of the skiff, and Daniel is pulling the dog in first."

Liza winced. "I hope there's room for all of them."

"I hope so, too. From the looks of it, I don't think that man will get in if he has to leave his friend behind."

"Daniel would never leave the dog," Liza said firmly. "He would put the dog in the boat and swim to shore himself, if that were the case."

Claire handed back the binoculars. "Yes, he would. But thankfully, that won't be necessary. He's got them both on board. The man looks exhausted. That's a lot of weight for Daniel to be rowing."

Liza stared through the binoculars again. The skiff was coming back toward the shore. A huge wave of relief washed over her heart—bigger than any ocean wave. The boat moved slower than it had when it headed out, weighed down now with two more on board.

"I hope he can make it back." Liza considered rushing into the water to try to help the boat somehow. But that was ridiculous. There was nothing she could do. She felt so frustrated and powerless, watching him.

Claire touched her arm. "Daniel will be all right. God is out there rowing with him."

Finally, the boat broke through the last line of waves and floated into the shallows. Liza splashed through the water and grabbed a line that dangled at the bow. She held on tight while Daniel jumped out. Together with Claire, they tugged and pushed the skiff loaded with its rescued passengers the rest of the way to solid ground.

"Daniel . . . I was so worried. I could hardly stand to watch." Liza stared into Daniel's eyes a moment, then quickly hugged him. His face and hair were dripping wet, raindrops trickling down his cheeks and strong jaw.

"I'm all right, sweetheart. Don't worry." He met her gaze for a moment with a look that connected them on the deepest level. "Help me get this man out. He's barely breathing."

Claire and Liza took the sailor's feet, and Daniel took his shoulders. Luckily, he was not a big man and seemed fit.

Still, it was difficult to carry him even a short distance.

"In the cave. He needs some cover." Led by Daniel, they carried the man up the beach and into the opening of one of the many caves at the base of the sandy cliff. They gently laid him down on the ground, and Daniel quickly knelt down and began working on him.

There was some light at the opening of the cave, but not much. Claire reached into her pocket and took out a small flashlight. She turned it on and pointed the beam of yellow light down at the sailor. "I grabbed this at the last minute. It's not much light, but it should help," she said quietly.

"It does help; keep it steady," Daniel replied as he quickly slipped off the sailor's life jacket and checked his pulse and eyes.

"He's not breathing. I need to give him mouth-to-mouth."

Liza knelt on the man's other side, waiting for Daniel's instruction. She had seen the dog jump out of the boat and suddenly realized the loyal pet had followed them. It stood right above its master and gently prodded the man's cheek with its nose.

"Here, boy." Claire grabbed the dog's collar and tugged him back. "You stay with me. Your master is in good hands. No one is going to hurt him."

The dog seemed to understand and allowed Claire to hold his collar. She gently petted his head, still holding the light steady with her other hand. A moment later, the dog lay down and sighed, his gaze fixed on their patient.

Daniel turned the man to his side and held his mouth open. Water poured out. "He swallowed half the ocean."

Daniel quickly cleared the man's mouth with his index finger. Then he set him on his back again, positioned his head, and breathed into his mouth . . . one, two, three breaths.

Liza watched, holding her own breath. Finally she saw the stranger's chest rise and fall as he took a breath on his own.

"He's breathing . . . Thank You, God," Claire said aloud.

Liza silently thanked God as well. She was so grateful that Daniel was here, alive and well and able to revive this poor man. Daniel had a gift for healing, there was no doubt.

Daniel leaned back, still kneeling at the man's side. When he finally looked up at Liza, she could see relief shining in his eyes. He sighed aloud. "That was close. I think he'll be all right now. He's just exhausted."

"He needs to be in dry clothes, in a warm bed," Claire said.

"Absolutely. But how will we ever get him up the steps?" Liza looked at Daniel, and then Claire. "Can we carry him together?"

"I have an idea," Claire said. "What if Daniel goes back to the inn, grabs some blankets, and drives his truck down to the boat launch? There's access there to the beach. He can drive here, and we'll put the man in the back of the truck and return the same way."

Daniel stood up and nodded. "I had the same thought. In the meantime, he should be covered. He could develop hypothermia." Daniel took off his slicker and tucked it around the stranger. "I'll be right back. Just watch him closely."

"We won't take our eyes off him," Liza promised.

"Neither will his friend." Claire rested her hand on the dog, who was now cuddled to the man's side, his big head resting on his paws.

Liza wondered if the man was aware of all that was going on—or of the dog's comforting presence at his side. Maybe on some level, he was. Maybe, even though it seemed he was barely conscious, it would help to say a few words to him.

Liza leaned over and spoke very softly. "Don't worry; you're going to be all right. Your dog is all right, too. He's right here beside you."

The man's eyelids fluttered, but his eyes didn't open. Liza wondered if she had just imagined it.

When she looked up, Claire was smiling softly. "That was a good idea. I think he can hear you . . . though I doubt he'll remember."

"I'm glad he survived. Another minute or two, and who knows what would have happened. What if I'd stayed inside this morning and answered e-mail? Or gone to Newburyport? No one would have seen him."

"No sense in dwelling on what-ifs. You did go out, thank goodness. Maybe you were meant to be there."

"Maybe," Liza quietly agreed. She looked down at the man again. He seemed to be resting more peacefully, with Daniel's yellow slicker tucked up to his chin. He breathed in a normal way, as if in a deep sleep.

She had not seen his arm move, but noticed that one hand now rested on the dog. Perhaps the familiar sensation had elicited the peaceful look that had settled on his face.

Following Claire's plan, the rescuers soon delivered both man and dog to the inn. They carried the stranger to a bedroom on the second floor, where Daniel took his vital signs again and examined him for any injuries he might have missed on the beach. Then Daniel cleaned him up, dressed him in some dry clothes he found in his truck, and tended to a few cuts and bruises.

Liza had slipped into her own room for a few minutes to change into dry clothes, too. The wind and rain had whipped her hair into a mass of wild brown curls, and she struggled to gather and pin it in a haphazard knot at the back of her head.

When she finally returned to the visitor's room, Claire was near the bed, drying the dog with an old towel. The dog looked very grateful for the attention and stood stone-still while she held his head in her hand and rubbed his thick fur.

"I called the Coast Guard back and told them what happened and how we handled it," Claire told the others. "They'd like some information about the boat and the sailor, to follow up."

"I'll get back to them," Daniel offered, "when we find all that out. Right now, I don't think our patient is up to any interviews."

Liza quietly walked over to Daniel, who was bandaging a small cut on the man's forehead. She noticed the box containing medical supplies that Daniel carried in his truck. The lid was open, and inside she could see gauze, tape, and antiseptic, a blood-pressure cuff and stethoscope, and some other instruments she didn't know by name. He kept them handy for his calls as a volunteer EMT at the medical clinic in the island's town center. The nearest doctor was in the village of Cape Light, and the nearest hospital was more than an hour away in Southport, so Daniel and the other island volunteers were kept busy.

But Liza knew that Daniel had been familiar with the tools of the medical trade long before he'd arrived on Angel Island, though that was something he almost never mentioned.

The stranger was now tucked under a thick pile of quilts, every part of him covered but his head and neck. He looked to be in his early sixties, with thick gray hair combed back straight from his forehead. It was a bit long, but perhaps he hadn't pulled into port to visit a barber for a while. A thick salt-and-pepper mustache covered his upper lip, and heavy eyebrows seemed at odds with his pleasantly rounded face, full cheeks, and ruddy pink skin. Something about his expression, even with his eyes closed, looked intelligent.

"Is he sleeping?" Liza asked quietly.

"He's in and out. He said a few words while I was cleaning him up. I don't think there's any need to take him to the hospital," Daniel said. "I was afraid he hit his head when the boat turned over, but he doesn't appear to have any contusions on his head, or any signs of concussion. His pulse is a bit erratic," he added with concern. "But he's not a young man. And he's still in shock."

"He has good color again in his complexion." Claire stood near the bed and studied the stranger.

Perhaps the man heard them talking. Liza watched his head toss from side to side, and his eyes slowly opened.

He stared up at them with bloodshot, blue-gray eyes. He looked alarmed for a moment, but Claire reached out and gently touched his shoulder.

"Don't be scared. We're here to help you. Your boat capsized in the storm. Do you remember?"

He stared at Claire and blinked, then ran his tongue over parched lips. He had not been out in the water long, but long enough to leave his mouth swollen, his lips sore and chapped.

"I do . . . I do now," he replied in a raspy voice. "The storm . . . it came up so suddenly. I wasn't ready. I should have headed for shore much sooner . . ."

"Don't trouble yourself. It's all over and done," Claire said quietly. "Daniel pulled you out. You're safe now."

The man nodded, his expression very grim. He swallowed

hard and suddenly seemed agitated, staring around and trying to sit up. "Edison . . . my dog . . . Did you see him? Is he all right?"

"He's fine. He's right here on the floor next to you. He hasn't left your side for a moment." Daniel pointed down to the place where Edison was resting. The ordeal had tired the faithful friend out, too. Claire had made him a bed from an old blanket and left a bowl of water for him. Now the dog was curled up on the blanket, snoring gently.

The man peered over the edge of his pillow, saw the dog, and sighed. A small smile formed on his lips. His eyes closed again, as if that simple act had taken a great effort.

"Can you tell us your name? I couldn't find any identification," Daniel said quickly, trying to get in one last question before the stranger fell asleep again.

"Nolan. Nolan Porter. I've been sailing down from Maine since late May," he murmured. "*Ariadne* . . . my boat. Did she go under?"

"She's taken on some water, but drifted toward the shore. She's in a protected spot, near a dock. The storm has almost passed. I might be able to pull your boat onto dry land, or at least tie it up."

"Could you?" Nolan's eyes opened again. He stared at Daniel with surprise and gratitude. "That would be . . . exceptionally kind." His words came out slowly, in a hoarse voice, each word requiring effort. "That vessel is all I have now in the world. My papers and belongings in the cabin. Very valuable . . . essential to me. Even if the boat is lost."

"I understand. I'll call a friend who has a fishing boat with a winch. We'll get your boat secured for you," Daniel promised.

Nolan sighed and nodded, his eyes still closed. His expression relaxed a bit, Liza thought. He'd spent what little energy he could summon.

Daniel signaled to Liza and Claire, and they followed him into the hall. He left the door open a crack, and when Liza looked back, the big dog was watching them, though he didn't stir.

"He'll probably sleep for a few hours. But you ought to check on him every twenty minutes or so."

"I'll check," Claire replied. "I'm going to put up some soup. It will take the chill out and give him strength."

Liza took Daniel's hand and looked up at him. "Do you want me to come with you? I can help with the boat."

"I know you can . . . But no sense in both of us getting soaked again." He smiled at Claire. "I will be looking for some of that soup when I get back, Claire."

"That's the least we can do, after you saved a man's life today . . . Now that I think of it, I guess you deserve some fresh biscuits and johnnycake, too." She smiled and nodded as she headed down the stairs.

Daniel laughed. "In that case, I won't be long," he promised, looking back at Liza.

"I hope so." She stood on tiptoe to kiss his cheek. "You did save that man's life. I'm very proud of you."

He put his arm around her shoulder as they walked to the staircase. "You and Claire did your part as well. We all helped to rescue him."

"But you got him breathing again. I don't think he would

have made it if you hadn't been there, Daniel. I know you love fixing old houses and broken furniture . . . but you have a real gift for fixing people, too." She took one of his big calloused hands in her own as they stood at the top of the stairs. "A gift for healing . . . You know that, don't you?"

He didn't exactly smile, but she saw a certain light in his eyes. Recollecting the moment he'd gotten Nolan Porter breathing again? Or other patients, too? "It's an amazing feeling, pulling someone back from the edge like that," he admitted quietly. "Like nothing else in the world, really. A humbling feeling, too," he added. "I know I can't take much credit for it. But I do feel privileged to help when I can."

Liza knew what he meant. It was really by the grace of God that Nolan Porter was alive right now. Daniel saw himself as a go-between; an instrument.

"You are privileged . . . and good at it, too," she added quickly.

He met her gaze briefly and smiled. Then he dropped a kiss in her hair. "See you later, gorgeous . . . Save me some biscuits."

Liza didn't answer, just leaned over the banister and watched him disappear down the hall. He knew very well that Claire would save him plenty. Maybe they would talk more about this later when they were alone. Liza hoped so.

She returned to Nolan Porter's room and glanced in at him one more time. At least they knew his name. She wondered who he was and where he was going. Was he from Maine, or had he only started his trip there? There must be someone they could contact. A wife or relative? A close friend?

And why did he tell them that the boat was all he had left in the world? That sounded so . . . extreme. So many people who came to the inn had interesting lives and backgrounds. She wondered about this visitor's story. She had a feeling it wasn't one she had heard before. Liza couldn't help but consider again the fragile circumstances that had spared the man's life. How she had almost skipped the beach this morning and how, even once she got down the steps, she had to persuade herself to stay. And how she was the only person on the beach for miles in any direction, and could have easily not even noticed the floundering sailboat. Or realized how dire its situation had been.

If any one of those factors had been different, this man and his dog would have both drowned.

Liza watched them for a moment from the door, both sleeping peacefully.

God works in mysterious ways, Claire always said. It certainly seemed true today.

Chapter Two

As Daniel had instructed, Claire and Liza took turns for the next few hours checking on Nolan and Edison. When the soup was done, Claire set a bowl of it on a tray, alongside a dish of fluffy biscuits and a small pot of tea.

Good, nourishing food and plenty of rest. A simple prescription, but that's what a body needed most of all to restore itself. Nature was remarkable. Claire believed the human system could heal and repair itself completely, given the right attention and encouragement. That was the way God made the world and every living thing in it.

As she quietly entered the room, observing man and dog, she sensed that they were already drawing peace and comfort from their surroundings. *Coming along nicely,* Claire thought, setting the tray on a bedside table. *Nolan Porter will be up and about by tomorrow. And the dog, even sooner.*

The big brown Lab had lifted his head to watch her, then

quietly beat his tail on the floor. *He likes me,* Claire realized. Feeling flattered, she bent down to pat Edison's head. *Must be the attention I gave him . . . or the dog bed. Or he smells the soup?*

When she stood up, Nolan was watching her. His eyes were open, though he had not lifted his head from the pillow.

"Hello, Nolan. Feeling any better?" Claire stood at the foot of the bed and smiled.

"I am, actually." He sat up and blinked, then whisked his hair back with his hand. "How long have I been sleeping?"

"Oh . . . an hour or two. Are you hungry? I've brought you some soup and biscuits . . . and some tea. Maybe your stomach is queasy from the seawater?"

"A bit," he admitted, tilting his head. "But that food sure smells good." He gazed at the tray with a hungry look Claire knew very well.

"Why don't you try some? Maybe just some soup to start." She had brought a lap tray for the bed and set it up for him, then carefully placed the food on it.

Nolan surveyed the offering with a pleased expression. He picked up the checkered cloth napkin and tucked it into the collar of the spare sweatshirt Daniel had found for him.

"Funny how drowning builds up an appetite," he joked as he dipped his spoon into the soup.

"It makes perfect sense. You were fighting the ocean for your life. The ocean is a formidable opponent. Bound to be tiring." Claire saw Nolan agree with a nod of his head as he bit into a biscuit.

"Hmm. Delicious . . . very fluffy. Are these homemade?"

"Fresh from the oven. We do all our cooking and baking right here at the inn."

"Is that where I've landed, at an inn?" He looked around at the room. "I thought it might be. But I wasn't sure."

"Sorry. We should have told you." Claire nearly laughed at the omission. She took a seat in the armchair near the bed and smoothed her apron over her lap. "The Inn at Angel Island. That's where you've landed. I'm the housekeeper and cook . . . and general second-in-command. Liza Martin is the owner and manager. She inherited the inn from her aunt, Elizabeth Dunne. I cooked for her, too, for many years."

"I see . . . And Daniel, the man who saved me . . . is he Liza's husband?"

Claire smiled again, a bit wider this time. *Not yet,* she might have answered. *Though all signs seemed to point that way.* Those two loved each other; had been in love for years, Claire was sure. But there were some questions yet to answer, obstacles to resolve. With love, hope, patience . . . and God's help . . . she prayed they would find their way.

Of course, she couldn't tell Nolan Porter all that right now. Instead she said, "No, Daniel and Liza are not married, though they've been dating for a while. Daniel helps around here a lot. He's a wonderful carpenter and can fix just about anything."

Nolan nodded and patted his chin with the napkin. "That's a fine and practical talent, fixing things. I'm pretty handy myself. Built my boat," he added with a hint of pride, and also a bit of sadness, Claire noted. Before she could comment, he added, "Any news of the vessel? Did Daniel find it?"

Claire sat up and leaned toward the bed. "He did. I should

have told you that first thing. He's not back yet, but he called and told Liza that he found the boat. He and a friend are trying to pull it up out of the water. I understand it's not far from here."

"That's good news. I might be able to recover some of my belongings."

"You might. We'll help you. Maybe tomorrow, when you feel stronger." Nolan didn't reply. He seemed lost in thought, staring down at the empty bowl.

"So you were sailing down from Maine? That's quite an ambitious trip, isn't it?"

He looked up again, called back from his wandering thoughts by her question. "I suppose. I didn't have any set destination in mind; just exploring. I'm a college professor—engineering and physics at Carlisle University. I have summers off and often take my boat out for a long cruise."

Claire nodded. She'd heard of Carlisle. It was a very good school with a strong slant toward technology, just outside of Portland. "Sounds wonderful. Summer is my busy season. Then again, living here, you feel as if you're on vacation all year long."

Nolan smiled briefly. "I suppose you might. I've heard of this island but never visited. I didn't even mean to visit this time," he added with a laugh. "I should have headed for port sooner, when I noticed the weather turning. I don't know what I was thinking . . . or not thinking. Of all people, I should know better. Sailing is all about energy. The universe is all about energy. Going with it. Or against it. Making it work for you . . . Now I've wrecked my boat, but I'm a better sailor than that. I really am," he added, as if pleading his case to her.

Claire nodded sympathetically. He was rambling a bit. She would tell Daniel. Maybe he had a fever or had struck his head.

Mainly, he'd had a shock, she realized, a grave shock. He had already told them that the boat was all he had left in the world. It was hard to wake up in a strange place and learn that you had nearly drowned and lost just about all of your possessions.

"I'm sure you're a very good sailor. You'd have to be to build a boat," she said with sympathy. "Daniel says it's not too badly damaged. A hole in the hull or something."

"And the mast for the mainsail is gone. I remember that. The wind snapped it like a toothpick." He sighed, his lips curled in a tight line, his shoulders sagging. "It's not just the boat . . . This is just like me. I've wrecked my life. Hard to explain, but . . . I create my own worst problems. Can't outrun the weather in time. Can't get out of my own way. I'm sure the world would not have given much notice if the sea had swallowed me up entirely." He leaned over and glanced fondly at his dog. "I don't know that anyone would miss me . . . except for good old Edison."

Claire was shocked by his words. She leaned forward and rested a comforting hand on his arm. "Now, now. Don't even say that, Nolan. You've had an awful shock, a harrowing experience. As for your boat and your troubles . . . believe me, there are few things in the world that can't be repaired or revised. If God's made a problem, He's made a solution to it, too. There's always some solution," she promised.

Nolan finally lifted his head and looked up at her. Though

he didn't reply, she felt her words had lit a tiny spark of encouragement.

"Is there anyone you'd like to call? A relative or a friend?" she asked.

Nolan carefully considered his answer, though Claire didn't see that the question required much thought. She knew who she would reach out to if she were in trouble. She had an entire list in her head. And in her purse, on a tiny note stuck right behind her license.

Most people did. But finally Nolan shook his head. "There's no one. I'm alone. Lost my wife a few years ago, and . . . there were no children."

He did sound quite solitary. Claire wondered about brothers or sisters, or even friends. But she didn't want to pry.

"All right. Just thought I'd ask. As for the rest of it, for now I think it's best if you put all your troubles out of your mind and get some more rest. Get your strength back. Things will look better when you feel like yourself again."

Nolan rubbed his stubbly chin with his hand. "Maybe. I do feel tired. I guess I will sleep some more."

As he began to slip down under the covers, Edison stood up and trotted over to the edge of the bed. He rested his head on the quilt, in between Claire and Nolan.

"Edison . . . you never give up on me, do you, old friend?" Nolan's expression suddenly brightened as he gently stroked the dog's soft head and ears. "Thank goodness I didn't lose my first mate. He's my best friend, adviser, and confidante," he told Claire. "Worth his weight in gold and then some."

"I can see that," Claire agreed. "I'm sure he doesn't know what he'd do without you, either. He hasn't let you out of his sight."

"We're a pair. Inseparable." He looked up at Claire. "I don't suppose you'd have any leftover bits down in the kitchen? He's not at all fussy, but he's probably hungry by now."

"Already thought of that. I put aside plenty of scraps from the soup. I never met a dog who didn't like chicken."

"You aren't about to, either," he replied with a laugh, patting Edison's head. "I don't know what we did to deserve such wonderful care and generosity. Are you sure I didn't drown . . . and this is some *better* place?"

Claire had to laugh at his question and the odd, almost serious look on his face. "No, sir. Nothing as mysterious as that going on, I promise you. Though they do say that when a person comes close to losing their life in the sea, it changes them. It's like a new beginning, a second chance, once you come out of the ocean's jaws."

"Really? I've never heard that before." Nolan's thick brows drew together.

"Just a bit of folklore." Claire shrugged and came to her feet. "But worth pondering."

"Yes . . . it is." He sighed and made himself comfortable under the covers again. Claire could see he was tired. "Thank you, Claire. And thank you for the soup . . . and the conversation. I appreciate your kind attentions."

Claire was in the doorway, carrying out the tray. "You're very welcome. It's the least we can do."

She wasn't sure he heard her. His eyes had already closed, and he might have already fallen back asleep.

As Claire left the room, she noticed Edison following her.

Had he actually understood her mention of the chicken scraps? Or was he simply following the scent of the empty soup bowl?

More where that came from, he might be thinking, applying some canine logic.

"Yes, there is something for you, down in the kitchen," Claire said aloud to the dog as they walked downstairs. "I even found you a bowl. And a spot where it won't be in the way."

Back in the kitchen, Claire set the tray down and quickly served Edison. He had very nice manners, she noticed, and sat at attention, waiting for her to set the food on the floor and step back. Once he started eating, she could see he was quite hungry.

"You enjoy that. You've had a rough time out in the water today, too. There's more for you later. And maybe I can find a bit of rope somewhere and take you out for some fresh air. The sun's come out already. I'm sure you wouldn't mind a little walk outside, right?"

Edison sat and looked at her with a dignified air. She was sure if he could talk, he would answer, and maybe even confide more about the problems that weighed so heavily on his master's heart.

Nolan's troubles drew her sympathy. But she was also sure that his survival today was something of a miracle. Daniel had fished Nolan out of the water, but it had really been God's

hand, dipping into the sea to save him. She knew in her heart
he'd been saved for some reason. A good reason.

SINCE there were no guests at the inn besides Nolan—and he
wasn't even a bona fide guest at that—Claire set the table in
the kitchen for dinner. The task of bringing Nolan's boat in had
proved more complicated than expected, and Daniel worked
with his friends for hours. Claire was just putting the finishing
touches on the table setting when Daniel finally returned,
walking into the kitchen through the back door.

"Well, it's all done, finally." He shrugged off his windbreaker and hung it on a hook in the mudroom. "The boat took
on a lot of water. But I've seen worse."

"Good job. But you must be chilled to the bone, out on the
water all day. Dinner in a minute. I'll make you a cup of tea."
Without waiting for Daniel's answer, Claire put on the kettle.

Liza walked in as Daniel was giving his news. "I just
checked on Nolan. He's awake. Maybe you should go up and
give him the news."

"Good idea. I'll go right up."

Before Liza could reply, a voice sounded from the doorway.
"No need. I'm right here."

Liza was the first to turn to him. "Nolan . . . I thought you
were going to stay in bed."

"I can bring your dinner up. No trouble at all," Claire
chimed in.

"No need to wait on me. I'm coming around. Better to get
some blood circulating in this old body than lie abed all day."

"As long as you feel up to it, it is better to get up." Daniel rose and pulled out a chair for Nolan to sit in. Edison padded softly behind his master, then curled up at his feet, beneath the table.

"Well, what's the verdict? Give it to me straight." Nolan's expression was solemn as he sat across from Daniel.

"Your boat took on a lot of water, Nolan. There's a large gash in the hull and the mast cracked off, about six feet above the deck."

"Yes . . . I remember that. Unfortunately."

"You didn't lose the sail," Daniel added, trying to strike a more positive note. "It was dragging behind on a line. We drained the cabin as best we could, and a lot of your belongings floated out. But there are still belongings inside to sift through. Some of it might be salvageable."

"There's a locked cupboard in the front cabin . . . It didn't open, did it?" Nolan asked eagerly.

Daniel thought for a moment. "Hard to say. I didn't go inside. But we pulled your boat up on dry land, near the dock down the road. I'll take you there tomorrow and you can check for yourself."

Nolan took a breath and sat back in his seat. "I would appreciate that."

"No problem. I'm happy to help," Daniel said sincerely.

Liza and Claire set out bowls and platters for dinner. Claire had made flounder roasted with lemon butter and capers, fresh spinach, and small, red roasted potatoes.

"This looks delicious, Claire. As usual," Daniel said.

"Yes, it does," Nolan agreed. He looked at Claire. "Thank

you for preparing this beautiful meal . . . and thank you all for rescuing me. I'm not sure if I ever said it, but I know I can't thank you all enough for your help. Or for your hospitality in this lovely place."

"You're welcome to stay as long as you like," Liza assured him. "I'm sure it will take a few days to look through your boat and get new identification . . . and get your life sorted out."

Nolan stared at her a moment and shook his head with a wry smile. "More than a few, I'm afraid. I don't have much money, and my entire life seems . . . well, at low tide right now."

"Because you damaged your boat?" Claire asked.

"Partly . . . but—" He paused and looked down at his dish, which was still empty. "When you asked what I did for a living this morning, I must confess, I didn't tell the entire truth. I am a college professor. I teach physics and I also hold a degree in engineering. But I'd have to clarify that I'm an unemployed professor right now. I was fired in May, when the semester ended."

Liza was surprised by the admission. "That's too bad. Didn't you have tenure?"

"I did. But that doesn't protect you entirely. It was department politics, more or less," he added with a sigh.

Liza sensed the admission embarrassed him, and that he didn't want to go into the details. But she guessed it had been more than department politics and that Nolan must have done something quite outrageous to have lost his tenured position. On the other hand, he seemed such a pleasant, even gentle, person. She couldn't imagine what his egregious misstep might have been.

"Losing my job would have been bad enough . . . but I also lost my home. My wife left me, too, at about the time I lost the house. She got quite frustrated with all the setbacks. All due to a certain situation . . . a legal situation that took over my life like a strangling vine, overtaking everything in sight . . ." He sighed heavily. Liza looked around at the others, but no one spoke, waiting for Nolan to continue. "I had a little workshop and laboratory on the property, in an old barn. That's where I built the *Ariadne*. I named her after the clever princess in the Greek myth about the Minotaur. She's the only one who figures out how to outsmart the monster so that her lover, Prince Theseus, can kill it and escape with his life."

"I remember that story. She gives Theseus a thread to lead him in and out of the winding passages in the labyrinth," Claire recalled.

"That's right. That's the myth exactly." Nolan nodded, suddenly looking very much like a teacher impressed by a student who had surprised him with her intelligence.

Perhaps he'd underestimated Claire, Liza thought. Many people did, because of her quiet, modest manner and her position as a cook and housekeeper. But Liza had made that mistake years ago. If Nolan stayed much longer, he would soon see that first impressions about Claire North were quite misleading.

"There's a labyrinth here, on the island," Claire added. "Though hardly the same kind that's in the legend. It's more of a stone path. But it serves its own purpose. Anyway . . . please go on with your story, Nolan. I'm sorry I interrupted. You were telling us about your workshop?"

"Yes . . . a perfect little workshop where I could concentrate, and carry out my research undisturbed. I miss that refuge the most of all. The lab and—" He suddenly stopped himself and didn't finish the sentence. He looked around the table and shook his head. "Let's just say my life was overturned. Capsized in a stormy sea, the way you found me today. But at least I still had my boat. So I set out with Edison a few weeks ago. Mainly due to necessity. I thought a long sail would clear my head and help me figure out my next move." Nolan shook his head, looking sick at heart. "But I didn't figure out a thing, and now my boat's gone, too."

"If you built it, Nolan, you can fix it," Daniel assured him.

"Perhaps . . . if I had the materials and a place to work," Nolan replied.

He seemed like such a nice man. Life had handed him a few rough turns recently, Liza thought. She didn't like to see him distressed and downhearted. "You're welcome to stay here until you sort it out, Nolan. For as long as you need to," she added.

"It's a lot to think about at once. And you're just back on your feet," Daniel noted. "Take it easy tonight. We'll help you tomorrow and go down to the boat as early as you like."

Nolan offered Liza a small smile, looking surprised at her offer. He looked over at Daniel, too. "Well, that's a plan. The first step is having one, I always say. I've always been an early bird . . . And believe it or not, I'm normally not the type to burden strangers with my problems. I do believe everyone has to take full responsibility for their actions, good or bad. I've landed at this lovely inn through sheer luck, but I'd never take advantage of your gracious hospitality."

"Liza and I are happy to help you. That's what we're here for," Claire said, meeting Nolan's glance. "Have you ever heard the Scripture 'Be not forgetful to entertain strangers: for thereby some have entertained angels unawares'?"

Nolan laughed. "I'm no angel . . . far from it. With all due respect, Claire, I know you're suggesting that God, or some divine power, is at work. But I'm a scientist first and foremost. The universe is a very random place. I've ended up here purely by chance. This time the wheel of fortune has stopped at a lucky space for me, but I easily could have ended up at the bottom of the ocean today. What possible plan could there be?"

Liza was about to taste another forkful of the flounder, but paused and glanced at Daniel a moment. She'd seen Claire challenged like this before and was always impressed by her artful rebuttals—neither proselytizing nor apologetic.

"Oh, I certainly don't know the answer to that," Claire replied. "But I'm sure it will become apparent by and by. I do know you've been given a second chance for a good reason, Nolan. And you should make the most of it."

Nolan politely dipped his head. "Good advice. Though we come from opposite sides of the faith spectrum, I will say that the closest thing I've ever known to a pure, sweet spirit and unconditional love is Edison." He glanced under the table, where his dog lay patiently at his feet.

Claire just smiled. "I'm sure that's true. Didn't you ever notice that the word 'dog' is 'God' spelled backward?"

She delivered this volley with a twinkle in her eye. Nolan laughed, and so did Liza and Daniel. It was clear that while Nolan did not share Claire's views about the universe, he did enjoy talking to her.

The conversation soon moved to lighter topics. Nolan was very interested in learning about the island—its history, topography, and population. He had the keen curiosity of a true scientist, and they all took turns answering his many questions.

The dinner concluded with a dessert of buttery shortcake covered with strawberries from the inn's garden, and fluffy whipped cream. Afterward, Liza was practically too full to move from the table.

Nolan rose first, clearing up the dishes and carrying them to the counter near the sink.

"Oh, you don't have to bother with that. Why don't you sit out on the porch and get some air?" Claire encouraged him.

"No bother. I'm happy to help. Makes me feel I'm earning my keep just a little," he said cheerfully. "That wonderful dinner revived me. Would you like me to wash those pots in the sink?"

Claire didn't answer for a moment. "If you really want to. The soap and scrub pads are on the left. I'll load the dishwasher."

Liza and Daniel began helping, too. But Claire was such an organized cook that, after a few moments, there wasn't much to do.

Claire looked over at them. "We don't need everyone in here to clean a few pots. Daniel's been working outside on the water all day. He's definitely exempt."

"Yes, he is. I'll take charge of him," Liza agreed. She took his arm and led him away from the sink. "I think the clouds have finally cleared. Let's sit out on the porch. Maybe we can go over that repair list," she suggested.

Daniel laughed. "Good idea . . . how romantic."

Liza didn't reply. He knew she was teasing him . . . and she knew he was teasing her back.

Out on the porch, the air was cool and dry, and the night sky was spread out like a dark blue velvet blanket covered with bits of sparkling diamond stars. The moon, almost full, hovered over the dark ocean, casting a shimmering light on the gently rolling waves.

Liza stood at the porch rail. "What a night. It's hard to believe the weather was so wild this morning . . . Or that we rescued a man from drowning."

Daniel stood behind her and put his arms around her waist, resting his cheek against her hair. "And just had some very lively dinner conversation with him. It has been a long, eventful day," he agreed. "Let's sit on the porch swing. I've hardly spent any time with you."

He had seen her much of the day. But Liza knew what he meant. They hadn't spent a moment alone together. It was all action—most of it having to do with Nolan.

Sitting by Liza's side on the swing, Daniel put his arm around her shoulder and pulled her close. Liza didn't speak. She didn't have to. It felt so good to be together this way, close and warm, with her cheek resting on Daniel's strong shoulder as she stared out at the sea and stars. It gave her a limitless feeling in her heart, a glimpse of infinity. It made her feel hopeful, as if anything were possible.

"Poor Nolan," Daniel said finally. "He's got a sad story to tell."

"He seems like such a nice man, and so intelligent. I bet he's a wonderful teacher. He's very interesting to talk to. He's hit a rough patch right now, but maybe we can help him in some way."

"You're certainly helping him by offering a room for as long as he likes."

"What else can I do? It sounds as if he doesn't have more than the clothes on his back. Which are actually your clothes, come to think of it."

"I know . . . I just hope you don't get too involved. It's slow at the inn right now. But you might need that room for paying customers in a week or two."

"It's all right. He can move to a smaller room on the third floor. We hardly ever rent those out. Jamie's old room would be good for him."

Daniel shook his head and laughed. "You and Claire are always taking in strays."

Liza knew what he meant. Jamie Carter had been their helper last summer. Claire had actually known him years before, when he was just a boy and she had worked in Boston at a settlement house. She had tried to help him then, but hadn't been able to. Then, last summer when he showed up on the island, he still needed help, even though he was in his early twenties.

"This was exactly the right place for Jamie," Liza said. "He's doing very well now . . . after some rough sledding. We can help Nolan, too," she added. "You helped him more than anyone. You fished him out of the water and got him breathing again."

"I did what I could," Daniel said. He smiled at her. "It's really not that extraordinary. Lots of people know how to perform mouth-to-mouth and CPR and all sorts of emergency procedures, thank goodness."

"I know. But when I saw you working on Nolan this morning, you just looked . . . I don't know, different. Totally in tune with who you are and what you're meant to do in the world. Totally . . . in a zone. Did it feel that way?"

Daniel didn't respond at first, then slowly nodded. "Yes. I felt . . . right. Though that doesn't describe it exactly. I enjoy carpentry. I like to build things or fix things. But the feeling I get from practicing medicine is different. It's satisfying in a deeper way. A more . . . solemn way, or something."

"Do you ever miss it?" Liza asked. "Do you miss being a doctor and having that feeling all the time?"

"I did today," he admitted. "And lots of times, when I help patients at the clinic, I miss doing more for them. What a real doctor does. Not just crisis intervention, patching them up and sending them to a hospital. But at least I'm still in touch with it."

"You are in touch," she agreed. "I just wondered if you ever thought of going back to it. As a career again."

They had skirted around the edges of this subject from time to time. But Liza had never asked Daniel so directly how he felt now about the medical career he had abandoned years ago. Maybe because the subject had always seemed so difficult for him. But for some reason, watching him today with Nolan and hearing his frank answers to her questions, she thought he might finally be ready to talk about it.

Daniel looked out at the sea and sky and smiled just a little. "Yes. From time to time, I have thought about it. But I'm not sure trying to pick up where I left off is the right thing to do. It's hard to retrace your steps in life and correct something that went wrong. It's hard to go back when you failed, Liza."

"I know what you mean," Liza said. "But you didn't fail, Daniel. You made one mistake, one misjudgment. No one said you couldn't be a doctor anymore."

"I know that," he said quietly. "I'm the one who chose to stop practicing. I blamed myself. And that was enough. But quitting medicine ultimately led me here, where I've had a chance to work things out. I believe now that God forgives me," he added. "So I guess I have to let myself off the hook."

"Yes, you do," Liza agreed. She felt as if she had been waiting for him to come to that conclusion for a very long time.

He studied her for a moment, and when he spoke again his voice was both serious and amused. "And what makes you so certain?"

"It's just that when I see that look on your face, the way you looked today helping Nolan," she continued, "I know that you're doing exactly what you were meant to do in the world. That's a rare thing, to find something you truly love to do and be so good at it. And I can't help but wonder if you would be happier going back to it." When he didn't answer, she added, "I wonder because I love you, Daniel, and I want you to be happy. Really happy."

"I am really happy." He squeezed her closer and kissed the top of her head. "I'm happy on this island, and being with you. I'm happy with my life just the way it is. Are you trying to tell me that patching a hole in the roof of this old place doesn't satisfy my soul?"

"Come on, Daniel. Be serious."

"I am being serious. Well, almost . . . I'm *absolutely* and *totally* happy with you. Is that serious enough?"

Liza felt herself blush and was grateful for the dim light. She could hardly object to that answer, or help smiling. "I like hearing that. But are you trying to get me off the subject?"

"I'm just answering your questions, thinking this through. I'd never want to move away if you were here. And as long as you run the inn, you're pretty much tied to this island."

It was true. As long as she owned the inn, she wasn't free to pick up and move wherever she wanted. She could barely get away to spend a day or two in Boston. "I am tied to the inn. But you could practice in the area . . ."

We wouldn't have to be apart is what she meant to say. But that was as far as she could go. They never spoke much about their future. Though she felt totally loved and secure in Daniel's commitment, neither of them had ever mentioned the word "marriage." It was definitely *not* the night to talk about that, too, she realized.

But Daniel picked up her meaning, as he usually did. "Being a doctor is hard on relationships, Liza. It broke up my last one."

Liza remembered that. He had told her once how his fiancée had felt ignored and underappreciated, and how she broke off their engagement, claiming Daniel was selfish and already married—to his work.

"I wouldn't be that way," she assured him. "I would never be that immature and demanding."

Daniel laughed and rubbed her shoulder. "You could never be anything like that. But the pressure—and the long hours— are real. That's something to consider."

Liza turned her head and caught his eye. "What else are you considering?"

Daniel shrugged. "Oh, I don't know . . . I've probably been away from real medicine too long and forgotten everything important."

"You passed all your tests once. You could study again," she said simply.

"Hey, I was a lot younger. With a lot more brainpower and more neurons firing." He smiled his charming, handsome smile and tapped his temple with an index finger. "All the fumes from the paint and wood stain have burned them out."

Liza knew that wasn't true. Daniel was as intelligent and sharp as anyone she had ever met. But maybe he was frightened. He'd made a huge error in judgment and had ordered the wrong procedures for an accident victim he'd been called in to the ER to treat. Daniel still held himself responsible for the man's coma and loss of faculties afterward.

Turning his back on medicine, Daniel had retreated to Angel Island, where he had spent summers as a boy. Here on the island, he immersed himself in building, painting, and carpentry, skills he had learned while working his way through school.

She glanced at him. "Well, aside from getting that flabby old brain back in shape, what else would you have to do?"

"Good question. I don't really know . . . I've never looked into it. I guess I could find out easily enough. There must be some place I can call, some certification board."

"I bet you could look it up on the Internet. It seems you can find the answer to anything if you just search the right question." When he didn't reply, she added, "How many years has it been? I forget."

"It was six years in May," he answered quickly, leading Liza to believe he thought of it far more than he would ever admit—and may have even known how many weeks and days. "I'd been living on the island for three years when you arrived. My lucky day."

"Mine, too. The day you walked into the inn and introduced yourself . . . and caught me looking like a dog's breakfast."

He laughed at her description. She had been cleaning the inn, from the attic to the basement, and looked a complete wreck. It was a wonder he hadn't turned and run straight out the door.

"A dog's *gourmet* breakfast," he corrected her kindly. Liza reached up and gently slugged his arm, and he laughed even louder.

"Ouch! That hurt—and was quite unnecessary, since you know I fell for you at first sight . . . And you always look beautiful to me."

Liza smiled slowly, feeling a bit penitent for her reaction. "Much better. Just what I like to hear."

He turned so that they were face-to-face and smiled into her eyes. "You know how to keep me in line, sweetheart. What would I ever do without you?"

Before Liza could say another word, Daniel pulled her close for a deep, sweet kiss.

Chapter Three

THE next morning, everyone was up early, even before the sun had burned away the smoky wisps of fog that drifted over the inn and the meadow next door, where the small, graceful goats of the Gilroys' farm were already out grazing.

Liza heard voices and activity downstairs as she dressed. She found Claire and Nolan in the kitchen, finishing a breakfast of hot coffee and warm blueberry muffins. She grabbed a muffin and filled a travel mug with coffee just as Daniel came through the back door.

He glanced over at the women. "Are you both coming to look at the boat?"

"Are you kidding? We're almost as curious as Nolan," Liza told him. "Besides, maybe we can help."

"All right . . . I guess we can all go in the truck if someone is willing to ride in the bed."

"I will," Nolan quickly volunteered. "I'll ride back there with Edison. He likes the open air."

Edison is coming as well? Liza nearly said that aloud, but from Nolan's serious expression, she could tell he wouldn't consider leaving the dog behind. He probably dreaded what he would find, and having his good friend with him was a comfort.

Daniel seemed to realize that, too. "It's a short ride. You can sit on some tarps. You'll be fine."

LIZA sat next to Daniel and glanced out the window at the sea as they drove down the main road to the dock. The fog was burning away, revealing a deep blue sky as the sun rose over the sea, promising a perfect summer day. No sign of foul weather marred the clear skies as long, smooth waves gently rolled toward the beach, breaking almost soundlessly.

What a difference a day makes, Liza thought. But that's the way the ocean was; "a fickle mistress," fishermen called it.

Moments later the truck drove down a short sandy road and pulled up next to the long wooden dock. Everyone jumped out, including Edison, and followed Daniel down to the beach.

They made their way down a slope covered with beach grass, and Liza soon spotted the boat, resting on the sand far enough back from the water to be clear of a high tide. Tilted on its side against a pile of gray boulders, it was partially covered with a huge blue tarp, and looked like an ailing patient in a hospital bed.

They all stopped and stared at it. Nolan pressed a hand to

his forehead. "My beautiful *Ariadne* . . . You poor thing . . . What did I do to you?"

Claire took a step toward him. "It was the storm, Nolan. It wasn't your fault. The wind and rain and the sheer strength of the ocean did it. One lone sailor isn't any match for that."

He glanced at her a moment, his expression bleak. Then he slowly set off toward his battered vessel, with Edison padding behind.

As they headed to the boat, Liza noticed some clothing, shoes, and other objects washed up on the shore. They could collect all that later. Perhaps some of it could be washed and dried. Considering Nolan's situation, it was certainly worth a try.

First they had to help Nolan search his boat. He had reached the *Ariadne* and was trying to pull off the big cover, though a strong breeze fought him even in that simple effort.

"Here, Nolan. Let me help." Daniel took one end of the tarp, and together they uncovered the boat. Nolan stepped back and gasped. The tarp had been covering a large gash in the hull, but now the damage was revealed.

"Oh dear, this is bad. Very bad . . ." He gingerly touched the torn wood with his fingertips, then glanced at Daniel. "I know you said there was a hole. But this is even worse than I expected."

"I'm sorry. I didn't mean to give you false hope. I still think you can repair it." Daniel's tone was encouraging.

Nolan sighed. "Guess I'll look inside. Can't get any worse than this."

Liza didn't know much about it, but guessed there was a

point where a boat wasn't worth fixing. That thought did raise a question. Did Nolan have any insurance on the boat? She hoped he did, though she didn't think this was the time to ask him.

Nolan scrambled up the rocks next to the vessel and hopped down to the deck. For an older man, he was quite nimble. So was Edison, who quickly followed.

Nolan turned and looked down at the others. "I won't be long. There's only one thing I really want to find in this mess— my papers and files. I hope they're still there."

Then he turned and disappeared down into the boat's cabin.

"I'll go help him," Daniel said, and set off after Nolan.

Liza and Claire followed as well, in a more careful manner. Liza climbed onto the deck first and held out a hand to help Claire. Edison was still on deck. He walked in impatient circles, then finally sat down at the far end of the boat, just managing to keep his balance, since the deck was tilting to one side.

They heard a lot of noise down in the cabin. Claire glanced at Liza. "Sounds like doors slamming?"

Liza peered below. "He's looking through all the latched cabinets and benches. Some of them are already open."

Down in the galley, Liza saw a tiny kitchen: a sink and a two-burner cooktop. There were portholes covered with short curtains along either side of the galley, with long wooden benches below. A small wooden table stood near the cooktop.

Liza thought it was a very nice boat . . . or had been. Right now it was a soggy mess. Water-soaked debris was strewn in all directions, most of it plastered to the floor and jammed in corners of the galley—clothing, cups, dishes, maps, seat cushions, a soggy box of oatmeal and cans of food, water goggles and melted copies of *American Inventor* magazine, and even a few books littered the floor of the cabin. Liza recognized the cover of one: *Leaves of Grass* by Walt Whitman.

It will take hours to sort through all that, she thought.

Nolan had bypassed the mess completely and made a bee-line for the most forward compartment. He stood at the wooden door, pulling and shaking it and making quite a racket.

"Can you see what he's doing now?" Claire asked.

Liza peered down again. "He's trying to open the door to a space at the front of the boat. Let's go down and see what's going on."

Liza led the way and Claire followed. Liza saw Edison staring down the steps; then the big dog scuttled down behind them. It was darker in the galley and, with the boat pitched to one side, difficult to walk. But they managed by holding on to the wooden counters and table, and made it to the middle of the space. Daniel stood next to Nolan, who had crouched down to examine a lock on a small door at the far end of the galley.

"Lost the key, of course," Nolan muttered, "along with everything else. Do you have a screwdriver in the truck? Maybe we can take the door off the hinges."

"I have a small one right here, on my key ring. A Swiss Army knife." Daniel leaned over and offered Nolan the tool. "Will that help?"

"It should do very well. I can use this thin blade and spring the lock."

Nolan's reply sounded to Liza like something a professional burglar might say. She wondered if he really could open a lock without a key that easily. But he was an engineer and doubtless knew how the mechanics of a simple lock worked. A few seconds later, she had her answer.

"There we go." Nolan sounded cheered, and Liza heard the heavy thud of the lock falling to the floor. "These locks aren't made very well. A child could spring them open," he said.

Claire turned to Liza with a surprised expression. "A very precocious child," she murmured.

Liza smiled. Nolan was quite a character. He could build a boat and spring open a lock with ease. What else could he do?

Nolan stepped aside, his hand on the small brass door handle. "Stand back. I hear water on the other side."

Nolan pulled the door open, and Liza heard a gushing sound as a small wave of seawater washed down from the compartment and right through the tilted galley, carrying bits of seaweed, sand, and shells.

Luckily, she and Claire were wearing rubber boots, which had been Claire's idea. Edison, of course, was not so lucky. He stood very still and looked down at the water as it rushed past his paws. Then he looked up with a confused expression.

The water had hardly drained before Nolan charged through the doorway. "There it is . . . thank goodness! If I lost this trunk, I would have to jump in the ocean right after it."

"And I'd have to jump in right after you, Nolan. So I'm glad you found it, too," Daniel said, making light of the desperate remark.

Nolan didn't seem to notice the touch of humor. "It's wedged to one side and full of water. Can you help me pull it out?"

"Let's see what we can do." Daniel slipped into the cabin,

too. Liza poked her head in the doorway and could just make out the edge of a battered black trunk trimmed with brass. The kind of trunk children take to summer camp or people used to take on long cruises.

Nolan had said something about papers and files. If that's what it contained, it was surely a waterlogged mess. The papers it contained might very well be illegible by now. But clearly Nolan had to have that trunk; he was acting as if it were filled with a pirate's treasure.

The two men worked hard, pushing and sliding the trunk to the cabin door, then tilting it sideways and shoving it toward the stairway that led to the deck. Claire and Liza began to help on the other end. Once it was all the way through the galley, Daniel got a plank and some rope from his truck, and they managed to get the trunk up onto the deck.

It was time for a break, and everyone stood on the deck, catching their breath and staring at the trunk. Edison circled it and sniffed at the bottom, where some water still dripped out.

"No need to try to get this out now, Nolan," Daniel said. "We'll put the boat up on the trailer and haul it back to the inn. You can open the trunk there and take out what you want."

"Yes, I know. But it's hard to wait. I just want to know if my documents have been soaked beyond recognition." The trunk was secured with a big combination lock, and Nolan hovered over it. He knelt down, took the lock in hand, and began twisting it around, whispering to himself as he tried to recall the combination. "Don't worry, I have it memorized, though sometimes it takes me a minute or two to remember . . . five to the left . . . thirty-three right . . ."

Edison stood very close to his master, and when Nolan looked up again, he and the dog were nose to nose. "The old address on Nutmeg Street?" Nolan asked his four-legged friend. "Or was it the phone number?"

Edison stared at Nolan. Even if he did remember, he had no way of telling. Nolan squinted down at the lock, then gazed at the sky. Then he shook his head and started again.

Daniel crossed his arms over his chest. Liza could tell he was growing impatient. They had started this expedition early enough, but she knew he had his own work to get to today.

Finally, Nolan looked up again. "I'm sorry. I can't seem to remember. So stupid of me. I usually keep a little card in my wallet, with the numbers written down. In code of course. But I don't have that, either."

"It will come to you," Claire promised. "Why don't we take the whole kit and caboodle back to the inn? I bet you'll remember the numbers as soon as you stop thinking about it."

Nolan took a deep breath, then nodded in agreement. "That's probably true. The mind will play tricks on you. My mind, anyway."

He came to his feet and rubbed his hands on the blue windbreaker Daniel had given him. "All right. Time to get this show on the road. How can I help you, Daniel? Tell me what to do."

Daniel brought the truck and trailer down to the beach, and with a bit more group effort, they managed to get the ailing *Ariadne* on the trailer and secured for the short ride back to the inn. While Nolan and Daniel finished loading the boat on the trailer, Claire and Liza walked down the beach and picked up everything they could find of Nolan's belongings, stuffing it all in large plastic bags.

Once again, Nolan and Edison rode in the back of the truck. Through her open window, Liza could hear Nolan talking to the dog, still trying to remember the combination. ". . . starts with my birthday, I'm sure of that much," she heard him say.

"What happens if Nolan doesn't remember?" Liza asked Daniel. "Can he break the lock?"

"I can try some metal clippers. But that lock is strong, and clippers might not work. I suppose he can call a locksmith. Let's just hope he remembers the combination," he added.

"Yes, let's say a prayer. He's gone through so much, and whatever is in that trunk is important to him," Claire added quietly.

Liza had to agree. She had to count her blessings when she saw what Nolan was going through. There was so much in her life she took for granted, so many comforts and advantages. Someone famous had once said that if the only prayer you ever say is "Thank you," it would be enough. Liza had a feeling that was true and resolved to be more grateful.

Back at the inn, Daniel left the boat at the back of the long gravel drive, near the barn. Liza and Claire went inside while the men covered the boat again, to keep out rain and enterprising animals looking for shelter.

Claire made some iced tea while Liza checked her laptop, trying to get oriented for the day. Her thoughts were broken by the sound of tapping at the back door. She saw Daniel and Nolan and wondered why they didn't just come in.

Claire walked to the door and opened it, then took a step back in alarm. Liza saw that they had carried the black trunk to the patio and had set it near the door.

"You don't plan on bringing that inside, do you?" Claire's tone was quiet and measured, but Liza sensed her sheer horror at the idea of it.

"Of course not," Daniel assured her. "We just need some rags to clean it off . . . if you have some handy?"

Claire's expression changed instantly. "I have plenty. I'll bring them right out for you . . . and some iced tea," she added. "That trunk looks heavy. It must have been hard to carry it all the way from the barn."

Daniel rolled his eyes. "It was" was all he said. Liza could only imagine. A huge trunk loaded with waterlogged papers. She glanced at Claire and then at Nolan.

"I just need to get the lock open," Nolan said, seeming unbothered by the trunk's weight. "I'll probably recall the numbers any minute now. Then I'll take out what I can salvage and put the rest in the trash." He glanced at Liza with a hopeful expression.

She forced a small smile. "As long as it's not in here when guests arrive. Maybe we can move it back into the barn by then if you can't get it open."

"Yes, I understand completely. It will be out of your way in no time," Nolan promised.

Liza hoped that was true. She stepped away from the door as Claire brought out a bucket of rags.

Edison watched the action, then laid down near the trunk, as if he felt a need to guard it.

"I'll go look for the metal shears," Daniel offered. "I'm not sure if they'll cut the lock. But we can try."

"And I need to get started on some phone calls. I guess I'll see you all later." Liza went back inside, heading for her office.

Though she was curious to see what was in the trunk, she also felt the need to get to work. If anything exciting popped out of the trunk—like a giant squid or a mermaid—she was sure someone would call her.

Liza had just settled down at her computer when Daniel appeared in the doorway. "I'm taking off now. Just wanted to say good-bye."

Liza stood up and walked over to him. "Not going to wait to see what pops out of Nolan's trunk?"

Daniel smiled. "I'll wait to read about it in the *Messenger*," he said, mentioning the name of the local newspaper. "I did want to let you know that I can't come back tomorrow to finish the step."

"Oh, that's okay. I'll just put up a sign or something to keep the guests off of it. They hardly ever go down to the drive that way anyway. Taking care of Nolan these last few days must have set you back with your work schedule."

"It has . . . but it's not that. I was thinking about that conversation we had last night, about what I would need to do to go back to medicine, and I started looking around online when I got home."

"Really?" Liza was surprised that he had researched the question so quickly. But maybe he really did want to go back and had just needed a little nudge in the right direction. "What did you find out?"

"Looks like a lot of tests," he said with a laugh. "But I made an appointment with someone at the medical certification board in Boston, and they're going to help me figure it out. Figure out if it's even feasible."

"I see. Well . . . I think that's really great. I mean, it's always better to know the answer to something like this, one way or the other, right?"

Daniel nodded. "Yes, it is. I guess I've wondered about it more than I've been willing to admit. It will be good to finally find out."

Liza gave him a tight hug. "I'm proud of you. I know it isn't easy to deal with this, and dredge up everything in the past. But I think you're doing the right thing, Daniel."

Daniel hugged her back. "Thanks . . . I think so, too."

CLAIRE had left Nolan alone with his trunk for a while, and now carried out a tray with a pitcher of iced tea, along with some tall glasses and a dish of oatmeal cookies. She placed it on the patio table and glanced at Nolan. He had just finished wiping off the trunk, and held a bunched wet rag in his hands.

"It won't be here long, Claire. I'm bound to remember the combination soon." Nolan crouched down in front of the trunk and started working on the lock again.

"When I have to remember something like that, I usually make up a clue or some little hint to remind me." She paused and watched him twisting the lock's dial around. "Would you like a glass of iced mint tea? It always gives me a boost of energy."

Nolan looked up at her. "I *would* like some tea, thank you."

Claire poured some cold tea into the tall glasses. The clinking ice cubes made an inviting sound. Nolan wiped his hands on a rag and took a glass from the tray. She took one, too. She loved mint tea the best. It refreshed her entire body and spirit and mind.

"Very invigorating," Nolan declared. "I can tell this is the real thing."

"Oh, it definitely is. I make it from my own mint. It grows like crazy in the herb garden."

"You have an herb garden, too? I guess that makes sense. You're obviously an expert cook," Nolan added, glancing out at the property behind the inn. "What's all that growing in the big garden? Vegetables? Flowers?"

"A mixture of both. It's a real kitchen garden. Though I don't just toss the rotten vegetables and such out the door and hope for the best," she said with a laugh. "That's what they did in the old days around here—Colonial times and even later, on farms. It was survival of the fittest for the plants. Low maintenance and usually a very good yield."

"But your method is far more orderly?"

"Yes, it is. I keep a careful record from year to year of the weather and what sort of fertilizer I've used. And which plants have thrived and where."

"Carefully observed, well documented." He nodded with approval. "Does that help?"

"Somewhat . . . but gardening is just like any other creative activity. You can apply your best and most consistent effort, but at a certain point, you have to let go and let the divine take over. That mysterious force that fuses through things, transforming a tiny seed into a watermelon, or a sunflower. There's only one real Gardener. I think of myself as a helper."

Nolan stared at her a moment, then took a cookie. She could tell by the set of his mouth as he slowly chewed a bite that he had considered a reply, a rebuttal probably, but had stopped himself.

"Interesting theory. It seems to work well for you," he added with a small smile.

Claire wasn't sure if it was a condescending smile or a friendly one. She actually didn't care. That's what she believed, and she didn't see any reason to be less than honest about it.

"It does work out well. Once we get deep into the summer, I can always find something to cook and serve growing out there—strawberries, asparagus, kale . . . Do you have a favorite summer fruit, Nolan?"

"I do. Quite a few, actually. I love peaches the best. Peach pie is my very favorite. My mother used to make it just perfectly and served it warm from the oven with vanilla ice cream. The peaches were soft and sweet and smelled like perfume, and the crust was so light and buttery . . ."

A dreamy look came over his face as he described the childhood treat. Peaches weren't in season yet, or Claire would have surprised him with a pie. Not to rival his mother's, of course; just to cheer him.

But before she could mention it, his eyes opened wide, and his mouth dropped open as well. He put his glass down and slapped himself on the forehead.

"That's it! That's it exactly . . . Four and twenty black birds.

Baked in a pie! . . . Four and twenty," he repeated. "And then just twenty-four." He said this last part nonchalantly, with a shrug, as if it should be perfectly obvious.

Claire just stared at him. Had the poor man gone mad from all the trauma and stress in his life? Perhaps they should call a doctor . . .

But when he ran to the trunk, crouched down, and deftly twisted the lock open, still reciting the rhyme, she knew what had happened.

Just as she had suspected, taking his mind off the question had brought the numbers bubbling up to the top of his mind. Or at least brought up the right clue.

But even with the lock tossed aside, Claire noticed that the lid wasn't opening very easily. She walked over, wondering how she could help. Edison was already there, standing next to Nolan, who was also down on all fours, crawling around the trunk, trying to figure out the problem.

"It's gotten dented on this side, see? And maybe jammed with some sand." Nolan grunted as he tried to pry and push the lid up.

Daniel had left, but Claire had some tools in the mudroom.

She went inside and grabbed the first thing she could find—a claw-shaped gardening trowel. She brought it out and offered it to him. "Will this help?"

Nolan looked pleased. "It might do. It might do very well."

He forced the sharp prongs under the rim of the lid at the dented spot and started to pry it open. When the trunk began to slide away under his force, Claire leaned over and held it steady.

"Thanks," Nolan said politely between grunts.

The metal edge slowly eased back, and Nolan used the tool again on the front of the trunk. Finally, the lid flipped open.

"Eureka!" he said aloud.

"Amen," Claire seconded as she stood up. Part of her felt the contents of the trunk were Nolan's private business. But another part of her was too curious after all this time—and after helping him open it—not to look inside. Besides, he hadn't asked for privacy.

Claire leaned over and looked in the trunk. From what she could see around Nolan—who knelt on the floor with both arms and most of his upper body inside of it—the mysterious and precious trunk was filled with soggy green file folders and piles of papers secured with rubber bands. There were also many long cardboard tubes with plastic seals on either end. Each tube was labeled and marked with scrawled handwriting. Claire didn't try to read the labels, realizing she couldn't decipher the handwriting anyway.

Nolan picked up one of the tubes and opened it. A roll of tissue-thin off-white paper slid out. It was water-stained on either edge but otherwise unharmed. He unrolled the large sheets, spread them between both hands, and quickly looked over the top sheet. Claire could tell it was a mechanical drawing of some kind, done on a grid with measurements, equations, swirling arrows, and handwritten notes scattered throughout.

"One of my inventions," he said briefly. "For a water purifier, solar powered."

"What a wonderful idea. People need clean water all over the world." And mostly in countries where there was little access to the huge power grids that everyone she knew took for granted.

"Never quite got the kinks out," he admitted, rolling up the drawing again. "But it's getting there. If someone else doesn't get there before me," he added with a sharp, self-deprecating laugh.

He slid the drawing back into the tube and sealed it, then gathered up a few others. "All of these tubes . . . my inventions. Or rough drafts—ideas in progress," he explained. "At least the tubes are airtight. Or should be."

"I hope the seals have done their job," Claire said sincerely. There were many drawings stored in the trunk. No wonder he'd been so worried. This really was a treasure chest; a treasure chest of creative ideas. Perhaps his entire life's work.

"Are all those tubes different inventions?"

"More or less. A few are revisions, or improved drawings. But most are different concepts."

"My goodness . . . you've thought of so many inventions."

"Yes, I have. But I've only sold a few. Even then, only one was ever produced on a mass scale. It's very difficult to bring an idea to market, to nurture it along from a mere thought in your own mind to a solid object. One that really works," he added with a small smile. "You know Edison—Thomas Alva, not my friend over there," he clarified, glancing at his dog. "Thomas Alva Edison tried ten thousand filaments before he found the right one to make a light bulb."

"Ten thousand? My . . . I didn't know that. Like looking for a needle in a haystack, wasn't it?"

"Exactly," Nolan agreed.

"But it does happen now and then, right? You do find that needle," she quipped.

"Now and then, for a lucky few, success. Happily ever after. But it's not all about luck. Or inspiration in the lab, or even technical expertise. There's an entire business side that's more important than any of those elements—a mysterious, hostile planet to me. I've learned that lesson the hard way. My best idea was stolen. Stolen right out from under my nose. I trusted the man ... Now see where that's gotten me. Betrayed. Ruined. Lost my laboratory, my business, my house ... my entire life." His voice grew a bit louder. "The most valuable idea I'll ever have in my lifetime. That's what really ruined me. Ruined my marriage, caused me to lose my house and my job, my good name and reputation ... everything."

His tone was suddenly harsh and bitter, even angry. Claire was surprised. She had not seen or suspected this side of Nolan. He seemed such a mild, easygoing man, despite his anxiety.

She didn't know what to say. But she was curious. "Your idea was stolen?" she asked. "How awful. How ... unfair. Was it another scientist? Another inventor?"

"Ha! No, not at all. That's the ironic thing about it; the cruelest cut. The man didn't know the first thing about engineering, about physics, about anything but making a dollar. He was a businessman. Called himself a financial angel, willing to provide the investment to produce my invention. Well, he didn't turn out to be an angel. Anything but. He left me high and dry and started making his own version of the product, with slight modifications to get around the patent laws. Clever, right?"

"Very clever. Not very ethical," she added.

"Not the least bit," Nolan agreed.

"Wasn't there something you could do?"

Nolan came to his feet, hovering over the trunk full of soggy documents. "I've tried. I've fought him tooth and nail. Tooth and nail," he insisted. "These are the files, all the letters about the lawsuit. I couldn't let that cheater get away with robbing me like that. All I want is justice, my fair share of the profits. Not a penny more . . . or less."

"That sounds . . . fair to me," Claire said carefully. It was hard to offer any opinion without hearing the details of the situation. But she could agree with the fundamental principle. She peered into the trunk at the stacks of files. "How long has the lawsuit been going on?"

"It will be five years in September. Sounds like a long time, I know, but it went by so quickly. I'm just a little gnat, buzzing around, bothering a giant. A minor annoyance he keeps trying to bat away. But he can't, see? I won't give up . . . just on principle," he insisted.

Five years? That was a long time to pursue such a situation. Claire guessed it took a lot of thought and energy, too. Thought and energy that Nolan might have otherwise put toward new ideas and inventions. She hardly knew him well enough to say that straight out, though.

And he did have a point. If someone had really stolen his idea, he deserved to be compensated. He shouldn't have to walk away with nothing. But life isn't always fair; Claire knew that very well. *It's not our experience that shapes our destiny. It's the way we deal with it.* It sounded to Claire as if Nolan was . . .

a bit stuck. For a good reason, to be sure. But perhaps he was so caught up in the injustice that had been done to him that he'd lost sight of the big picture. His life was passing him by.

He picked up a file folder and opened it. "The wheels of justice grind slowly," he said.

"I've never been involved in a lawsuit," Claire admitted. "But I've heard that's true."

"Take my advice—steer clear if you're able." He sighed. "What can I do with all these papers? I suppose some of them will have to be thrown out now. But I do need to keep the important ones."

Claire considered the problem a moment. "We have a clothesline back behind the barn. You can hang them out there. It's such a fair day, they might dry in an hour or two."

"Excellent idea!" Nolan smiled with appreciation, making Claire feel very clever. "Where do I find the clothespins?"

"They're in a net bag on the line. There are more down in the laundry room." Claire headed for the basement, sure that Nolan would need all the clothespins she had . . . and then some. "I can help you. That will make it go faster."

"Would you? That would be a great help. I have to make sure I'm not throwing away anything important."

"Of course. You don't want to do that," Claire agreed.

She had some work to do today, but not a very heavy schedule, since the inn was still a day or so away from new guests arriving.

She was sure Liza would not mind it if she helped Nolan with this job. It would lighten the load in the big trunk, and they would be able to move it up to his room and out of sight before guests arrived. And Claire did feel sorry for him after hearing more of his story. He had gone through more than losing his boat or even losing his position at Carlisle. He had been sailing through rough waters for years now.

While Nolan examined the documents and sorted them into either a "dry out" basket or a "toss out" plastic bag, Claire carried the papers outside and carefully clipped them to a double-row clothesline that extended from the back of the barn to a large oak tree.

Nolan was tossing out a good part of the trunk's contents, but saving a great deal as well. Claire didn't mean to read the documents, but it was hard not to notice that many were copies of letters from Nolan to other parties involved: to the patent office, various attorneys and judges, and even to the Better Business Bureau.

Twenty minutes later, Claire was standing outside studying the clothesline and wondering where she would fit in any more papers if Nolan needed to save more, when he trotted out of the house with a few more pages in hand and Edison following close behind.

"This is the last of it, I promise. You've done a wonderful job out here. I could have never managed to get this all up so quickly . . . and carefully. I think a few of these might be dry already," he said, examining a few sheets at the start of the line.

"That would be a good thing. Then we'll have room for the rest." Claire took the wet papers from his hands and set them in her laundry basket. As Nolan removed a few dry sheets of paper, she hung up the wet ones.

"Tell me, Nolan. What does your attorney think about this lawsuit? Does he think it should be going on this long?"

"He claims he's working on this night and day, claims we're making progress. But there are always delays. Delays and delays. It could be settled soon, he tells me. He says that they're going to give in and present me with an offer, a good offer. Nothing to laugh at, like before," Nolan added with a scornful sniff. "Terms that won't insult me. By the end of the summer. Well, that's what my attorney tells me."

Claire was pleased to hear that the situation wasn't so grim. "There's a light at the end of the tunnel then, isn't there?"

"There is, if it comes through. I've gotten my hopes up before. Still, if my lawyer is right, I'll have some funds to set up a new lab and get back to work. That's the most important thing, getting back to work," he insisted heartily. "I've been so . . . distracted by this battle. It's used up all my energy. Drained me dry, like an old battery," he confessed.

"I can understand how that could happen." It was just as Claire suspected. "I bet you have a lot of wonderful new ideas once you turn away from this distraction. Maybe you should start on something new while you're waiting," she suggested mildly.

He had thought of one good idea, Claire reasoned. Surely he could think of others? He might already have more than one hidden in those tubes of mechanical drawings. Maybe Nolan couldn't see the valuable diamond in the rough right under his nose because he was so focused on what he had lost.

Nolan sighed and sat on a bench in the shade of the tree.

"It's not a matter of time, but of focus, of attention. It's very hard to do that sort of work when you're distracted and your mind is going every which way at once," he tried to explain. "Even with a lawyer representing my case, I still need to put a lot of time into it. Working on our strategy, keeping up with correspondence to the patent office and invention societies and . . . whatnot. It takes a lot of time, a lot of thought. Nobody's going to watch over my interests as well as I can. I've learned that the hard way."

Claire could not debate that point. Though she still thought her advice made sense. She knew that no one had an unlimited time on earth, and it seemed foolish to her to waste even a minute on anger and resentment and revenge.

Nolan got up off the bench and examined some of the documents that hung from the clothesline. He did have a lot of energy, Claire noticed; restless energy. He was not one to sit still for long.

Claire stepped back to admire her handiwork. The long rows of paper, drying in the sun, looked very pretty. "They look like flags, fluttering in the breeze," she said to Nolan.

He looked up from the sheet he was reading and took a wider view for a moment, too. "Yes, they do. But not white flags of surrender. Believe me, you'll never see me raise those colors."

Claire forced a smile, but didn't reply. His mind was made up. He would see this fight to the finish, no matter what it cost him.

Chapter Four

By Friday, when guests were due to arrive, the trunk had been carried up to Nolan's room and all the damp documents had thoroughly dried and been removed from the clothesline. Claire was relieved to see that.

Nolan was still at the inn, working on having his identification replaced and getting access to his bank accounts and credit cards. Not that he had a large amount of funds to fall back on, he had told Claire. He tried to take the wreck of the *Ariadne* in stride, but Claire could see that it undermined him. He did have the boat insured, however, and an insurance agent was coming out soon to assess the damage.

"It's not the best coverage one can buy, but I'll get something toward repairs—or toward just going forward in some fashion," he confided.

Claire knew Nolan would prefer to fix the boat and not turn it over to a boatyard for scrap. She hoped he would be able to do that. The project would give him a goal, a new direction—one he so sorely needed, in her estimation.

And how long would he stay at the inn? It had already been three nights. The weekend was not fully booked, and Liza had no objection to him staying longer. But Claire could tell that Nolan was getting restless and feeling he had already over-stayed his welcome. He was a proud man, not one who accepted help easily, and not one to take advantage of generosity.

Claire had overheard him a few times making calls to friends and casually mentioning his dilemma. Hinting around about needing a place to stay, ". . . just till things get sorted out." Claire wasn't sure exactly which situation he meant. His boat? His lawsuit? His lack of a job? Nolan had many situations to sort out, that was for sure.

On Friday morning he was in the kitchen, in the midst of another one of these calls, while Claire prepared dishes for the lunch that would be served to the incoming guests—clam chowder, lobster rolls, and homemade strawberry ice cream and butter cookies. She had already put up the chowder and was working on the lobster salad.

Nolan seemed to have a friend willing to let him stay. His tone sounded suddenly bright and excited. "Yes, I can come tomorrow. I'll take the train. I can get into Boston easily from here . . . That would be great. I can't tell you how much I appreciate . . ."

Claire didn't mean to eavesdrop, but he was talking right near her and not trying to keep his conversation private in any way.

"The dog? You mean Edison? Yes, he's still with me. He's a loyal old fellow. You should see him now, a little gray around the muzzle but still very spry . . . Oh, they don't? That's too bad."

Nolan's voice went from chipper and bright as he described Edison to suddenly downcast.

". . . Oh no. I'd never do that . . . No, there's no one who could mind him for all that time. I wouldn't even think of it. I couldn't leave him, Jack. He's just . . . Well, Edison and I are a package deal," he added with a forced laugh. "Thanks for the offer. I'll keep in touch. You enjoy your sabbatical . . ."

Nolan hung up and let out a long, sad sigh. Claire couldn't help but turn to him. "Bad news?" she asked.

"A friend offered to let me house-sit his apartment while he's traveling for a few months. Perfect, right? But I can't bring Edison. So it's out of the question."

"I see . . . Too bad it didn't work out." Claire wondered if she should offer to watch Edison. The dog seemed happy at the inn and seemed to like her. She would have to ask Liza first. But it seemed that even if Liza agreed, Nolan would not want to leave the dog. She'd discerned that much from his side of the conversation.

Before she could say another word, Liza came up from the basement and burst into the kitchen. "The hot water heater has gone berserk! It's spewing out steam and water all over the place. It looks like it might explode!"

"Oh dear . . . That's awful. Did you call Daniel?"

"He's in Boston. I tried a plumber in Cape Light, but he's not picking up." Liza held her cell phone in one hand and began scanning the tiny screen. "I guess I could try another . . ."

Daniel was in the city for the day without Liza? That was unusual. But Claire didn't have time to ask any questions.

Nolan jumped up from his seat. "Let me take a look. I might be able to help."

Liza did not look entirely comforted by the offer. "Do you know anything about hot water heaters, Nolan?"

"Oh, I can tame most mechanical things. It's just a knack I have. They call me the . . . the Hot Water Heater Whisperer," he joked.

"Okay, then. Give it a try. What do we have to lose?" Liza led the way downstairs to the furnace room. Claire went into the mudroom and grabbed the toolbox. She brought it down to them, along with a flashlight. The hot water heater was indeed on a rampage. Claire blinked at the spraying water, then left the tools and flashlight with Nolan and returned to her cooking. She did have a feeling Nolan could fix this little glitch in the machinery—just by the way he stared at it with such an intrigued expression.

It would be good for him if he was successful. He had been so eager to help the last few days, to do any job that he saw needed doing, from folding linens to watering the garden or taking out the trash. Claire had joked with him, saying she wondered if he was trying to steal her job away. But Nolan insisted that he wanted to make himself useful; he was so grateful to Liza for putting him up the last few days. Fixing a hot water heater would be proving himself very useful. And it would be a big savings for Liza.

Claire was simmering the strawberry mixture that would be cooled and blended with cream in the ice-cream maker when Liza ran back up the stairs.

"Did he fix it?" Claire peered at her over her reading glasses.

"He's getting there. He knew what was wrong with it right away, and the darn thing doesn't sound like it's going to explode anymore." Liza smiled with surprise. "He sent me up for some wire, duct tape, and rags for a temporary fix. He thinks he can get the part that needs replacing at most any plumbing supply house, and knows how to install it, too. There's a plumbing place right in Cape Light, I think."

"That's a relief. It's fortunate Nolan was around today."

"Yes, very lucky." Liza glanced at her watch. "By the time our guests want to shower before dinner—all at once, of course—we should have plenty of hot water again."

"A weekend at the shore without hot showers would not be very enjoyable—or encourage good reviews." Claire turned off the burner under the melted strawberries and set the pot to the side to cool.

"I would hate fielding that complaint." Liza had gathered the items Nolan needed from the mudroom, and now she ran back downstairs.

A few minutes later, Nolan emerged, with Liza following close behind. Claire could see he'd been working hard. A sheen of sweat covered his face, and his T-shirt and even his cheek were smeared with grease. But a victorious expression lit his face.

"Just a bad valve. I had a feeling." He held up the offending part.

"The plumbing supply place is just outside the village. You can take my car. I'll write down the directions." Liza started scribbling on a pad. "We have an account there, so you can just charge it."

"I'd better call first, see if they have the part. They might need to order it, or we can try somewhere else."

"Good point. Here's their phone number. You'd better call. I have no idea what to ask for. And if you need to look for another place, you can use my computer. It's right on the kitchen table."

Nolan took the slip of paper with the phone number. "Will do."

"Will the heater keep working if you can't find the part today?" Liza asked. Claire noticed a hint of apprehension in her tone.

"The patch will hold, no worries," Nolan promised. "You could put off a new valve for a few weeks, though I wouldn't recommend it."

"I wouldn't dream of that," Liza said, sounding relieved. She smiled again at Nolan. "I can't tell you how much I appreciate you jumping in to fix this. You really saved the day."

"It was nothing at all. It's the least I can do for you after all you've done for me these past few days."

"Really, Nolan," Liza said. "A plumber would have charged me a small fortune for what you just did. I want to pay you something for the work. Please?"

Nolan shook his head, his long gray hair flopping out of place. "Thank you, Liza, but I won't hear of it. You've been too kind. As I said before, it's the least I can do." He seemed suddenly self-conscious, and ducked his head again. "If you ladies will excuse me, I'm going to wash up before I make these calls."

After they heard Nolan go upstairs, Liza turned to Claire. "I wish he would take some payment. He saved me a fortune, and he can certainly use the money."

"Nolan has a lot of pride. And you've done a lot for him, letting him stay here," Claire reminded her.

Liza shrugged. "That's no big deal. I'll think of some way to repay the favor, sooner or later."

"I'm sure you will," Claire said sincerely. Liza had such a good heart. If someone did her a good turn, she never forgot, and always repaid it a hundredfold.

"How is lunch coming? The Millers should be here soon." Liza checked her watch. The little emergency hadn't taken that long, but enough to fall behind a bit in their schedule.

Liza had prepared for guests hundreds of times by now, maybe even thousands, Claire reflected. But there was still a certain edge of excitement before their arrival—and a certain tension, too.

"All the food is ready, and the table is set out back. I was just going to give the rooms a final check," Claire added as she took her apron off. "I cut some nice hydrangeas this morning. I'll arrange them and bring them up in a minute."

"Great. Room number three needs more towels. I'll grab a few from the laundry room."

Liza hurried off in one direction and Claire in another, each of them looking forward to having the inn once more filled with guests.

LIZA was busy taking care of her guests for the rest of the day—two older couples and a young family with a five-year-old girl. But her thoughts did drift toward Daniel, even in the midst of her duties. She wondered how he was doing on his quest to research reentry into medicine. She wondered what answers he had found and if this entire idea was even possible.

She certainly hoped he had not been discouraged, and felt almost breathless with anticipation when she finally saw his truck pull in the drive later that evening. It was almost nine. Dinner had been served and cleared hours ago, and most of the guests had dispersed, taking walks on the beach or a drive into Cape Light.

Liza stood on the porch, watching as he jumped out of the truck. She squinted in the dim light. The sun was just going down behind the ocean, painting the horizon with brilliant hues of purple and rose and gold.

But Liza was totally focused on Daniel. She would know the entire story of his day in one instant—the moment she saw his face and his gaze met hers. She would know if this was going to work out—or not.

Daniel walked toward her slowly and raised one hand in greeting.

Was he smiling? It was hard to say. He wasn't frowning; that was a good sign. She met his gaze and held it. And she could tell, just from the way he held her gaze and didn't look away.

She let out a long breath that she didn't even realize she'd been holding.

He had worn a dark blue suit today, with a white dress shirt and a red silk tie. Liza could count on one hand the number of times she had seen Daniel in a suit. His tie was already unknotted, hanging loose, and his jacket was off, but he still looked incredibly handsome.

He walked up the steps and kissed her. Liza kissed him

back and then tilted her head back. "Excuse me . . . have we met? You really remind me of somebody . . ."

Daniel laughed. "Cute. Did the suit and tie throw you off? Is that what you're saying?"

She looked at him a moment and snapped her fingers. "That's it. Not bad. I could get used to this," she added with a nod of approval. "Though I love you in jeans and sweatshirts just as well."

"Good to know." Daniel still had his arms around her waist, and he leaned back and gazed at her. "Do you really want to talk about my wardrobe?"

"Not really," she said honestly. "How did it go? Did you find out what you wanted to know?"

"I have good news and bad." Daniel put his arm around her shoulder, and they walked over to the porch swing and sat down together. "I didn't let my license expire, which is very important. Working at the clinic all these years, and as an EMT, helps, too. It shows direct contact with patients, and that makes it easier to return."

"That sounds great. What else do you need to do?"

"Well . . . a lot. I haven't kept up with board certification. I couldn't just go back into ER work. But I don't necessarily want to. I could practice as a GP after taking some courses and exams. I would have to be interviewed by a board . . . and I'd need to be totally transparent about the reason I left in the first place," he said finally. Now his expression and tone did darken, just as the sun dropped below the horizon.

Liza didn't answer right away. "Of course you'd be honest

about that. There's nothing to hide. The hospital reviewed the case and never sanctioned you."

"Yes, I know. And there are certainly physicians who have messed up far worse and kept practicing. Not that I'm saying that's ideal."

She knew what he was saying. Maybe he was finally coming around to see that he'd been too hard on himself.

"It's a lot to think about. At least you have all the information now, and you can just take your time to figure it out."

He glanced at her. "I have been thinking about it, the whole time I was driving home. And the adviser I spoke to was very encouraging," he added. "The thing is, all the tests I need to take are offered this summer—and they won't be offered again for almost a year. So he advised that if I wanted to recertify, I should get on the ball and go for it. I might not pass the exams the first time."

Liza was surprised by his answer. Things were suddenly moving quickly, but that was good, wasn't it? She wanted to see Daniel happy, using all the amazing talents and gifts he had been blessed with.

"I think that's good advice," she said. "You seem excited by the idea. Waiting and putting it off might dampen your enthusiasm."

"I was thinking the same thing," he agreed. "Why put it off? I've already lost over six years. I'm not getting any younger."

"So what do you do next?"

"Besides fill out a pile of forms? I have to sign up for some courses, and take some tough exams when they're done. They're given this summer, starting July eighth. The exams are in the middle of August."

"July eighth? That's not very long from now—a little over a week."

"Yes, I know. If I want to do this, I have to register online by Monday."

"Can you take the classes online, too?"

Daniel shook his head. "No, I have to be in Boston for those, and honestly, I'm wondering how I'll have enough time to take the courses and study and work, too. From what the adviser told me, they're going to be intense."

"You'll just have to put your work on hold for a few weeks. Do you have a lot of jobs lined up between now and the middle of August?"

"Only two so far. I could pass those off to Sam Morgan," he added, mentioning a well-known carpenter in Cape Light. "He's got a big crew working for him now, and my clients probably wouldn't mind."

"That's a good idea. So you've cleared the decks. That wasn't so hard," she pointed out.

"No, but . . . it did feel strange to be back in the city. I went over to Mass General to ask for copies of some records of my time there. It felt so . . . odd to be in a hospital again; thinking of myself as a doctor again, I mean."

Liza smiled. "That's not surprising. You've been out of that environment a long time. But you don't have to practice in a big hospital again, Daniel. Or even in Boston."

Though he actually could, since the city wasn't that far. But that might mean he would be away from the island a few days a week, Liza realized with a pang. For a brief, selfish moment, she couldn't help hoping it wouldn't come to that.

As if reading her thoughts, Daniel said, "No, I wouldn't want to practice in the city again. I'm sure of that. I've had enough of Boston, even if I can get my certification back."

"Of course you'll get it back," Liza said, feeling a surge of relief. "One step at a time. You made the most important one today. You got all the information, and now you know it's possible and what you have to do."

"I think I want to try," Daniel said quietly. "It's just all coming up so fast. And money—I have some savings, but this is my prime season for work. It will be hard not to work at all."

"Oh, if that's all you're worried about, you can eat here—or rent your cottage for the summer and stay here, too."

Daniel laughed. "You keep giving the rooms away to strays, Liza. You have to save a few for paying guests."

"Don't worry; there are more than enough."

"I might take you up on that. Though you might have me taking care of that repair list during my study breaks."

"No way. I'm not going to give you any excuses to skip your homework. I'll just have to find ten handymen to take your place, that's all." Liza knew how spoiled she was by Daniel's ability to fix just about anything that went wrong at the inn. And in the grand old Victorian building, there was always something in need of repair.

"Oh, guess what?" she said. "The hot water heater broke down today, and Nolan fixed it. Isn't that great? He picked up a new part in Cape Light and has already installed it."

Daniel didn't seem surprised. "He's a very smart guy. I

expect he understands how most mechanical things work—and knows how to fix them when they don't."

"I really wanted to pay him something, but he wouldn't take it. He says he feels better earning his way at least a little bit. Isn't that sweet of him?"

"It's more than sweet . . . I think you've found my replacement around here already."

Liza felt a spark of encouragement at his reply. "Do I really need a replacement? I thought you were going to think it over for the weekend."

Daniel let out a long sigh, but he was smiling. "What does Claire always say? 'A task begun is half done'? I started this today, and I admit, I'm afraid to go back to classes and studying and tests. But I'm more afraid that if I put it off, I won't do it at all. So might as well just jump in the deep end."

"You need to go for it," Liza agreed, "even if it has come upon you in a rush. But sometimes things just happen that way." She felt a genuine happiness for Daniel. "I'll tell you something else Claire always says: 'If you take the first step in faith, God will be there to help you the rest of the way.'"

"I thought about that, too," Daniel admitted. "I do have a gut feeling this is the right thing for me to do, to at least give it try. So I don't look back and have any regrets. So why wait until Sunday to decide? I'm going to register for classes tonight."

"Excellent decision," Liza said approvingly. "Because waiting the whole weekend to see what you'd say was going to kill me. I could hardly wait the few hours for you to get back from Boston."

Daniel laughed at her and hugged her close. "It's easy to jump into the ring when I have you in my corner."

Liza smiled softly at him. "No worries; I'll always be there."

Daniel kissed her quickly, and Liza sighed. She rested her head on his shoulder. He'd made a big decision tonight. Her own head was spinning. But it felt good. She knew something good would come of this.

"Now that you've officially given up your post of resident handyman," she said finally, "do you think I should offer Nolan the job?"

"I think he'd be perfect."

"I do, too. But I wonder if he'll stay. Our first wave of guests will hit on July Fourth weekend. I'm going to need someone for the whole summer. Do you think Nolan will stay that long?"

"He needs to fix his boat. It's much easier for him to work on it here than to move it up to Maine or into Boston," Daniel reminded her. "I already told him I'm going to loan him some tools and put him together with Harry Reilly," Daniel said, mentioning a friend who owned a boatyard. "Harry can help him get some materials for a good price. Nolan was happy to hear that."

"I bet he was. I think I will offer him the job. But first I need to talk to Claire. Can I tell her why you won't be working here this summer?"

"I don't want to broadcast it yet. But sure, you can tell Claire. She already knows I was once a doctor, though I didn't tell her why I gave it up."

Knowing Claire, she had not pried or judged him, Liza

thought. "Well, she's going to be curious when I mention hiring Nolan. She's the one who will have to work with him most closely, and even supervise him some of the time."

"I doubt she'll object. Nolan and Claire get along pretty well. He's a physicist and she's a housekeeper and cook . . . but I hear them talking about everything from gardening to quantum theory."

Liza laughed. "I noticed that, too. They both have a very simple, straightforward way of looking at the world. I think that helps. They do disagree about spiritual matters, like the other night at the dinner table," she reminded him. "But it's not really arguing. I think they enjoy those debates, too."

"Oh, I think they enjoy those conversations the most. I don't think either of them will mind working together this summer at all."

Liza thought that was true. She would tell Claire her idea tomorrow morning and, hopefully, offer Nolan the job tomorrow, too.

CLAIRE was much in favor of the idea of hiring Nolan. "I know we need an extra hand around here in the busy season. But doing repairs, too? What about Daniel? Is he going away for some big project again?"

Daniel had been up in Maine for most of the summer last year, helping to build a summerhouse for a friend of his. Liza wasn't sure she should tell Claire about Daniel's decision to return to medicine.

But it was hard not to confide in Claire, who had become

one of her closest friends—practically family—these past years. And she knew Claire loved Daniel, too, and would be excited for him.

"You know that Daniel used to be a doctor, before he came to live here," Liza began.

Claire nodded. "Yes, I do. He told me a long time ago, before you came to the island."

"Well, he's decided that he wants to go back to medicine, and he found out what he needs to do. That's why he went into the city yesterday. He had to visit the medical board and some other places."

"He did? Oh, that's wonderful news. I'm so happy for him . . . for both of you," she added.

Liza offered a hopeful smile in return. "It's not an easy road. He needs to take some heavy courses and study for the next month and a half. He's going to take the summer off from work and give it his full attention . . . and he'd rather not let everyone know right now," she added. "I think he needs to start the courses and see if it's really going to work out for him."

"I understand completely." Claire nodded. "Thank you for confiding in me. But I won't say a word about it."

Liza trusted Claire to be discreet, though she could tell from her expression that Claire's thoughts were already leaping ahead, wondering what this development meant for Liza and Daniel as a couple.

The truth was, Liza didn't really know. Though deep inside, she felt something was changing, moving forward. Not just for Daniel, but for both of them.

Chapter Five

CLAIRE dropped Nolan off at Reilly's Boatyard on Sunday morning on her way to church. "The service ends around eleven. I'll come back and pick you up. Or you can walk up to the village green and wait for me there," she suggested. "The park is shady and has a nice view."

Claire had pointed out a few sights on their way, including the church and the green. Nolan had been with them almost a week and hadn't seen much of Cape Light, except for the plumbing supply shop.

"I showed you the green, remember? Just backtrack along this street that runs along the water. You can't miss it."

"We'll find each other, don't worry." Nolan smiled as he jumped out of the Jeep. "Thanks for the lift. See you later."

He was a happy man this morning, Claire noted as she drove away. Quite a different man than the one they had pulled out of the sea last Monday.

He had been surprised by Liza's job offer yesterday, but had accepted immediately. Liza and Claire had both wondered if he might think the position demeaning and a blow to his dignity. After all, he held advanced degrees in engineering and physics, and his usual job descriptions were college professor and inventor. He was clearly overqualified to unstuff the drains at the inn or tote luggage up and down the stairs.

But it didn't appear that such an objection had crossed Nolan's mind. He was eager to repair the *Ariadne*, and working at the inn gave him both the means and the perfect place to accomplish that. Daniel had put him in touch with a boatyard that could supply materials at bargain prices, so Nolan was the happiest man in town this morning, Claire guessed. He deserved a break or two. She'd been praying for him, and would continue to.

A short time later, she sat in a rear pew of the old stone church and listened to Reverend Ben's sermon. He was talking about the same Scripture she had quoted to Nolan on his first night at the inn: *Be not forgetful to entertain strangers: for thereby some have entertained angels unawares.*

Quite a coincidence, Claire thought. Though the truth was, there were no coincidences, not really. The verses of Scripture offered a wonderful lesson, worth remembering every day, in every encounter.

"The Gospel urges us to see one another the way that God sees us," Reverend Ben explained. "Everyone we meet, kin, friend, and stranger, are of equal worth, equal value—regardless of their outward appearance. We are all God's children, perfect in His sight. And everyone is deserving of respect, and of a helping hand if they were to appear, unexpected and uninvited, at our door . . ."

Someone had come in late and sat down right next to her. Claire was focused on the sermon and hardly noticed. But when she heard a polite throat-clearing, she turned her head.

Nolan met her glance and offered a small smile. Then he opened his bulletin and glanced at the pages with curiosity, as if he were visiting some distant, exotic culture—or making observations for an experiment.

As Reverend Ben concluded and left the pulpit, the choir began to sing the anthem. Claire leaned over to Nolan. "I thought you were going to wait in the park."

"You seem quite devoted. It got me curious. Thought I'd see what goes on here," he whispered back.

Claire noticed people looking at them; church friends she knew well. Had they overheard the conversation? Well, what if they had? She would have to field some questions—or avoid them.

Claire rarely came to church with anyone. Certainly not a friend like Nolan.

She felt her cheeks grow red, though she wasn't sure why she felt so flustered. The big, lazy ceiling fan offered some breeze, but was not really up to the job of cooling the sanctuary on a hot summer day, and she fanned herself with her church bulletin.

Nolan sat attentively for the rest of the service, even rising to sing the hymns. He had a good voice, she noticed, deep and strong; though he did not recite the prayer responses, which Claire thought was perfectly appropriate, all things considered.

When the service was over, Claire assumed they would slip out the side door and avoid the congregants waiting to chat with Reverend Ben. But Nolan had other ideas and steered her toward the line.

"I'd like to meet your minister. Is there some reason you would rather not introduce me?"

"Of course not. I didn't think you'd be interested," she replied honestly.

"I liked his sermon, what I heard of it. I haven't been inside a church in years. Might as well get the full treatment, right?"

Claire didn't know how to answer. His remark sounded a bit flip, but she didn't think Nolan meant any offense. "If you like, we'll wait to meet him."

As they took a place in line, Vera Plante, an old friend of Claire's, walked over to greet her. Vera was a retired school-teacher who took in boarders at her big house in the village. Claire could tell she was curious about Nolan, and hoped she didn't ask too many questions.

Claire wasn't sure if Nolan would feel comfortable talking about his boating accident and being rescued by Daniel in the storm. In fact, she had a feeling he wouldn't like that at all. There was no time to ask him, so she decided not to mention it.

"Morning, Claire. Have you brought a friend to church today?"

Claire forced a smile. She was going to be the talk of coffee hour whether she liked it or not. "This is Nolan Porter, Vera. He's working at the inn this summer. He was interested in visiting our church." *He was interested in observing the activity from a scientific point of view* would have been a more accurate report, but that would have sounded a little clinical, Claire decided.

Nolan politely extended his hand. "It's a pleasure to meet you."

"Thank you, same here," the older woman said with a smile. "Well, I hope you enjoyed the service and hope you two have a lovely day. Do something fun and enjoy this beautiful weather—a real treat after all the rain last week."

Claire's eyebrows jumped a notch, but she tried not to show much reaction. Vera made it sound as if they were out on a date and the church service was the first stop.

"It is perfect weather. But we'll both be working at the inn. We have quite a few guests there this weekend."

"Yes, very busy at the inn," Nolan chimed in, though Claire could see that the way he said it made Vera think he was covering up something.

But before the conversation could be continued—and confused even further—it was time for Claire and Nolan to greet Reverend Ben.

"Good to see you, Claire." Reverend Ben greeted her with a smile and a brief hug.

"This is Nolan Porter, Reverend. He's just started working at the inn. He heard your sermon and wanted to meet you."

Reverend Ben turned to Nolan with a pleased expression. "How do you do, Nolan? Thanks for coming this morning."

"I was just curious," Nolan admitted. "I'm not a church-goer; never have been. But Claire seems to set a great store by her beliefs. I was interested to see what inspires her."

"Really?" Reverend Ben seemed surprised by that reply. "Did you figure it out?"

"Haven't had enough time to observe and consider the question, Reverend. But it is a fascinating one."

"It certainly is. When you've figured it out, please let me know," the reverend added in his typical offhand way.

"I will, sir. Nice to meet you."

"It was very nice to meet you, Nolan. Come observe us again, anytime," Reverend Ben replied sincerely. Then he met Claire's gaze again with a small smile and nodded a silent good-bye.

Thank You, God, for blessing me with a minister with a good sense of humor. And one who isn't so full of himself that he can't appreciate the way Your hand has crafted us each with lovely eccentricities that make us all interesting and unique.

Nolan was certainly unique in the way he viewed the world and acted in it. Claire had to admit that at times her first impulse was to judge him. She wondered now if he had been delivered into her life as some sort of lesson in learning how to restrain judgment and simply enjoy and appreciate a personality and perspective so different from her own. He was refreshing company, even if he had embarrassed her a bit this morning. *Though Vera's curious looks and assumptions are really not his fault,* she quickly reminded herself.

If they talked this week on the phone—and Claire was almost certain Vera would call—she would have to straighten out any misconceptions.

"It is a beautiful day, even if we do have to spend the better part of it working," Nolan said as they walked out of the church and onto the green.

"It doesn't seem fair sometimes," Claire admitted. "But you'll have plenty of time off. Just not on Saturdays and Sundays, like everyone else. You'll get used to it."

"I'm happy to be on any schedule at all. I find it a little disorienting to have my time so unstructured I can't even tell what day of the week it is. That's the way I felt out on the boat," he admitted. "A bit lost at sea. It's good to be back on solid ground and have honest work for my hands to do. How long have you been at the inn, Claire? You mentioned once that you worked there even before Liza came?"

Claire was surprised that he remembered. She had told him that the first day, when he was still in bed recovering from the near-drowning.

"I worked for Liza's aunt, Elizabeth Dunne," Claire explained as she and Nolan got into her Jeep and she started back to the island. "Elizabeth and her husband, Clive, opened the inn, oh, let's see . . . almost fifty years ago now. They were both artists who had come from the city to live on the island but also needed steady income. They did a fine job with the inn. But when Clive died and Elizabeth was running the place by herself, she needed some help. That's when I came on. Later when she got sick . . . well, I helped keep things running and helped her, too."

"You nursed her, you mean?"

Claire nodded. "She had a weak heart and caught pneumonia one winter. We thought she was getting better and brought her home from the hospital. But she could never quite shake it."

It was a difficult subject to talk about; it brought back so many memories, most of them happy, but some painful. Claire tried to lighten the conversation. "Elizabeth was a good artist; watercolors, mostly. Artistic talent seems to run in that family. Liza was a graphic artist and worked for an advertising agency before she moved out here. She still has many of her aunt's paintings hanging up in the rooms."

"I've noticed a few. I've noticed the signature. 'E. Dunne.'" Nolan nodded. "And what about you? Were you raised in New England?"

"Me? Whatever gives you that idea?" Claire asked innocently. When he laughed, she couldn't help laughing, too. "Yes, in New England. Right here on the island."

They had come to the land bridge. The gate was up, and they started to cross.

"Angel Island, really? That's amazing. It must have been an unusual childhood, growing up out here."

Claire shrugged. "I don't have anything to compare it with. So it seemed very normal to me."

Nolan laughed again. Claire was just being honest, but he seemed to enjoy her frankness.

"So you've never lived anywhere else? You've never traveled?"

"Oh, I've seen a bit of the world. I traveled through Europe in my twenties, and have been around many parts of the U.S. I lived in Boston for a year or two," she added, "working at a settlement house. It was very gratifying. But when my father took sick, there was no one else to take care of him, so I came back home. And here I am, still," she concluded. "What was it

Henry Thoreau said? 'I've traveled widely in Concord'? Well, I've traveled widely on Angel Island and in Cape Light. It's fine for me, for now."

"You seem satisfied with your life. That's worth more than gold," Nolan said as he gazed out the window.

The Jeep was skimming along the narrow road that connected the mainland with the island. Blue waves lapped at the piles of rocks on either side of the road, and seabirds swooped and dipped overhead.

"It's a beautiful place, as perfect as any on earth. I'm very blessed to live here. I give thanks every morning," she replied honestly.

Nolan glanced at her. "Then you're one of the few people I've ever met who are wise enough to know when they're content, myself not included. But I'm trying to do better," he added quietly.

"Tell me about yourself, Nolan. Were you raised in Maine?"

"Yes, up north, near Bar Harbor. I had a younger brother, but he died quite young. My mother never really recovered. She stayed at home and took care of me, was quite devoted . . . and protective, as you might imagine. My father was a science teacher. A great influence on me," he added. "He taught me to observe and appreciate the natural world. He built a little cabin on a lake for the family, and I helped him. It wasn't much, barely had indoor plumbing. But I loved our visits there. I could go out in the woods all day and collect insects and toads or lizards. I could fish, or just watch the fish. That water was so clear," he added in a wistful tone. "I would watch an anthill or the clouds passing for hours," he recalled. "While growing up,

I spent a lot of time alone, I guess. But nature was my companion, and a very entertaining one."

"That sounds like a perfect childhood," Claire said. "Apart from being an only child, I mean. When did you decide that you wanted to be a scientist and an inventor?"

"Oh, I was always interested in how things worked. How a kite could stay up in the air or why you hear a sound if you put your ear to a seashell. I was always making little gadgets from odds and ends I'd find . . . or pilfer. Most of them didn't work, but I had some good ideas. I once took the engine of my father's car apart," he recalled. "He was furious, of course. But I was able to put it back together, and it ran even better than before. Soon he started bragging to all his friends about my mechanical abilities," Nolan said with a laugh. "My father was very proud of my accomplishments. Though I wish he'd lived to see me create some truly great invention."

"I'm sure he's still watching over you and cheering you on."

Nolan turned to her. "I don't know what happens when we die. Most of the time, I don't believe anything does. I don't believe in a soul, some gauzy little shadow that floats out of your body when you take your last breath . . . I don't believe in an afterlife, either. But it is nice to think about what you've just said. Even though I know it isn't true."

"But you're still curious about church and what goes on there," she pointed out, recalling his surprising appearance beside her in the pew.

Nolan shrugged and grinned. She could tell she had cornered him.

"I suppose I am. I was today anyway." He turned to her a

moment, then looked out the window again. "Perhaps nearly drowning last week persuaded me to hedge my bets? I didn't think a few prayers could hurt, no matter what's really up there," he added, glancing at the blue sky outside the window. "You know what they say about soldiers on a battlefield: 'There are no atheists in foxholes.'"

Claire had to laugh at his rebuttal. "Well, do the research and keep an open mind. You might discover something that you missed the first time around."

They had arrived at the inn. A few of the guests lingered on the porch, reading the newspaper. Claire noticed Liza watering the flowers, and Daniel sitting out there as well. Claire drove her Jeep to the back of the property and parked near the barn.

"I like to park back here, so my Jeep won't be in the way of any of the guests going in and out," she explained. "I also prefer to come and go through the kitchen, so I can avoid folks who keep stopping me to ask about the day's menu."

Nolan laughed. "I don't blame them. I told Liza a major benefit of my new job is your cooking. I just hope I have enough outdoor work to burn off the calories."

"We'll keep you busy. This weekend is fairly slow in comparison with what's to come. Next weekend, July Fourth, that's the real test."

Nolan shrugged. "Don't worry, I'll be up to it."

She could tell he didn't believe her. It really was four days that could feel like four weeks. Especially if the guests were demanding or they hit little unpredictable snags or—heaven forbid—bad weather.

As they got out of the Jeep and headed toward the kitchen, Claire noticed Nolan looking back wistfully at the barn. She guessed he was thinking of his boat. But he couldn't visit the *Ariadne* until he had at least finished his morning tasks, like mowing the lawn and cleaning off the patio.

"How did it go at the boatyard? I forgot to ask," she said as they walked toward the back door.

"I've ordered some supplies that I need. Daniel's friend Harry Reilly is giving me a good price. He's going to call when everything is ready to be picked up."

"You know your way now. You're welcome to take my Jeep any time you need it. I bet you're eager to get started."

"I am, once I have some free time from my new job," he added quickly. "I think I can work on the boat at night if I rig up some strong shop lights."

"Liza probably won't mind some better lights in the barn," Claire replied—though she doubted the inn's owner would encourage sanding machines and power drills running after dark. The guests would certainly complain about that.

But Claire didn't want to dampen his enthusiasm. It was good to see Nolan looking ahead.

"So, what's on the schedule for today?" Nolan rubbed his hands together.

Claire opened the back door and entered the kitchen, and Nolan followed. "Some lunch to start. Then I'll give you a list of chores."

"I'm at your service, ma'am," he replied.

"I hope you're this cheerful a week from now. You're start-ing off on one of our biggest weeks of the season," she warned him. "It will be like trying to ride the Tour de France when you're just getting training wheels off."

Nolan laughed at the comparison. "I thrive on a challenge. Now, how can I help with lunch? You don't need to wait on me hand and foot. In fact, I'd prefer it if you would stop treating me like a guest. I have two hands and two legs, and I also know how to cook."

Claire laughed at his complaint, though it pleased her as well. It was a refreshing attitude. She had rarely met a man who didn't expect to be waited upon, guest or otherwise.

"I'm not sure this kitchen is big enough for two cooks," she answered quickly as she gathered some food from the refrigerator. "But I will appreciate the helping hands—and feet—in all other ways. Here's some cold chicken. There are garden tomatoes in the blue bowl on the counter. I can make some sandwiches if you like."

"I would like that. But why don't I make the sandwiches?"

Claire was tying her apron, and stopped short. It took her a moment to process his suggestion. But why not? It seemed as if it would make him happy . . . and he'd already started. After washing his hands, he had begun slicing a tomato on a cutting board.

"I'd like mine with some lettuce, please," she told him as she took out a head of lettuce and a pitcher of iced tea. "And a dab of mayo and Dijon mustard."

"Will do. I wouldn't mind some of that potato salad from yesterday, if there's any left over."

"Oh yes, plenty. I'll take some out for you."

A few moments later, everything was set out, and Nolan

served the sandwiches while Claire sat, politely waiting. It was a distinctly different feeling; she felt a little uneasy at first, but she realized she didn't mind it a bit.

"How is it?" he asked after her first bite.

"Very good," she said sincerely. He did know his way around a kitchen, enough to make a very tasty sandwich, though her enjoyment at being waited on did improve the flavor.

After the meal, Nolan cleaned up the kitchen while Claire explained and wrote out a list of his assignments for the day. As he headed off to mow the lawn, Claire hoped that his positive attitude and energy would hold up over the week ahead.

If he's half as chipper next Sunday, we'll be okay, she decided.

By Monday afternoon, all the weekend guests were gone. Liza, Claire, and Nolan were free to prepare for the big rush, but barely had forty-eight hours to do so. Fourth of July fell on Thursday this year, and guests would start arriving on Wednesday afternoon and stay through the weekend.

Just about all of the rooms were booked, and the trio rushed to get everything done—cleaning, shopping, and washing. Making beds and arranging the bedrooms and common rooms in the most inviting way, with dishes of special soaps and fresh flowers, appealing magazines, games, and other amusements. Plus plenty of maps and brochures for sightseeing and menus of local restaurants.

Even the empty rooms on the third floor would be occupied. This was the floor where Claire stayed when she didn't go home to her own cottage and where Nolan had been moved to a small, cozy room at the opposite end of the hall from Claire's.

Liza and Claire always prepared the menus well in advance so Claire could get a jump start on baking and prepping dishes—as much as she could without compromising her exceptionally high standards. That part was difficult; she still liked to make everything right before it was served and didn't believe in freezing and reheating. There were many reasons guests returned to the inn year after year, and everyone knew that one of them was Claire's cooking.

Nolan's spirits and energy held up well for the preamble, she noticed. When guests began to arrive on Wednesday, he greeted them with a jovial manner and quickly helped them with their bags. Claire often overheard him engaged in conversation with their visitors while he watered the porch flowers or helped serve a meal. She could tell that his quirky personality and colorful stories charmed the guests, even if he often talked to himself as well, especially when he was trying to work out some new idea in his head. But with Edison always at his master's heels, this little quirk was easily masked.

"But what if the base was doubled, Edison? Then it would easily support the weight. With a larger diameter on the wheels, of course," Nolan might say.

Edison, in his wise, dignified way, always looked as if he were considering these suggestions very thoughtfully . . . and agreeing, of course. The big brown dog was also a hit with the guests, and Claire had no doubt that Edison would be the official inn mascot before the summer was out.

But while Edison seemed to know instinctively that the

customer was always right, Nolan was sometimes too blunt with his opinions. Nolan being Nolan, however, he hardly noticed when guests bristled. "Yes, your room is three flights up. But you can certainly use the exercise," Claire had overheard him say to a somewhat portly guest one day.

Or when a couple came down very late for breakfast and were annoyed that the buffet had been cleared: "Isn't the clock in your room working? It's nearly time for lunch."

Claire chalked up this overly honest trait to his scientific perspective, which filtered out most everything but the facts. Nolan often saw social niceties as a time-wasting nuisance, a needless inefficiency. She wasn't sure if any guests had complained, but hoped Liza would give him a pass on that, especially since he was very amenable to the requests of the guests and didn't seem to feel belittled at all by providing service. Yet he could be quite forgetful, setting out to fix a leaky faucet or stuffed drain and getting distracted by the articles in the newspaper he'd spread out to keep the floor clean. Or he might deliver luggage to the wrong room because he'd stopped in the hallway to jot down an idea on one of the many index cards that he stuffed in his shirt and pants pockets. One visitor actually drove off with the wrong set of luggage after one of Nolan's lapses, but fortunately discovered the mix-up in time and quickly backtracked. Nolan felt quite contrite and explained to Liza he had been lost in thought, trying to figure out how he could rig a rope-and-pulley system off the back of the building to lower and raise bags very quickly and with far less effort.

Claire skipped church on Sunday. She was far too busy

preparing for and serving breakfast to their throng of guests. She wondered if Nolan noticed or had given any thought to returning to church. If he had, he didn't mention it.

By Monday night, the inn was quiet again, and vacant except for the intrepid trio. Claire fixed a light dinner from an array of leftover foods, and they sat together in the kitchen, recapping their efforts.

"You did very well overall, Nolan, especially with those unexpected repairs," Liza said. "Though there are a few areas you could work on—dealing with the guests, mainly."

"I suppose you mean I could have a better bedside manner. Nice talk has never been my strong suit."

Claire had to hide a smile. Nolan was pleasant and polite enough with her and Liza, but he wasn't the type who could suffer fools gladly, and, well . . . for better or worse . . . some of the guests could get under one's skin. If you let them.

"I have a little book upstairs, *The Innkeeper's Companion*, or something like that. It covers all those sticky situations dealing with guests, when you need to draw on your patience," Claire explained. Of course Claire knew that most of Nolan's faux pas had not arisen from sticky situations but mainly from his own blunt way of speaking. But at least he might read the book and get the idea of how to soften his style. "I can loan it to you if you like, Nolan."

"I'd appreciate that, Claire. I'm sure I can get up to speed on this innkeeper-speak quickly."

Liza smiled. "A book on the topic is a great idea, Nolan. You can just flip through whenever you get a chance. Do you have any questions at all for me?"

Nolan thought a moment. "Just one. Now that all the visitors are gone, I'd like to get started on my boat. I hope it's all right with you if I work in the barn at night—if I don't make too much noise."

Claire was not surprised by the request, though she was surprised that Nolan had a drop of energy left after the pace they had kept the last few days. She was exhausted. A cup of tea then up to bed with a good book and her knitting was her plan for the rest of the evening.

She and Nolan had gotten into the habit of spending time together in the evening, playing Scrabble and even chess. She usually beat him handily at the former and held her own at the latter. Sometimes they just sat together out on the porch, reading. Nolan even had a special system for brewing tea and liked to prepare the pot for them. Again, it was an unusual switch of roles for Claire, but she liked his tea almost better than her own. And she had to admit, it felt nice to be served at the end of a long, hard day.

But tonight it was best if Nolan went out to his boat and she went up to her room. It had been Daniel's first day of classes, and he would be home late from the city, so Claire also thought it best to give the couple some time alone. They had hardly seen each other over the long weekend.

"Why don't you go out and work on it right now, Nolan? While it's still light?" Liza suggested. "Oh, but don't forget the trash. All the recyclables need to be sorted before it goes out on the road—or we'll get fined."

Claire could see that Liza was reluctant to remind him of this one last task for the day and deter him from the *Ariadne*. It took time to sort out the trash and get it out in proper order—precious time he would want for working on his boat.

But Nolan sprang up from his chair with a cheerful grin. "Already taken care of that. I rigged up a little system with some plastic piping to sort things quickly, and the newspapers have their own chute. They just need to be tied. It's all set up on some planks that I nailed together. I attached them to an old bike, with one wheel in front and the pedal part in the back, so I can get it down to the road quickly. Just some odds and ends I found around the barn. I hope you don't mind that I used them," he added quickly.

"Um, no, I don't mind." Liza's brow knit together as she tried to picture this trash-sorting-conveyance contraption. Claire's did, too. She had heard hammering and whistling out in the barn a few days ago, but she thought Nolan had just stolen a few minutes to work on his boat. She didn't realize he was inventing something.

"I'd be very interested to see that," Liza said.

"So would I," Claire added.

"I'll be riding it down to the road in a minute. The first official run, though I have tested it once or twice."

He tested this contraption? Claire wondered how she had missed it.

"Take a peek out the window," he suggested as he picked up his dish and brought it to the sink. "And thanks for another fine dinner, Claire. A bit of a hodgepodge," he admitted. "But delicious as always."

It had been a hodgepodge with all the leftovers, that much was true. Though most people wouldn't have mentioned that, you could count on Nolan to be honest. Claire appreciated that about him, too.

Liza and Claire began to clear the table and soon heard a loud rattling sound coming from the back of the house. They ran out the back door just in time to see Nolan riding his trash-sorter. It was a strange, ungainly-looking vehicle: a wooden platform, attached to bike wheels at the two rear corners, with half a bicycle—he'd somehow sawed off the back—attached to the front. Nolan was pedaling for all he was worth, propelling the platform along. The platform held several large plastic barrels, which were attached to long chutes made of flexible plastic pipe, the type Claire had noticed at the back of the clothes dryer, but a bit wider. The chutes swirled up to a board on the far side of the vehicle that had large round holes. Each hole was labeled—glass, clear plastic, opaque plastic, tin foil, cans, food waste, and so on . . . all the different categories of trash-sorting the township required. There was some other sort of contraption at the rear of the platform, as well, with a large spool of hemp twine attached to a modified plastic milk crate that caught and piled old newspapers in a tidy, even stack. Bunches of newspaper were also on the platform, neatly packed and tied.

As Nolan pedaled past, he lifted his hand and waved. "Evening, ladies. Just delivering this load to the roadside. Be right back."

Claire waved back, smiling. "I wish I had a camera," she murmured. "I've never seen anything like that."

"No one has," Liza said, struggling to hold back her laughter. "It looks a little shaky to me. I hope it doesn't fall apart midway down the drive . . . Oh, I wish Daniel were here. He wouldn't believe this."

"I think it looks quite solid," Claire said. "And it does the job nicely."

Before they could say more, Nolan appeared again, pedaling back up toward the barn. He stopped, smiling proudly. "So, what do you think? I must have saved at least an hour of labor tonight. Not to mention time I would have spent sorting during the week without that chute system and newspaper piler."

"It's . . . remarkable," Liza said sincerely. "I'm very impressed."

"So am I, Nolan," Claire added. "You've saved a good deal of time to work on your boat, that's for sure."

"And I'm going to get right to it. Good night, ladies. See you tomorrow." Nolan waved and started pedaling again, dragging along his recycling mobile. The big doors of the barn were open, and he drove it inside. He had already installed bright lights for working, and now the barn doorway framed a bright yellow square at the back of the property.

That cheerful square of light signaled to Claire optimism . . . challenges met, and inspiration answering problems. Nolan didn't see himself as a spiritual person. But she knew he was touched and inspired by some greater intelligence all the time. Of that, Claire could not be more sure.

CLAIRE had gone up to bed and Nolan was still working in the barn when Daniel's truck finally appeared. Liza felt her heartbeat quicken at the sight, as if he had been away a long time, not just one day. But it had been an important one: his first day of classes in Boston. Liza was eager to hear how it went, though she knew you couldn't tell much from a first day of something like this, good or bad.

You're acting like he's a little boy and had his first full day of school, she mocked herself. *He's a grown man and will have to deal with some ups and downs in this process. You can't do it for him.*

She knew she had to remember that. But she loved him, and if Daniel was happy, she was happy. Wasn't that the way it was supposed to be?

He walked up to the porch, and she flung her arms around his neck, greeting him with a long, sweet kiss. She was determined not to blurt out, *"So, how did it go?"*

"I missed you today," she said instead.

"I missed you, too." He answered her embrace with another hug, then he pulled back and grinned down at her. "Anything to eat around here?"

"Oh, right, enough of this goopy romantic stuff. You are a guy, after all," Liza said, laughing at him. "Don't worry, I think we can find a few crumbs for your dinner." She took his hand and led him through the house to the kitchen, where she had saved him some dinner.

Daniel sat at the table and poured himself a tall glass of iced tea as Liza began to set covered dishes on the table. "We have quite a selection," she told him. "Leftovers from the weekend. The lobster salad is amazing."

"It all looks great," Daniel said. "I was so busy today, I skipped lunch." He dug in quickly and was soon talking around a mouthful of food.

Liza sat across from him. The kitchen was dim and cozy, with only the low lights over the sink and under the cabinets turned on.

"You must be starving. How did you make it through class this afternoon? Snack machine?"

Daniel took a forkful of lobster salad, trying not to laugh. "They do have some healthy choices in those vending machines these days. But mostly, I drank coffee. It's the only way to get through those classes. I'd forgotten just how dense medical texts can be."

"I can imagine. Actually, I can't imagine," she said more truthfully. "I bet I wouldn't understand a word of it."

"It is like a foreign language at times, partly because there's so much Latin in the terminology. But I've been there before. I should remember this stuff."

"I'm sure it will come back to you. The first day is always the hardest, right?"

Daniel nodded, helping himself to more food. "That's what they tell me. The teacher seems tough, but maybe he's just trying to scare us. Weed out the weak links," he added with a small smile. He looked at her seriously. "I'm going to have to spend a lot of time studying if I'm going to have any hope of passing these exams."

Liza nodded. "I know. And it doesn't help that you have to spend what—four or five hours every day?—driving back and forth from Boston."

"Just five days a week," Daniel said with a grin. "But I met up with a guy who lives out past Worcester. He's rented a little studio apartment in the city, and we talked about chipping in on it. If I bunk with him a few nights a week, I'll have more time to study. And it looks like I'm definitely going to need it."

Liza hadn't expected that solution. It made perfect sense, and it was lucky for Daniel to have figured it out so quickly. But it meant he would be away for most of the week. Maybe all of the week. *You've been separated before,* she reminded herself. Daniel had been away last summer in Maine, building a house with a friend. But that had felt . . . different. His evenings were free for long phone calls, and he came home frequently. She had a feeling the next two months were not going to be like that.

"Good idea," she said quickly. "When will you start doing that? Next week?"

Daniel looked surprised. "I'm going to start tomorrow. I'm packing up some stuff tonight and will get more on the weekend. The sooner, the better. We already have a test at the end of this week."

He was going to move to Boston tomorrow? Liza tried to hide her shock. She picked up a few dirty dishes and got up from the table. "Well, you were lucky to meet up with him," she said finally. "He sounds pretty friendly."

"Yeah, well, we're all in the same boat, so people in the classes are pretty friendly, though most of them are much younger than me." He practically winced as he noted that last observation.

"Maybe, but I bet you're the cutest returning doc there . . . Not too many women in that class, I hope?" she asked with mock concern.

He smiled at her, tiny lines around his eyes crinkling in a

way that never failed to make Liza's pulse quicken. "Oh . . . I guess there are a few. More women go to medical school these days than men. Did you know that?"

Liza's eyes widened. "No, I didn't. If I had, I may have told you to rethink this back-to-school plan."

Daniel laughed, looking pleased at her concern. "If there are any women in my classes, I didn't notice them. I'll check tomorrow and get back to you."

"Good plan. I'd like a full report, please. Or I'll have to stop by and check for myself."

Daniel laughed at her. "Does that mean you're going to miss me?"

She had found a blueberry pie Claire had left on the counter and looked around for some small dishes and a knife. "A little, I guess. But I'm so busy around here this time of year. And we do have a new handyman signed on, thank goodness."

"Just a little?" Now it was Daniel's turn to look bemused. "I've been so easily replaced. It's positively frightening."

Liza put her arms around his shoulders and her cheek close to his, feeling his rough stubble. He obviously hadn't taken time to shave that morning. "Of course I'm going to miss you, silly. I'll miss you like crazy. But I understand you need time for studying instead of spending four or five hours on the road."

"I know you get it. And I know the apartment is a good idea. But I am going to miss you like crazy, too." Daniel pushed his chair out and pulled her down to sit on his lap. He buried his face in the crook of her neck. "This is going to be hard, Liza.

No two ways about it. Hard for me and hard on our relationship. I told you it wasn't easy to be in a relationship with a doctor. This is just the start of it," he warned her.

"I can't say I'm happy about you staying in the city all that time. You know I'm not," she admitted honestly. "But it's for a good reason, and it's only until the middle of August. We just have to take it one day at a time. I think we'll be fine . . . I know we will," she added, trying to sound more sure of that.

He nodded and sighed, then pressed his cheek to hers. "I was sitting in class today, remembering how I felt as a young med student. I wanted it so badly . . . If the professor had told me to come down in front of the lecture hall and walk on hot coals, I would have done it." He pulled his head back and looked up at her. "I still want it, but . . . I'm just older. I've been through things. I know I won't die if I'm not a doctor. Do you know what I mean?"

Liza nodded slowly. "I understand. You don't have that fire in your belly anymore. You have some perspective. Which is generally a good thing."

"Generally," he agreed. "But maybe not in this case. You have to be so . . . single-minded to scale this mountain. Even a second time. I was looking around at the other students in my class, wondering about their stories. I watched them listening to the lecture and tried to guess which of them wants it the most. Which of them will make it across the line. I can almost tell," he added.

"What about you? What would you guess if you looked at yourself the same way?" she asked, curious.

He didn't answer for a moment. "I don't know . . . but I'm willing to find out. I've been there, and I know what being a doctor really is . . . and what it's not. So it's different for me. I can't have the same naive, blind ambition, you know? Maybe it's just a low-key thing that will build as I get closer and remember more and more how much I loved it."

"You did love it, didn't you?" she asked softly. She'd never heard him admit it before.

He met her gaze and slowly nodded. "I did. And I think I can love it again." He touched her cheek with his hand. "But I know one thing I've never stopped loving . . . You, Liza. I love you."

He pulled her closer and kissed her deeply. Liza clung to him. She loved him so. Sometimes she felt she wanted his happiness even more than her own. Maybe that's what really loving someone meant.

After Daniel finished his dinner, including a huge slice of pie, they sat on the porch swing awhile, just holding each other and looking out at the night sky.

Daniel covered a big yawn with his hand. "I'd better get going. I still have some homework to do," he said with a youthful grin. "Can you believe that? A grown man is telling you he has to leave you here on this beautiful summer night because he has to do homework? Is that pathetic or what?"

Liza laughed and stood up, then held out her hand to pull him up, too. "I have to go in anyway. It's almost past my curfew," she joked back.

They kissed again, and Liza reluctantly let Daniel go. She

watched as his truck pulled out of the drive and disappeared on the black ribbon of road.

She lingered on the porch, gazing out at the sea and starry sky. Like most worthwhile endeavors, the initial excitement was wearing off and the hard, tough work was beginning. This was going to be a hard road for Daniel, no doubt.

And hard for her, too. Hard in ways she hadn't expected— and maybe didn't even know about yet.

She already missed him, staring at the place where his truck had disappeared down the road. She felt an empty place inside her and knew she would need time to adjust to the fact that she wouldn't see him tomorrow morning, or during the day . . . or even tomorrow night. He wasn't just a text or a phone call away anymore.

When Daniel had told her about the way his ex-fiancée had grown so frustrated with him for the time he spent away from her and how much they had fought about his job, Liza had always assumed that the unknown woman was self-centered and selfish.

But now you're getting just a little taste of that, and you don't like it much, do you? she asked herself honestly.

But she had to keep her eye on the big picture. Once Daniel passed his exams and started practicing again, their life would go back to normal. Or some new normal that would be comfortable for both of them, and not so different as this, she decided.

They were in a committed relationship, and each had to make a few sacrifices now for a better future. Missing him during the week this summer might be the worst of it, Liza comforted herself. She would look back at this time and see how silly it had been to worry about this.

She felt a great calm spreading through her as she gazed out at the night sky and heard the sound of the waves breaking on the shore. She had faith in God and faith in the love she and Daniel shared. They had nothing to fear.

Chapter Six

LIZA wanted to call the trash-sorter and conveyor Nolan's Recycling-Cycle. But Claire liked her name better—the Green Machine. Though it wasn't quite as clever as Liza's and didn't entirely make sense—since Nolan had not painted it green—she liked the name because it made their efforts to be mindful of recycling and ecology sound efficient and even cool.

Being cool was not a state that Claire usually worried about, but she did feel strongly that the ecology movement wasn't just for young people. Any effort to respect and protect the beautiful planet and the natural, abundant world God created was a spiritual act, Claire felt—though she was sure Nolan wouldn't agree.

The Green Machine was just the first of his innovations.

It seemed that any mundane chore on Nolan's to-do list was an opportunity for him to devise a more efficient strategy, one that usually included rigging up an odd-looking home-made apparatus.

Days after the unveiling of Nolan's trash collection invention, Claire and Liza stepped outside one morning to check the progress of the tomato plants. Liza wanted Claire to try a new recipe, a tomato avocado salsa that could be served as a side dish or topping for grilled fish or poultry.

Claire wasn't sure if enough tomatoes would be ripe in time or if Liza should pick some up at the farm stand. "They won't go to waste if you do buy some," Claire noted as they stepped out the back door. "There's a thousand ways to serve a tomato in the summertime."

Watering the garden was now one of Nolan's jobs, and Claire had shown him how to work the tall pole sprinklers, which needed to be moved around the garden at intervals.

As the two women stepped outside, Claire heard the water spraying, and even felt a light mist carried in the air and settling on her cheeks and hair. But when she turned to the garden, she didn't see the pole sprinklers, or any sign of them.

The first thing she saw was . . . a rainbow, arcing over the garden as droplets of water were caught in bright rays of morning light. It appeared to be raining, as if Nolan had engineered a mini rainstorm over one special square of the property. Water poured down from the hoses onto the rows of plants, while a shimmering mist rose straight above them in the sun-warmed air.

"For goodness' sake . . . he's created a tiny rain shower . . ."

"Complete with a rainbow. I wonder if I should pay him extra for that." Liza laughed.

"Rainbow-making, or even rainmaking, was not on Nolan's to-do list this morning," Claire noted. "How did he do it, is the question. He's rigged up some sort of new watering system. I've got to see this close-up. No time to get my umbrella," she added with another laugh.

Liza followed as Claire quickly walked out to the garden. She could see that lengths of garden hose had been strung around the top of the high chicken-wire fence, which kept the deer, rabbits, and other hungry creatures from feasting on the vegetables at night.

The hose was pierced with tiny holes, and long streams of water arced out over the rows of plants—just on the plants, nowhere else. Claire wondered how he had gotten the trajectory of water to spray so accurately. But he *was* an engineer and a physicist.

"Just what the garden needs, a nice soaking of rain every day. At just the right time in the morning, too," Claire observed.

Liza looked pleased and amazed by the apparatus, too. "Nolan is so overqualified for this job, it's scary. I hope he doesn't take all these gadgets with him when he goes. We could definitely use a few."

"I'm sure he'll leave us with one or two. They might turn out to be very valuable; the first models of some new inventions— like the watering rainbow-maker."

"That's a good name for it. You could help Nolan name his inventions, Claire. You could help him with a lot of things. You two make a good pair," Liza said lightly. "Even Daniel noticed."

Was it something in Liza's smile—or just her tone—that made Claire blush and look away?

Claire smoothed down her apron, feeling flustered by the comment. "We've become good friends, if that's what you're trying to say."

"I know that you're friends. You've been very kind and patient with him. I would have never been able to manage him so patiently," Liza admitted. "But your personalities balance each other perfectly. You've been very good for Nolan and . . . he's been very good for you, too," Liza said, surprising her. "I guess what I'm trying to say is, I think he likes you as more than a friend . . . and I suspect the feelings are mutual. Are they?"

"Well . . . I . . . I don't know why you would say such a thing. I'm really not sure . . . I've never thought of it that way." Claire knew she was rambling but couldn't help it. She finally stopped and just shook her head. Liza's words had struck a clear-sounding bell that seemed to resonate inside Claire's heart. She knew it was true.

She did feel more for Nolan than friendship, or even sympathy for a nice man down on his luck. She looked forward to seeing him each day and spending time with him in the evening, when he wasn't busy working on his boat. She enjoyed their conversations and his curious, active mind. She admired and respected him, his talent and intelligence and persevering personality. Even his odd quirks.

Feelings were blossoming inside her that she hadn't felt in a long time. Had Liza seen that happening before she had even admitted it to herself?

"How do you think Nolan has been good for me?" she asked quietly as they headed back to the house. "I'm just curious," she added quickly.

"Well, let's see . . . For one thing, he's very considerate of you. I've seen him help you do your work and even serve you breakfast or lunch. Or bring you a cup of tea at night when you're knitting," Liza reminded her. "I think you enjoy his attention. And," Liza continued before Claire could respond, "I've noticed that you're looking especially lovely lately. The way you've been fixing your hair and wearing a little lipstick in the morning. You—"

"Enough said. I get the idea." Claire quickly cut her off with a laugh. "My hair has been just the same for years," she insisted. "As for the rest . . . well, wouldn't you just chalk that up to having a new employee around the inn?"

"Nope. Sorry. Even without the lipstick, Claire. There's been a certain . . . glow," Liza added with a small smile. "You can't get that from a bottle of face cream, even if you want to."

"Oh, stop teasing me now, Liza." Claire blushed again and began attacking a dirty frying pan with a scouring pad.

"I'm not teasing, honestly." Liza gently touched her shoulder. "I think it's sweet. You deserve some attention from a nice man like Nolan. You deserve some companionship, don't you think?"

Claire didn't know what to say. "I suppose so, but . . . it's been so long since I've been involved with anyone. It's all a bit . . . unexpected. I don't know what to think of any of this."

Liza smiled gently. "Just relax and enjoy it."

"All right . . . I will try," Claire said quietly, hoping Nolan was nowhere around to overhear their girl talk. What else could she call it?

Claire focused on the burnt pan. Oh dear, it was worse than she had imagined. The pan and . . . the way she was acting around Nolan. Glowing, was she? How embarrassing. Did Nolan notice? She certainly hoped not. Claire was suddenly thankful for his absentmindedness. Perhaps she could get control of this glowing, blossoming situation, and he would never know. She was so unused to these feelings at this stage in life . . . It was all a bit . . . confusing.

One thing she knew for sure: Even if Nolan was harboring feelings for her, he was still sticking to his plan of leaving once his boat was repaired. The *Ariadne* would always be his one true love. Claire knew she was no competition for the boat.

In the meantime, maybe she could be of some help to him—an encouraging influence, at least. He was remarkably talented and brimming with imaginative solutions to all kinds of problems. It made Claire wonder why he had gotten so stuck on his lawsuit—the invention he said had been stolen from him.

Could this lost idea have been so much better than all the others he came up with all the time? Better than the new inventions he was capable of creating? It was like seeing someone sitting on an untapped gold mine and mourning over one lost silver dollar.

God never closes a door without opening a window. She had often heard Reverend Ben say that. And he usually added that most people are too stuck staring at the closed door to notice.

Maybe Nolan's time at the inn creating all these little gadgets and inventions would help him see that. She certainly hoped so.

WHEN Daniel pulled up to the inn on Friday night, he heard music playing and saw the porch and front lawn filled with guests. There was laughing and talking and even some dancing and shouting. A party was definitely going on, and as he parked his truck on the drive he realized the partying group was all women. Then he remembered Liza had told him the inn was fully booked this weekend with a twenty-year reunion of sorority sisters.

He decided to avoid wandering through that group and went around to the back door instead. Luckily, Liza was in the kitchen, filling an ice bucket. She stepped out from behind the freezer door, put the bucket down, and ran to greet him.

He pulled her into his arms and kissed her hungrily. She felt so soft and warm and smelled so good. It was the moment he had waited for all week. When she pulled back and smiled up at him, he kissed the tip of her nose. "How's it going with the sorority? Looks like everyone is having fun."

Liza rolled her eyes. "I think they're trying to make up for lost time. In fact, I know they are. I'm just glad they booked the whole inn. Otherwise, I'd be fielding some complaints tomorrow morning."

Daniel laughed and leaned back, his arms looped around her slim waist. "Yeah, I think you would. Good planning. What's going on, disco night?" he joked.

"Almost. It's a dance party right now . . . and in a little while"—she glanced at her watch—"we'll be moving on to pj's, chick flicks, and late-night snacks."

Daniel laughed. "Enough said. I'm out of here."

Liza made a face. "Already? I've hardly seen you for five minutes."

"Liza, can I help you with that ice?" a woman's voice called from the hallway.

Liza winced and turned to call back over her shoulder, "I'll be right there, Melinda."

"Sorry, sweetie. I think you have your hands full. And I'm totally beat," he confessed, which was true. "I was only going to stop by for a few minutes anyway and then head back to the cottage. I'll see you bright and early tomorrow?"

Liza sighed and nodded. He could tell she wasn't happy with his quick departure, but he was certain she understood. "Okay, but not too early," she added. "I have a feeling this is going to be a late night."

"Taking part in the pj's and chick flicks?" he asked innocently.

She sighed. "Even if I go upstairs to my room, I'm sure the giggling will keep me up all night."

"Well, good luck. I hope they pick some movies you like."

He kissed her quickly and headed for the door. "And that sort of gets me off the hook for tomorrow night," he realized, thinking of how he and Liza usually settled down with a movie on Saturday evenings.

"We'll see" was all Liza said as she headed in the opposite direction with the ice bucket.

Daniel really did feel sorry for her. But he also felt exhausted, and a bit relieved to be going back to his cottage and avoiding Liza's inevitable questions about this past week at school. It had more or less been a disaster, and he wasn't ready to talk about it yet—even with his best friend and sweetheart.

When he returned on Saturday morning, the inn was quiet, though it was well past nine. He saw Claire on the front porch, dragging a large black trash bag as she cleaned up the remnants of the previous night's revelry.

"Good morning, Daniel. Liza's still sleeping. Would you like some coffee or breakfast?"

Daniel smiled and shook his head. He had carried a pile of books up to the porch and set them on a wicker table. "I'm fine. Would you like some help? I can sweep and wash down the porch," he offered.

Claire looked very happy to hear that. "Would you? That would be a great help. I really have to get back to the kitchen, and Nolan is out back, trying to fix the fence at the back of the property before it gets too hot."

"Go ahead back inside. I don't mind at all. I've been sitting all week. I'd love to do an outdoor job or two."

Claire laughed. "I have more than two for you, if you're interested. See me later," she suggested.

Daniel took the bag from her hand and finished the trash collection. Then he moved all the wicker furniture out on the lawn and swept and sprayed down the porch, being careful not to turn on the water too hard and chip the floor paint.

He was just watering the hanging plants when Liza appeared in the doorway, looking a bit groggy and totally adorable.

"Sleeping Beauty . . . your prince awaits."

Liza smiled. "You look more like Cinderella today. Did Claire forget that we hired Nolan to do those jobs now?"

"Nolan is fixing the fence. I offered to help out a bit. It feels good, working outside in the fresh air. No complicated formulas or long Latin terms to think about."

Liza laughed. "That's one way of looking at it. I bet when you were working here all the time, you didn't find these little odd jobs quite so wonderful."

Daniel had never really done the little jobs like sweeping the porch or watering the plants. But he knew what Liza was talking about. "It's true. You don't realize how good you have it sometimes, until life changes."

He delivered the philosophical insight with a shrug and a smile, but deep down he knew the words were really true. At least it felt that way to him this morning. He suddenly felt wistful for the days of having nothing more pressing on his mind than Liza's to-do list, or running off to the other side of the island to fix a broken gutter. Once again, he wondered if he had made a big mistake going back for this medical certification. The question had kept him up all night every night this week.

Liza came out with a mug of coffee and sat on the porch steps, gazing out at the ocean. He kept watering the plants but wondered when he should talk to her about this. And if he even should talk to her about it.

After all the excitement and buildup, it seemed so . . . cowardly to admit he was starting to think it was too much pressure, too much work. He was starting to wonder if he could really cut it . . . and why did he want to do this, after all?

He was starting to question everything. He had done very poorly in his classes this week and practically failed a test. Everyone in his class except him seemed to understand the material. As much as he studied and tried to remember, he did very poorly on the take-home work and the pop quizzes in class.

Daniel wasn't sure what to think or what to do. He glanced at Liza, who seemed lost in her own thoughts right now, glancing at her laptop and answering e-mails. He wondered if this was a good time to talk to her. Maybe it was best to just get it over with?

"There you are." One of the guests came out on to the porch and walked over to Liza. "A group of us are going to head up to Newburyport for some shopping. Claire said you could tell us where the best stores are."

Liza stood up and smiled. "Sure thing. Let's go inside. I have a map that shows all the shops and restaurants."

The woman went inside, and Liza followed, pausing at the doorway to look over her shoulder and smile back at Daniel. "See you later. And you're still my prince. I was only kidding about the Cinderella thing."

"I know. You're still my Sleeping Beauty," he said quietly. He meant it, too.

After Daniel put the furniture back in place, he found his books and settled down in the far corner of the porch to study. At least he could see the ocean and be outdoors here. It was much better than his stuffy little Boston apartment, or even the medical library.

But it wasn't long before a bunch of sorority sisters emerged and settled in the wicker chairs and love seats. They were trying to figure out whether to go into the town of Cape Light, head down to the beach, or ride bikes around the island. Daniel turned his chair around so that the back of his seat was facing them. It helped a bit, but he still wished he had brought a pair of earplugs. He didn't want to go inside but was thinking that if they didn't decide in a few minutes, he would have to retreat.

But before he could figure out what to do, Nolan appeared. He had come around the side of the building and stood near the porch, talking to Daniel over the railing. "There you are. Claire said you still might be out here. I was wondering if you could help me out back for a few minutes. I'm trying to set some new fence posts, and it really would go much faster with some help."

Nolan looked tired and sweaty, Daniel noticed, with dirt streaking his shirt and face. Daniel was happy to help him; happy to take over the job if the older man would let him. It was a warm morning, and he didn't think Nolan should be working so hard outside today.

"At your service, Nolan." Daniel set his books aside in a neat pile and felt his spirits lighten. He glanced over the group of women, who now blocked the steps, then grabbed hold of the porch rail and neatly hopped over onto the lawn.

He heard one of the women gasp and another one giggle.

"Oh, my! Did you see that?" one of them said.

Nolan laughed. "Well done."

"Thanks, Nolan. I enjoyed that," he admitted, feeling like a horse that had just jumped the fence. "Let me get my work gloves and some tools from the truck. I'll meet you back at the fence."

It was almost three hours later when Daniel finished the job. He had persuaded Nolan to leave him after the first hour; the sun was growing so strong. Now the fence was repaired from one end of the property to the other, standing solid and strong. Daniel felt a familiar, quiet sense of pride and satisfaction looking over the work he had done. There was something to be said for this type of work. There was no reason to be embarrassed about making your living this way, Daniel decided.

When he went back inside the inn, Claire fussed over him, as he expected she would. He found a huge sandwich and fresh lemonade ready and waiting and quickly inhaled all of it. Liza had run into Cape Light, and all the sorority sisters had fanned out in different directions. It would be quiet enough for some studying, at least until dinnertime. Daniel settled on the porch with his books again but soon found his thoughts wandering.

What was the use? Who was he kidding? He could memorize all these books, and he still wouldn't earn back his medical certification. It took more than studying; he already knew that. It took real grit, a real edge. Something he didn't seem to have anymore.

The ocean was calm today, in contrast with his emotions. The gentle repetition of the waves soothed him. Called to him.

He put his books aside again and decided to take a walk on the beach.

Maybe that's what he needed today. He was entitled to a little downtime. All this studying was going to burn out his brain.

He walked across the lawn, crossed the road, and started down the wooden steps to the sandy shoreline.

How could he come back to the island and not come down here on such a picture-perfect summer day? Daniel stood at the bottom of the steps a moment, taking in the sight of the dark blue ocean and the smooth, soft sand that stretched down to the stone jetty.

Living in the city this past week had made him more conscious and appreciative of the island. When he returned, he could hardly believe he'd been living here every day and taking all this natural beauty for granted.

He started off, walking toward the jetty, his hands sunk into the pockets of his cargo shorts, his thoughts troubled. He wondered if he would pass a few of the guests from the inn, but the beach was almost empty. He did make out a lone figure not too far away: a fisherman with a few poles stuck in the sand who had waded in over his knees, fly casting.

Daniel drew closer, wondering if it was Matt Harding, a doctor in town, whom he was friendly with. Matt liked to fish in his spare time and sometimes came to this spot.

But as Daniel drew closer, he realized it wasn't Matt but another familiar face from Cape Light, Reverend Ben Lewis, who came to the island to fish year-round, though Daniel could never recall seeing the minister catch anything. Perhaps he did and threw the fish back, Daniel thought as he drew closer to the minister. Maybe that soothed his conscience. He wondered if he could ever ask Reverend Ben that question. He had a feeling the reverend would just laugh and answer him honestly.

When he wasn't too far away, Daniel stood on the shore near the minister, watching him reel in his line. Finally, Reverend Ben noticed him. He turned and squinted at Daniel, then smiled.

"Hello there, Daniel. How are you? Doing any fishing?"

Daniel shook his head. "Not today. Just down for a walk. Catch anything yet?"

"No, not yet. I hear the stripers are running," he said hopefully.

"It's about that time of year," Daniel agreed.

Reverend Ben stuck his pole in the soft sand and walked closer. "What are you up to these days? Do you have a lot of projects going on?"

Daniel knew the reverend wasn't prying, just making small talk. Still, with the reverend, Daniel knew he could never lie, or even give an evasive answer. There was something very open and accepting about Reverend Ben that always made Daniel want to be open in kind.

"I'm not doing any carpentry this summer. I've gone back to school," he admitted.

Reverend Ben looked surprised. "Really? Good for you. What are you studying?"

Daniel smiled grimly. He wasn't sure what else to say, how much he wanted to disclose. Finally he said, "I'm studying medicine, trying to get recertified. I used to be a doctor before I came to the island. But I . . . I gave it up."

Reverend Ben's expression changed to a serious look. His thick brows knitted together, and he removed his glasses and cleaned them with a handkerchief. "That's very interesting. So you've gone back to school so you can practice medicine again?"

"More or less . . . less, in my case," he added glumly.

"Oh, how do you mean?" Ben put his wire-rimmed glasses on again and stared back at Daniel.

"Well . . . it's hard to explain. But I was all gung ho at first. The idea just took me over. A couple of weeks ago, I guess, Liza and I started talking about it, and I checked things out on the Internet, to see what I'd have to do to be recertified. A few days later, I decided to try it. It was as if some part of my mind had been thinking about this for years, and the other part of my mind had never asked."

Ben nodded with a small smile. "It can happen like that sometimes."

"Maybe for other people, Reverend. But not for me. It's never happened like that for me. So I'm back in classes, trying to review four years of medical school in five and a half weeks. And this week, I started to think I moved too fast on this. I should have waited and thought it through."

"You're doubting you made the right decision to go back to medicine. Is that it?"

Daniel nodded. "It's complicated," he began. "It's not just going back to medicine. The reason I left in the first place . . . I made a big mistake. That's why I quit and wound up here. I'm starting to think that I'm trying to go back to the past, to that exact place, to make things right again. But maybe that's not possible."

Reverend Ben didn't answer for a moment. "What sort of mistake? Can you tell me the whole story? Only if you want to, I mean."

Daniel met his glance and took a breath. "Sure, I can tell you. I was an emergency room doctor at Mass General," he began. "It can be a crazy place to work on busy nights. I was out of the hospital, on call, one Saturday night. It was pretty late, after midnight, when they asked me to come in. I was tired and stressed. I'd just had a huge fight with my girlfriend. We were engaged, and she broke up with me. I guess you could say I wasn't really at my best and should have admitted that. I'd even had a beer that night. But I was too . . . macho or something. In medical school they make a big thing about toughening up, and I didn't want to admit I couldn't shake off this personal stuff and just go in and do my job."

"I understand." Reverend Ben nodded. "So you went into work that night to handle an emergency?"

"It was a bad case—a multicar accident. The patient they gave me wasn't in good shape to begin with. A middle-aged man with a bad gall bladder. He needed surgery and had quite a few complications; diabetes, a bad heart, a weak liver, you name it. I ordered the wrong procedures, and he went into a coma. It was a mistake. I wasn't thinking clearly. There were two other doctors on the case, and neither of them overruled me. Or spoke against me afterward. But later we all realized that he hadn't been evaluated completely before we started treating him. That happens a lot in the ER. You just don't have time to get the full story. You have to work a lot on instinct, and mine was not that sharp that night."

"It's amazingly difficult work. Did the man die?" Reverend Ben asked quietly.

Daniel shook his head. "He was in the coma for three days and finally came out of it. But he'd lost some of his faculties for speech and movement. It was needless . . . A tragedy for his family." Daniel had been staring out at the sea, remembering. He looked back at Reverend Ben. "The family filed a complaint against me, but they never tried to sue. The hospital reviewed the case. I was questioned and reprimanded, but they never suspended me or took my license. I was free to keep practicing. But I felt responsible. I couldn't just shake it off and go on as if it had never happened."

"Which is what you were advised to do?" Ben asked.

Daniel nodded. "Yeah, advised a lot. By the other docs in the case especially. But I knew that I shouldn't have gone in that night. It was really my fault. I can't blame anybody else."

"So you've carried this around for a long time."

"It's been more than seven years. I thought I was ready to go back and try again. But I had a terrible week in my classes . . . I failed a test. I can't even tell Liza. She's been great. Really in my corner on this all the way. She'll be so disappointed."

"She might be," Reverend Ben agreed. "But you can't worry about disappointing Liza. You're the one who has to live with the decision and feel sure of it. In your heart. Everything follows from that."

Daniel looked up at him. "I did feel sure of it. At least I

thought I did. Now I'm not so sure. Now I'm all confused about it," he admitted.

"Because you failed a test? Do you think that's a sign that this isn't the right path for you after all?"

Daniel shrugged. "Well . . . it could be."

"Just because a path we've chosen is suddenly hard going, it doesn't mean God is trying to say you made the wrong choice. He just might be saying you need to work harder. Ever think of it that way?" Reverend Ben wasn't sarcastic. In fact, his tone was quiet and kind.

"I guess I didn't. Not this time."

"Think of Moses and the Israelites. They wandered forty years before they crossed the desert. That was some tough going. I'm sure they had their doubts about their mission at times. But they didn't turn around and go back to Egypt."

"No . . . they didn't. I get your point. But I sure hope it doesn't take me forty years to pass these exams."

Reverend Ben smiled but looked thoughtful again. "Daniel . . . I think when you felt ready to go back to medicine, you felt ready to forgive yourself. And you should forgive yourself. God does," he added with certainty. "If He does, you should, too."

Daniel didn't answer. Liza had said the same thing, more or less. He had brushed her words off, but now he felt them. Thought about them.

"You felt you had healed and were ready to go back to the fight," Reverend Ben continued. "Now you're actually out on the road, moving toward your goal, and it's harder than you thought. That doesn't mean you should revert to your old way of thinking, of blaming yourself. Or feeling you shouldn't be forgiven. Or that you don't deserve to be a doctor again. Is that what you're really thinking? Is that why you failed that test? Maybe to prove to yourself that you don't deserve this, after all?"

Daniel heard a big wave crash on the shore and felt the spray. But he was so stunned by Reverend Ben's question and how it resonated within that he couldn't answer for a moment.

"That's a good question, Reverend. I have to think about it," he said honestly.

"All right. Fair enough. But you know, I've come to see that people are really only limited by their beliefs. Or should I say, misconceptions? God has given us all infinite gifts. After all, we're made in His image. We can really do just about anything we set our minds—and hearts—to do. Sometimes the goals we want most are the hardest to reach. But when you put your heart into it, the universe has a way of cooperating. God has a way of smoothing a path for you. When you expect to get there, and ask Him for help, you do."

Daniel nodded. He let out a long breath. Maybe, deep down inside, he was still conflicted, feeling he shouldn't follow this impulse, this drive. That he should still deprive himself because of the incident that happened so long ago.

But maybe the past wasn't what was really holding him back. Maybe after all this time, he was plain scared. Scared that he couldn't do all this studying again and pass these exams. Scared of practicing medicine again.

"Maybe I'm trying to trick myself. If I fail the exams, I'm

off the hook. I can say, '*Well, at least I tried, and I couldn't do it,*'" he admitted.

"Yes, but you'll always know deep inside that isn't true."

"I would know. I wouldn't be able to fool myself. Or Liza," he added. "Well, I have a lot to think about now," he said finally.

Reverend Ben reached out and touched his shoulder. "I hope I've helped you—and haven't just confused you more?"

Daniel laughed. "No, sir, not one bit. I'm going to walk some more and think about what you've said. I thought I had made this decision. But maybe I have to dig in a little deeper, see what I'm really made of."

Ben smiled and nodded. "Maybe. I hope you feel at peace with your decision. Whatever that turns out to be," he said sincerely.

Reverend Ben soon returned to his fishing poles to check the lines. He waved at Daniel as he continued down the beach.

Daniel walked to the jetty and sat on the rocks while the waves swirled around him. Reverend Ben had been right. Life was all a matter of perspective; this situation was, anyway. As long as he continued to think he didn't deserve to be a doctor, he would continue to undermine himself. To mess up his tests and blow off his studying.

But that was wrong thinking. He could see that now. He had made a mistake long ago, a lapse in judgment. But he was only human. No one was perfect. No one was infallible.

God forgave him. It was time to forgive himself, wasn't it?

All these years out of medicine, he hadn't really felt his true self. It was more like he was taking a break, playing a role.

Always thinking it was only temporary. Did he really want to go back to that now that he had woken up to the truth?

I could do a lot of good if I can get back to being a doc. I know I can. That has to count for something, Daniel told himself. *I have to think of the good I can do, instead of the one time I messed up. That's what I have to remember. That's why I have to do this,* he finally decided as he rose and headed back to the inn. He would try to find some time alone with Liza tonight and have a quiet dinner together. But he would head back to Boston early tomorrow and straight for the library. Liza wouldn't be pleased, but she would understand.

God, if You can hear me, I have something to say, he began to pray silently as he walked along the soft, smooth sand. *You put this thought in my head about being a doctor again, and I went with it. But I've been going at it only halfheartedly these last few weeks. Now I really have to dig in. I know it's win or go home. I've got to give it my all—or live to regret it. But I need Your help. I don't think I can get there without You.*

WEDNESDAY was often a slow day at the inn, especially if there was rain in the forecast. Though most of the rooms were booked weeks in advance, there were always the last-minute arrivals in good weather that filled the place to the brim—and in bad weather, some people canceled.

Claire didn't mind a little rain once in a while. She enjoyed the cozy feeling in the dimly lit rooms and the fresh, cool scent of the air. The garden needed rain, as careful as Nolan had been this summer to water it. And a rainy day was perfect for cooking, too. It cooled down the kitchen nicely when she needed to bake or roast something in the oven.

She had finished a large batch of banana and blueberry muffins for the weekend breakfasts and decided to get a breath of air outside. The mail had arrived; she trotted down the drive with an umbrella to retrieve it.

She was expecting a card or letter from Jamie. During their last call, he mentioned he was sending her something. She had her own address at her cottage, of course. But during the summer months, he would know to send it here.

Jamie was still in his twenties, and he teased Claire about not using e-mail. But she just couldn't get the hang of it and didn't own a computer. She would have to use Liza's or go to the library in Cape Light, and both seemed far too much trouble. She preferred a good old-fashioned phone call, and if not that, a short note. *Just let me know you're all right*, she would tell him. *That's all I need.* He was like a son to her, and Jamie looked upon her as the mother he'd never had. So he did indulge her this simple wish, calling almost every week, and sending a card or note from time to time, as well.

Best of all were the visits. Since Jamie had settled in Portland last fall, he had come to the inn for Thanksgiving and Christmas, and she knew he would come again this year. She was just about his only family, and he was her only family, too.

What would Jamie make of Nolan? she wondered as she pulled out a thick stack of mail. Jamie would probably be intimidated at first. He had just about finished high school, but had graduated with a GED.

But after some initial awkwardness, he would like Nolan very much, Claire thought. He would be intrigued by his inventions, that was for sure. Jamie was mechanically minded, too, and wonderful with electronics and computers. That was what he had decided to study, and it was proving to be a perfect career path for him.

Claire ran back up to the porch with the mail tucked under her arm. Once under cover, she shook out the umbrella and set it to the side of the door to dry. She quickly leafed through the envelopes, all addressed to Liza or the Inn at Angel Island except for one thick manila envelope at the bottom of the stack. It was very official looking and was addressed to Dr. Nolan Porter. He had a PhD, so that was his correct title, Claire reasoned. The return address looked like the name of a big law firm, with several surnames strung together. She picked up her umbrella again and quickly walked to the barn. The barn doors were open just a crack, and she heard the sanding machine running. Daniel had helped Nolan get the boat up on metal supports that held it steady and upright, high enough off the ground so he could repair it. Nolan had to climb a ladder now to get on the deck and work inside—and to reach most of the outside, for that matter. The boat looked much bigger in the barn than it had in the water, or even out on the beach.

Nolan was on the ladder, wearing goggles and some sort of earmuff contraption. The machine was going, and he didn't hear her approach.

"Nolan? There's a letter for you." Claire waited a moment. When he didn't answer, she knocked on the side of the boat.

Nolan suddenly glanced down, looking alarmed. Then his expression eased into a warm smile.

"Sorry, I didn't hear you. Were you waiting down there a long time?" He yanked off his headgear and came down the ladder.

"Not long. This came in the mail for you," she said, holding out the letter. "It looks important. I thought you might want to see it."

She had not even finished speaking when Nolan took the envelope from her hand. He stared at it long and hard, pulling on the reading glasses that hung from a cord around his neck and then tearing open the package.

"I've been waiting for this. Thank you, Claire, for bringing it out to me. This could be it. Should be it. From what my attorney told me last time we spoke, it's the settlement. He said that he finally reached an agreement with the scoundrel I've been suing. All he needed to do was finalize a few details and get it signed on the dotted line."

Nolan was talking so quickly and excitedly, Claire could barely keep up with him. But he did seem very happy. Finally. She watched as he held the thick sheaf of pages in his hand, the uppermost being a letter with fancy letterhead on cream-colored stationery with crisp black type. From what she could see, the body of the letter was just a few lines long.

That's all it takes to turn things around in a person's life at times. A few lines of good news. Claire smiled to herself, feeling happy for Nolan that his problem was resolved.

But as Nolan scanned the page, his happy expression melted into confusion and distress. He shook his head, then read the letter again, then examined the back of the page, which was blank, as if he must have missed something. He finally looked back at her, pale and upset—and quite shocked.

"What is it, Nolan? What's the matter? Isn't it good news?"

"It was supposed to be. But . . ." He sighed heavily and sat down on a wooden crate, then passed his hand through his long hair. "Everything's changed. The deal is off. My attorney didn't get an agreement after all."

"But you said it was all decided. How could they go back on their word?"

Nolan swallowed hard. "Well, they can and they did. The lawyers for that crook who stole my idea threw in a monkey wrench and delayed this again. Set us back a giant step." Nolan shook his head with dismay and distress. Edison trotted over to him, sat near his leg, and leaned against his body. Nolan hardly noticed, absently patting the dog's head.

"Oh, my . . . that's not fair. That's not fair at all." Claire's words were quietly spoken. "Have they turned you away entirely?"

"They've made some counteroffer." He waved the pile of pages. "A very paltry one; just not acceptable. Not acceptable at all," he repeated with an angry edge to his voice. He suddenly stood up and faced her.

"This is just a tactic. They think they'll wear me down and I'll just give in. But I'll never give in. There's no question that I'm in the right here. It's shameless how they twist everything and try to get around the law. I don't know how they get up in the morning and face themselves in the mirror."

His complexion had gone from pale as paper to bright red. His hand was shaking as he held out the letter, and Claire was worried about him.

"It's stuffy in this barn, Nolan," she said gently. "The rain has stopped. Why don't you get some air?" He looked at her, seemingly unable to answer. But Claire took his arm and led him slowly out of the barn. "How about a glass of water? You must be thirsty," she said, leading him toward the back door.

"A glass of water would be good," he said finally.

She guessed that he didn't feel well, but didn't want to admit it. Edison followed close behind, and Claire had the feeling that the loyal dog was concerned about Nolan, too.

Nolan sat down at the table with a heavy sigh and dropped the papers in front of him. Claire quickly poured him a glass of cold water. He drank it down thirstily, though his expression remained bleak when he was done.

"Can I get you something else? Something to eat, maybe?" She wanted to do something for him, but felt so helpless. All she could offer was food and drink.

"I'm not hungry. Maybe later." He rose from the seat and grabbed his papers. "If Liza doesn't need me right now, I'm going up to my room. I need to write my attorney a strong letter. He obviously doesn't know how to handle these people. I have to tell him exactly what to do, what to say . . ." He sighed again. "I'd better get to work. This is going to take some time and thinking."

"Yes, of course. I'll tell Liza what's happened. I'm sure she'll understand."

Claire watched Nolan go, with Edison padding after his master.

Claire felt a bit shaky herself after witnessing Nolan's receipt of bad news. She put on her apron and began cleaning some kale that Nolan had picked for her earlier in the day. The wet weather had made the leaves extra muddy, and she had to rinse them several times in the big deep sink. She didn't even notice that Liza had come into the kitchen until she was standing right next to her.

"What's wrong with Nolan? I passed him going upstairs. He didn't even notice me. Doesn't he feel well?"

"He's not sick, exactly. But he's had a shock," Claire began to explain. "He got a letter today. He was expecting good news from his attorney, papers to sign agreeing to a settlement on his claim. But he was sent a counteroffer instead that made him very upset. It was a terrible blow."

"How awful for him, poor man. Did he go up to rest?"

Claire shook her head, lifting the kale, leaf by leaf, into a strainer. "He wants to write a letter to his attorney, telling him what to do, how to handle this development . . . He said to tell you that if you need him, he'll come right down and get back to work again."

Liza considered the offer. "It's all right. He's all caught up on his work. He even had time today to work on his boat. Maybe he'll feel better once he gets his thoughts down on paper," she said. "It sounds as if he was very angry."

"Oh, he was—and sort of crushed at the same time. It was quite upsetting to witness," Claire admitted. "It will be good for him to write that letter. A letter that he may never mail," she added, knowing Nolan's propensity for not editing his feelings.

"We've all written a few of those," Liza agreed. "Let's give him some space for the afternoon. He'll probably have things in better perspective by this evening."

Claire certainly hoped so. If he didn't come down eventually for some lunch, she would fix him a tray—maybe just some fruit and cheese—so he wouldn't get a headache from being too hungry on top of all the stress.

She felt a sharp tug in her heart, thinking of his distress. It hurt her, too. That's how she knew that it was true, what Liza had said a few days ago—she had come to care for Nolan. His hurt was her hurt. She wished she could help him let go of this lawsuit and focus on some project or goal that was more positive and productive.

Nolan claimed he would never give up the fight, sounding so noble. But how was this noble quest serving him? By his own admission, he had already wasted at least five years and come away with nothing. As one grew older, time was so precious. How much more would he waste in this pointless fight?

Claire suddenly took a step back, knowing she was judging too much now. She didn't even know the entire story; only what Nolan had told her so far. Clearly, he had to work through this in his own way. All she could do was stand by and pray that he did work through it, that something good would come of this battle and all these delays.

Dear God, please help Nolan today. He's so distraught. If he's supposed to learn something from this drawn-out lawsuit, please let him learn it. Please help him get past this grievance and move forward.

NOLAN did not come down for lunch, or even for dinner. Claire was concerned and brought him trays of food for both meals. But he hardly touched a bite. When she stood in the doorway of his room that night, to take away the dinner tray, his room looked as if it had been hit by a private snowstorm; the balls of wadded-up paper covering the floor were that deep.

He didn't seem to notice, sitting at a desk near the window, just as she'd seen him all day, writing and writing, page after page. Hunched over the desktop, his reading glasses slipping down his nose, while many files, retrieved from the black trunk, were spread about all around him, on the bed and bedside table. He wrote and wrote, and often cast the sheets off and onto the floor.

Claire had to practically wade through the balls of wadded-up, rejected pages in order to pick up the tray on the night table.

"How's it going?" she asked finally.

Nolan barely raised his head. "Hard to set the right tone. I want to back up what I say with the facts of the case, of course. The facts are the important thing. The rest is just posturing, roosters in a barnyard, squawking and flapping their wings. I won't be fooled by that. The facts of the matter are in my favor entirely," he insisted. "And so are the legal precedents. I've researched this thoroughly, even better than my attorney."

Claire nodded. "Good for you. Sounds like a good strategy."

"It is," he assured her, returning to his writing. "Please tell Liza I'll be back to work tomorrow without fail. But perhaps I can borrow your Jeep to run this letter down to the post office at some point during the day?"

"I'm going into town tomorrow afternoon. I can mail it for you," Claire offered.

"I'm sure you could, but I prefer to see it off myself. I'll hitch a ride if that's all right."

"That would be fine."

Claire welcomed his company, though she hoped his mood would be evened out by the next day. He did seem a little calmer and more himself already, she thought as she left the room and closed the door.

Nolan was already working outside by the time Claire came down to make breakfast the next morning. Guests were scheduled to arrive that evening, after dinner, so it wasn't a terribly rushed day.

She was glad to see Nolan up and out and hoped he had shaken off his dark mood of the day before. When he came in for lunch, he did seem more cheerful. A short time later, after all was prepared for the new guests, they set off for town. Edison jumped in the backseat, and Nolan's letter sat in his lap in a large manila envelope, addressed to the law firm in bold, black letters.

The package looked very substantial, Claire thought; the letter had to be many pages long. He had not asked to borrow Liza's laptop, so it had been handwritten. Claire wondered if his attorney would balk at reading it. From what she'd seen so far of Nolan's penmanship, it was more like a secret code than commonly known letters.

She dropped Nolan at the post office and did her shopping, then picked him up a short time later. He looked happy and satisfied, and that made her feel happy, too.

"That letter will give him something to think about," Nolan said as they drove through the village and headed back to the island. "He's a smart young man, my attorney. But his head is still stuck in schoolbooks. He hasn't had any life experience and doesn't think outside the box. I know he appreciates my perspective."

Claire wondered if that was true. It was probably irksome to receive fifty-page letters from your client telling you how to do your job. Maybe the young man was just too polite to object.

She waited for a good opportunity to tell Nolan what she had been thinking about—that he ought to consider giving up this case, or just giving it over to some higher power and allowing whatever will happen to just happen. Meanwhile, his energy and focus would be free to work on new ideas. And he clearly had so many of them.

But Nolan talked on and on about the letter and what might happen next, as if it were all some elaborate chess game. Claire couldn't quite find a good moment to introduce her perspective.

As they headed back toward the inn, she had an inspiration. She passed their turn and took another route, the only other big road on the island, which led to the north side. Nolan didn't seem to notice, until suddenly he stopped talking.

"Aren't we going back to the inn? This isn't the usual way."

"I thought we might take the long way around. You've never seen the famous cliffs—the reason the island got its name. This is the perfect time of day for viewing them."

It actually was, a bright and mild summer day, not too hot

at all, even in the strong sun. It was late afternoon, too, when the light on the rock formations would be absolutely breathtaking and really show the curves and wind-worn grooves that had given the cliffs their name.

"Oh, you mean the cliffs shaped like angels' wings?" Nolan turned to her. His tone wasn't scoffing . . . but almost.

Claire remained calm. "Those are the only cliffs we have around here, and well worth a little drive out of your way, believe me."

Nolan shrugged. "I'd like to see them. I've heard enough talk about them by now."

He had heard talk. Not just from Claire, but from the many guests at the inn who would ask about the cliffs, go out to see them, then report their visit at the breakfast or dinner table, usually showing off their photos.

"I've seen so many pictures by now, I feel as if I have visited them," Nolan complained good-naturedly.

"Photographs don't really do the cliffs justice. Not like a firsthand viewing. It's more of . . . an experience. As well as a beautiful view."

Nolan glanced at her but didn't reply. He stared ahead and then suddenly sat up straight in his seat.

Claire steered the Jeep around the last bend in the road, and the legendary cliffs—jagged, gold-colored sandstone, came into full view.

They looked quite majestic today, Claire thought. As if someone knew that this extraordinary sight was about to be scrutinized by a scientist—and a skeptic.

It was nearly four, and the sun was starting to sink toward

the sea. The late-afternoon light reflected on the rolling blue waters and on the feathery curves of gold sand.

The road inclined uphill and she pulled the Jeep over to the sandy shoulder. The jagged outline stood out in stark contrast to a backdrop of dark blue sky. The cliffs did indeed look like wings, crescent-shaped and cupped, a point flaring out at the bottom, like a long feather.

Before Nolan could say anything, Claire opened her door. "Let's get out and walk a bit. So you can get the entire view."

"All right, good idea." He got out of the Jeep but gently pushed Edison back inside and told him to stay. The lookout point was very high, and the dog was not on a leash, as usual. Claire was relieved she didn't have to worry about him.

Nolan followed Claire along a narrow path to a space where they could stand and look out over the rocks and crashing water.

She waited for Nolan to say something, curious to hear his impressions of the place, whatever they might be.

"Very unusual," he said finally. "People keep yammering about a legend. What is that again?"

"Back in the late sixteen hundreds, the first colonists to settle in Cape Light were struck by a plague of sorts during their first winter. The illness was so contagious, the town fathers decided that all who took sick had to be quarantined out here, on this island. There was no real name for it then, and it was completely uninhabited."

"So they were left out here to die. Very cruel, but thought to be for the greater good," he reasoned.

"I believe that was their reasoning. The sick ones were visited from time to time by folks from the village, who came out on boats with food and supplies. But the winter set in harsh and cold, with many storms. The harbor froze, and no one could visit for many, many weeks. When spring came, it was assumed that everyone out here had died. A search group was sent from the village to see what had happened and bring back any remains for burial. But when they arrived they were astonished. The sick ones had all recovered and were perfectly healthy. They claimed they had been visited by beautifully dressed men and women, who ministered to them in the worst of the winter and cured them with a healing touch. And so these cliffs, with their winglike shape, drew their name. The survivors of the plague, and all the townsfolk who heard the story, believed the sick ones had been visited by angels."

Nolan nodded, his mouth a thin line. She couldn't tell if he was trying to hold back laughter or trying not to interrupt her with some objective, fact-filled rebuttal on how and why this story was simply not possible.

"Visited by angels. What a lovely thought. What a lovely tale," he added. "It's perfectly obvious that the rocks have been carved by the unceasing friction of the wind and water, resulting in these pretty, arched formations." He pointed at the golden sandstone. "I'd be interested to see the oldest pictures or images of these cliffs. I'll bet they looked quite different then. And decades to come from now, well, these curvatures of stone will all be worn away. The angels' wings will be clipped," he said abruptly. "Though that sweet story will probably live on, as such fairy tales do."

"You're not the first to make that assertion, Nolan. Though

it is a thoughtful one," she granted him. "The thing is, very early drawings of these cliffs, dating back to the Colonial era, show them exactly as they are now. With no loss of the rock or change in the shape over the centuries. In fact, geologists have been out here studying the cliffs and the wind patterns and tides and just about any physical factor. And it's been verified. The rocks simply do not change."

Nolan cast a doubtful look in her direction. "Really? I'd like to see some of those studies."

"Maybe we can find them on Liza's computer tonight. I know they have copies at the Cape Light Historical Society."

"I'll take a look sometime. Facts are facts, Claire. Facts don't lie. It's the one thing you can depend on. Not people," she heard him murmur. He suddenly looked over at her. "You don't really believe all that . . . that fairy story, do you?"

Claire knew very well what he thought of the story, and could only guess what he thought of people who believed it. But at the risk of losing his good opinion and even having him think less of her intelligence, she had to be truthful.

"I do," Claire said bluntly. "But you're free to come to your own conclusions."

"I certainly am," he said with a laugh. "I'd say those Colonial settlers felt very remorseful about what they had done to their sick relatives and neighbors. So they concocted that tall tale to ease their conscience. And it was a culture that would explain just about any natural phenomenon with some supernatural cause."

"By supernatural, you mean God?"

He tilted his head. "Yes, I suppose I mean God and angels and all that. No offense," he quickly added.

"No offense taken." Claire shrugged. This wasn't going at all as she had hoped. Then again, she didn't know exactly what she had been hoping for. That Nolan would have a more open mind about the cliffs and the legend? She already knew he would only see the scientific explanation.

Still, she felt something had to be said. Something about his lawsuit and the way he was so focused on this quest that he was missing out on the wonderful ideas and inventions he could be developing. "Nolan, I'm sorry you don't believe in God. But even so, I have to tell you that I've been praying for you," she confessed.

Nolan looked at her with surprise. Instead of the condescension she expected, a certain softness came into his glance. "You have? Praying for what, may I ask? That I stop insulting Liza's guests and mixing up the dinner orders?"

Claire had to laugh. "I've been asking God to help you let go of your struggle. To help you step back and see that you have so many wonderful ideas for inventions to develop, you can't waste your best years fighting over that one you lost."

"I see." He nodded curtly. "Has God answered you yet? Or was that letter I received the other day the answer, do you think?"

Claire had never thought of the letter that way. And she wasn't about to answer his question, either. "I think that God sent you to this island to help you. To help you out of this rut that you've dug yourself into. There now, I've said it. I'm usually not so blunt, but . . . well, you talk that way sometimes. Now you know what it sounds like."

Nolan looked shocked. Then leaned his head back and laughed.

"I do talk like that. It does sound pretty . . . rude." He sighed. "I understand your point, Claire. But I don't think you fully understand my side of it, what I've been through, what I'm fighting for. This man betrayed me, cheated me. I can't just shrug it off and walk away. I know I act extreme at times, but I have to persevere. If I give up, I won't be able to live with myself."

"I see." Claire nodded, thinking she had gone too far, said too much. "I shouldn't have spoken out of turn like that. You're right; I don't really know the whole story."

He met her glance and smiled at her. "I'm not a praying man, you know that about me. I don't believe that God is speaking to me through rainbows and four-leaf clovers and shooting stars." He waved his hand at the sky. "But I am honored and deeply touched to know that someone as kind and good and true as you are, Claire North, has said a prayer or two for me."

Claire was touched by his words. She didn't know what to say, and was even more surprised when he took her hand and twined it into the crook of his arm.

"We'd better get back to the inn. Liza will be wondering what's happened to us," he said. "Watch your step. It's quite slippery up here. I'm not sure the angels are fast enough to catch us if we take a tumble. Are you going to argue with me about that, too?"

Claire was so shocked by Nolan's show of affection, she didn't answer, just shook her head. It felt quite comfortable and natural to be led along by him on the stony path. She felt . . . cared for. It seemed he did care for her, just as Liza had said. Claire's heart did a little flip as he politely opened the car door for her and helped her inside.

When Nolan went to the other side of the Jeep to open the passenger door, she noticed that he had left his hat on the seat.

It was a dark blue Red Sox baseball cap, turned upside down. She was about to pick it up and take it out of the way, so he wouldn't sit on it, when she noticed a curious sight.

"Wait, Nolan . . . your hat."

She pointed at the hat but didn't touch it.

"I was afraid it might blow off in the wind, so I left it." He picked up the hat, put it on his lap, and slid into his spot.

She pointed down to the cap again, to the contents within. "What's that?" she asked, even though she knew full well what was stuck inside.

He looked down, too, and pulled out a pure white feather. He studied it a moment, then looked at her.

"I didn't put it there," she said, though he had not accused her.

"I don't believe you did. I was with you every minute outside the car. Unless you're a magician, adept at sleight of hand."

The accusation was so silly, she didn't address it. She was sure that he was teasing her, anyway.

"A bird must have flown by, and the feather drifted in. Simple explanation," he said.

"I didn't see one bird while we were out here. No less, one that flew over the car. Did you?" she challenged him.

He shrugged. "Maybe we didn't notice. We were talking. Not bird-watching."

Claire thought a moment. "Edison's been in the Jeep the whole time, and he didn't bark. If a bird flew that close to the Jeep, don't you think he would have gotten excited?"

Considering the way Edison carried on when he spotted even a tiny sparrow, Claire could not imagine the retriever sitting still for a bird that approached that near to him.

Nolan shook his head, as if flustered by her counterarguments. "You would have made a good scientist, Claire. You do consider all the variables. Maybe the feather just drifted in on the wind. That's possible, too, don't you think?"

"I suppose," Claire replied. Though she thought the chance of that was very unlikely. She knew where the feather had come from.

Claire drove toward the inn and let the matter drop. As they traveled in silence, she noticed that Nolan started to toss the feather out the window. Then he pulled his hand back and slipped the feather into his shirt pocket when he thought she wasn't looking.

She smiled to herself, facing the road again. She did find the small gesture encouraging.

Chapter Seven

Daniel needed to study for a practice exam that was going to be given on Tuesday, and decided he couldn't return to the island for the weekend. Liza tried hard not to sound disappointed when he told her on Friday afternoon. After all, he needed to focus on his studies and not worry about her, too. And it was nearly the third week of July, smack in the middle of her busy season, and she had an inn full of guests to take care of, didn't she? It wasn't as if they got to see each other all that much on weekends, anyway.

But she did miss him and did look forward to their phone calls—which were small consolation at times like this, when Daniel had to fit them in during study breaks, and sounded so tired and distracted.

Liza tried not to worry about it. A situation like this was bound to put some strain on a relationship, even a strong relationship. She didn't really worry about him getting interested in other women while he was away. Though she did like to tease him about it. And she was sure all the women in his classes had noticed him. *What woman wouldn't?* she wondered.

It was mainly that she missed him. It made her feel sad and tired and even short-tempered at times. It made her work at the inn seem so lackluster and routine, wishing the days would pass quickly until Daniel was back on the island again.

She missed his unpredictable visits and moving through the day with a feeling of expectation, knowing that any moment, his truck might come rolling down the drive and she would see his brilliant smile and slip off to spend a few stolen moments with him.

This separation phase wouldn't last long, she kept reminding herself. It just felt that way. She wasn't sure if he was counting the days until his exams. But she certainly was.

On Tuesday night, Daniel sounded a bit more relaxed during their evening phone call. His test was over and he was able to talk a little longer than usual.

"Hey, do you know what Friday is?" she asked him.

"Give me a minute. I can get this . . . Friday is the day I get sprung from this study dungeon and spend the weekend with you?"

"Well, that, too. But that's not what I was thinking of exactly."

He thought a moment. "I know it's not your birthday."

"Right, that's in October." She heard the worried tone in his voice and thought it very cute. She was sitting outside on a wicker love seat, her legs curled beneath her.

"It's not our anniversary," he said, more definitively. "Do we even have an anniversary?"

Liza laughed. "Sometimes we celebrate our first date. But that's really hard to calculate," she admitted. They had spent a lot of time together as friends before their first "official" date.

Daniel had once found her on her bike, riding in the rain, and brought her to Daisy Winkler's teahouse in the island's village center. They had spent a few romantic hours in the dim little cottage, sipping tea and eating cakes with the rain pattering on the roof and windows and no one in the entire world knowing where to find them. It was one of Liza's favorite memories.

But their first official and bona fide date had to be the night Daniel made dinner for her and served it out behind his cottage, overlooking the sea and a sky full of stars and a brilliant full moon. That had been one of the most romantic nights of her life. "Okay, I give up. What are we celebrating?"

"You'll be halfway through your review courses," she reminded him. "July twenty-sixth, to be exact."

"I get it. Right. Three weeks down, three to go."

"It went by fast, don't you think?" It hadn't really gone all that fast for her, but she was trying to stay positive.

"Fast for you, maybe. Torturously slow for me . . . Maybe because I miss you so much."

"I miss you, too," she said quietly. "Very much. But when you get back, we'll do something fun. We'll celebrate. I think there are some meteor showers passing this weekend. Maybe we can go down to the beach and watch them."

"Great idea. I'd love to have a midnight picnic on the beach with you."

Liza liked that idea, too. More than she wanted to say.

"Hey, I have some news," he said, suddenly changing the subject. "I was roaming around the web last night, trying to track down some former colleagues. Wow, some of those guys have done pretty well for themselves. I was impressed . . . well, intimidated, actually," he admitted. He was laughing, so he wasn't *that* intimidated, Liza thought. Why were men so competitive? It had to be a genetic thing; survival of the fittest and all that.

"Did you find anyone who might help you?" Liza knew that Daniel had been looking for former colleagues who might recommend him for a job opening.

"I did find someone. Someone I knew very well, who was a big influence on me. Jim Mitchell, another ER doc, was a bit older than me and helped me when I was a resident. And later, when I decided to leave medicine," Daniel added in a more serious voice. "I don't remember how we fell out of touch. He's out in Arizona now, working on a reservation."

"Really? How interesting. Did you send him an e-mail or something?"

"I did, and he answered right away. He's coming to Boston for a conference in August and we made plans to get together."

It was good to hear Daniel sounding so excited and happy. All this studying and homework was monotonous and wearing on him. At least he had something to look forward to.

"Where will he be staying? In Boston?"

"Yes, the conference is at a hotel in the city and runs for three days. But he and his wife want to drive around New England for a week or so after that, for a little vacation."

"Really? Why don't you ask them if they want to come

here? I'd be happy to have them stay over, as my guests, of course," she added.

"Liza, that's so sweet, but you don't have to do that. I bet you're booked solid."

"Let me see. I'll just check right now. What's the date, do you know?" Her laptop was handy, and she clicked to the reservations list.

"I'm not sure. I have to check on it. It's after my exams, that's all I can remember."

"That's a good thing. You'll be able to relax and have a good visit with him. If Dr. Mitchell was that great an influence on you, I'd really like to meet him."

"All right. I'll send him a note tonight and let you know what he says. It could be great visiting with him at the inn. We could have a lot of time together to talk. I bet he has some good advice for me. He always did."

They said good night a short time later, trading fake kisses over the phone. It was sweet, but . . . no substitute for the real thing, Liza thought as she ended the call. Three short weeks and this would be over. And Daniel would have to take his certification exams.

One question would be answered, and many others would take its place.

Liza wanted to surprise Daniel with a special dinner on Friday—lobster, his favorite. Claire didn't mind. A lobster dinner with chowder and steamers to start, corn, coleslaw, hot rolls, and blueberry pie à la mode for dessert was one of the easiest in the world to cook, even for a houseful of guests, as well. And that is what they would be dealing with this weekend.

On Wednesday morning, Claire looked over the menus for the weekend, then searched for the lobster crackers. She climbed up on a stepladder so she could check the top shelf in the pantry. They would need at least fifteen. She hoped those essential tools were not misplaced, or she would have to send Nolan to town to buy more.

Nolan found her just as she started to climb down from the stepladder. He offered his hand, and she finished her descent like a lady disembarking from a coach-and-four. "Thank you," she said with a smile.

"My pleasure. What were you looking for up there?"

"Lobster crackers, the extra sets. You might need to buy some in town." She noticed he had set a stack of envelopes and a small cardboard box on the kitchen table. "You can leave Liza's mail in her office today. I don't think she'll have time to look at it."

Ever since Nolan had sent off his letter, he had taken over the job of bringing in the mail. Claire couldn't blame him. There were few things worse than waiting for a letter; she knew that from her own experience.

Nolan handed the small cardboard box to her. "This one is for you."

Claire was not expecting a package. She sometimes bought items by mail order. Shopping was so limited in Cape Light, and pretty much nonexistent on the island. But she hadn't ordered anything in a long time.

"Let's see." She checked the return address as she pulled off a piece of tape. "It's from Jamie. He said he was sending me something," she recollected. Her birthday was in early June, but Jamie was not that good with dates. The important thing was that he remembered and took the trouble to send her a gift.

They were in the kitchen. Nolan was drinking a glass of water. He left the glass in the sink and headed back out to the garden. "I'll leave you to enjoy your surprise," he said. "I have some weeding to do."

Claire looked up, the package half open. "You haven't invented some little robot yet to do that for you?"

"Not yet . . . but that's not a bad idea," he replied, rubbing his chin.

Claire laughed, imagining the sight. Then she pulled back the last bit of tape and took out the gift. It felt heavy and was wrapped in sheets of newspaper. When she uncovered it she found a mug, a very lovely handmade piece decorated with dark blue glaze and a yellow sunflower on a gray background.

Claire already knew it was a special type of stoneware pottery, one she collected. A tag hanging from the handle confirmed that the salt-glaze and cobalt-blue color were unique to New England. Jamie had remembered her collection, and she was touched by the way he had tried to please her.

There was a card inside, a birthday card with birds and a happy saying. Jamie had written a short note:

When I saw this cup I thought of you and your garden. Hope you like it and hope you had a great birthday.

Love, Jamie

How sweet, Claire thought. She was eager to call him. She loved the mug. Jamie really knew her taste. He had given her a necklace last year made of sea glass—a piece he found on the beach—and she rarely took it off.

Claire set the mug on a shelf right above the sink, where she could see it all the time. Then she gathered up the sheets of newspaper. She was just about to throw them out when a headline and photo caught her eye.

LOCAL COLLEGE PROFESSOR MISSING—DAUGHTER OFFERS REWARD

She peered down at the smeared newsprint and blurry photo, then grabbed for her reading glasses on the table. She quickly read the article, though a piece had been torn off.

Nolan Porter, former professor of engineering at Carlisle University and a professional inventor, has been missing for nearly a month. Porter was last seen embarking on an extended sailing trip begun on May 23.

His daughter, Fiona Porter, age 25, contacted police last week, after efforts to contact him by cell phone and ship-to-shore radio failed, causing her to believe he's met with hazardous circumstances. Police are currently working to retrace Porter's path on the coastal waters. His last radio contact was sent from a point about five miles offshore of Rockport, at the tip of the Cape Ann peninsula.

His daughter is offering a reward for any information leading to his return. "My father is an excellent sailor. I'm afraid something has happened to him at sea. I hope that he's been rescued and is recuperating somewhere. I welcome any information that can help me find him."

Fiona Porter's phone number and e-mail address appeared below the article. Her picture was there too, holding up a photograph of what appeared to be the *Ariadne.*

There was a picture of Nolan, too, taken on the deck of his boat, the mainsail billowing out behind him, the wind lifting his hair. It could only be Nolan; Edison stood pressed against his leg.

His daughter? Nolan had said he didn't have any children. Claire recalled that very clearly. The poor young woman looked beside herself with worry. She seemed to have faith that her father was alive and hadn't drowned at sea. At least it seemed so from her quote. But she must have her doubts and plenty of worries.

Claire thought back, and realized that Nolan's boat went down several weeks ago. Almost a month to the day, she noticed, glancing at the calendar.

She took the scrap of newspaper and headed outside, not even bothering to remove her apron or the glasses hanging around her neck.

Nolan was on his hands and knees, weeding the garden. He looked up as she marched toward him. Then he stood up and rubbed some dirt from his gloves. She often brought him a cold drink around this time of day, and she guessed he would be surprised to see she was empty-handed—except for the piece of old newsprint.

"Something wrong?" He ducked his head, his thick brows knitted together.

Claire was so flustered she could hardly speak. "Your picture was in the *Portland Times*. I thought you would want to see it."

Nolan took the piece of newspaper and read it quickly, his eyes widening with surprise and then growing a little glassy. He looked back up at Claire, his expression unreadable. "Where did you find this?"

"That box you gave me. There was a gift inside from a friend who lives in Portland. He wrapped it in old newspapers. I just happened to notice your photo. And your daughter's," she added, not meaning to be sarcastic. "Why did you tell me that you don't have any children, Nolan?"

Nolan drew in a sharp breath. He stared down at the ground and shook his head. "Oh . . . I don't know. It seemed simpler that way. Under the circumstances."

He was embarrassed, she realized. But at least he didn't deny that he had lied to her.

"What circumstances? What do you mean by that?"

"Fiona and I haven't been in touch for a long time. I didn't think she would want to hear from me."

"Even after nearly drowning and wrecking your boat?"

"Especially after that." He sighed and looked up at her again. "She was sympathetic when my invention was stolen and I lost my business and the house and all that. But after a while— when I could no longer get along with her mother—she lost patience with me. I could see she thought I was a failure and an old windbag . . . and the cause of all my own problems. Harsh words were said, very harsh words." He looked away again as a pained expression crossed his face. "I don't know if I can ever forgive her for the way she spoke to me. And I don't think she can ever forgive me."

"But she must have forgiven you . . . or at least is willing to put the past aside. She's been looking for you, Nolan. She has the police involved. The Coast Guard may be involved, too," Claire realized. "We called them the day you were rescued, when we saw your boat floundering."

"Did you give them my name and the name of my boat?" he asked quickly.

"I couldn't on the first call. We had no idea who you were. Daniel was the one who followed up. I'm not sure what information he gave them, aside from the fact that you had survived." Claire paused and gazed at him. "The point is, your daughter is very worried about you, Nolan. She's doing everything she can to find out if you're even alive. Never mind what she said in the heat of an argument—don't her actions now count for something?"

Nolan sighed and looked at the clipping she held in her hand, but he didn't ask to see it again.

"I have to think about this," he said at last. "Part of me knows what you're saying is true. But in that argument we had . . . Fiona told me she never wanted to see me again, and that she was ashamed of me. If she feels guilty now and has regrets . . . well, maybe that's what she deserves."

"Maybe," Claire said carefully, "but we all have our faults, and we all hurt each other from time to time. It's not our place to judge, Nolan. It's not our place to punish. She's young. She has a lot to learn," she reminded him.

"Do you have any children, Claire? I don't think I ever asked you." She knew what he was trying to say. If she wasn't a parent, how could she know what he was going through?

"No, I never had children of my own. But I am blessed with a young man I think of as a son. I couldn't love him more if he were my own child. That's Jamie, in Portland, who sent the package," she explained. "He's in his early twenties now, but I met him when he was just a boy, at a settlement house in Boston. We grew very close, and I wanted to foster or adopt him. But I had to come back to the island to take care of my father, and we fell out of touch. I tried to find him a few times. But finally, last year, he found me." Claire paused, wondering if she was going on too long. But Nolan was listening attentively. "He was in trouble, of course. He stayed here for the summer, and we had our differences. I nearly gave up on him. I wanted to help him so badly, but he had to help himself. He left here after a terrible argument. But somehow, he found a good path for himself up in Portland and is making a good life. We patched up our differences and we're still very close. I'm just about his only family, and he's just about all of mine."

"I'm glad it worked out for you," Nolan said. "But Fiona and I . . . I don't think we'll ever patch up our differences."

"Do you love her, Nolan?" Claire persisted.

His head sagged a bit, and his lower lip trembled. "Of course I do. She's my only child," he said huskily.

"Then that's all that matters. The rest is just . . . static on the line," she insisted. "It wasn't easy to forgive Jamie for our argument and the trouble he'd caused here," she confessed. "But I managed to get there. I had to remember that God forgave Jamie. So I had to forgive him, too. It was just easier that way. You're all for efficiency, Nolan, aren't you? Think how much time and energy you'll save by letting go of this heavy baggage."

He shook his head. "I had a feeling you'd bring the *supernatural* into this." He caught her gaze with his twinkling blue eyes. His tone was not mocking, but warm and amused, and Claire did not take offense. He couldn't bring himself to say "God," she noticed, but she got his meaning.

"Well, even if you can't forgive her yet, you can at least be kind. It's cruel to keep her worrying, wondering whether you're alive or dead. Isn't there some way you can let her know you didn't end up at the bottom of the ocean?"

He shook his head and picked up the bushel of weeds he'd pulled and the basket of gardening tools. "I'm not sure. I have to think about this." He glanced over at Claire. "You're not going to get in touch with her on your own now, are you?"

That option had not occurred to Claire, though all the information she needed was there, at the bottom of the article. She could tell Nolan's daughter where he was if she wanted to.

"I'm not sure . . . I have to think about it," she replied, echoing his words. "I might call the paper to see how large that reward is."

He looked surprised at her sassy comeback, then amused again. "Claire North, I'm learning to never underestimate you.

You are the very definition of the phrase 'still waters run deep.' Did you know that?"

Claire shrugged. "I'm not sure what you mean by that. But I'll take it as a compliment."

She turned and headed to the house. Edison had been sunning himself on the lawn nearby and suddenly jumped up. He looked from Nolan to Claire, then back at his master. Then he decided to follow Claire, after all. Claire knew the dog probably wanted some cold water after helping in the garden all morning. She often put ice cubes in his dish on a hot day like this. Nolan, who had watched the dog's decision-making process, stood dumbfounded, then, with an exasperated sigh, headed for the barn.

Claire filled Edison's bowl, plunked a few ice cubes in, and set it on the kitchen floor. The dog lapped noisily while Claire thought about Nolan. He was a proud man who had a knack for holding a grudge. But this was more than that, she sensed. Fiona had hurt him; he had taken his daughter's hurtful words to heart. He must feel he had to prove Fiona wrong before he got in touch again. He had to show his only child that he wasn't a failure or "an old windbag." But how did he think he was going to do that?

With a successful conclusion to his lawsuit? Perhaps. Maybe that's why this legal decision meant so much to him. Claire paused a moment, surprised at that insight. Winning back his daughter's respect could very well be at the bottom of his drive to be vindicated by the lawsuit. It had not only cost him his business and home, his marriage, and his self-respect . . . but the love of his only child.

If Nolan finally found justice, he could show everyone—Fiona most of all—and return home in glory. While Claire could understand why he felt this way, it was really very sad that he didn't believe he had true worth in his daughter's eyes—or the world's—without this material symbol.

Claire knew she would never get in touch with Fiona Porter behind Nolan's back. But she wondered now if she and Liza were doing him a favor by letting him hide out at the inn. That's what it looked like to her now. Still, what good would it do to meddle? It wasn't her place to decide who knew Nolan's whereabouts and who didn't. It was only Nolan's business.

Claire was sorry she and Nolan had had words, but she had to be honest. Wasn't he that way himself?

NOLAN was very brusque with her for the rest of the morning and into the afternoon. Usually so loquacious, he confined his communication to monosyllables, or ignored her entirely, even avoiding eye contact if he walked into a room where she happened to be working.

All right, act like I'm invisible. Nothing I can do about that, Claire said to herself. Though his cool attitude did sting, more than a little.

Just before dinner, as she bustled to put finishing touches on the meal, Nolan came through the back door carrying a bushel of freshly picked strawberries. He set them on the table, but she didn't turn from the stove or pay him any special notice.

"I should have picked these this morning," he said finally. "Guess I rushed off after our . . . conversation."

Claire finally looked at the offering. He had thought to rinse the berries outside, she noticed, which was a help to her. "Thank you, Nolan. I'll serve them at breakfast tomorrow."

He stood by the back door, watching her store the berries in the refrigerator and return to the stove. She could tell he had something more to say. She turned down a burner under the chowder pot and looked over at him.

"I want you to know I've considered your advice, Claire. And perhaps you're right. There's no need for Fiona to worry. I'll send a message through my attorney to let her know I'm alive and kicking . . . But I'm still not ready to see her."

Claire thought the solution was a step in the right direction. "I'm sure she'll be relieved to know you're all right. That's a good idea."

"It just came to me. Seems a good compromise . . . I'm sorry we had words. I do value your friendship and your opinion. Even when we disagree," he added.

Claire was touched by his apology and his compliment. "I'm sorry for my sharp words, too," she admitted. "Please forgive me for meddling. It wasn't any of my business."

He smiled at her warmly, looking pleased and relieved that they had made amends. "Well, maybe not. But since I lied to you about having a daughter, you had a perfect right to call me out," he admitted frankly. "I guess you'll miss out on that reward now."

"I guess I will. But I think it's worked out even better." For Nolan and his daughter—and for herself and Nolan, too. They had managed to navigate this rough patch and come out with an even closer bond. That was a fine reward right there.

She reached into her apron pocket and handed him the article, folded into a neat square. "You can have this now. You might need the information on the bottom," she added quietly.

He knew what she meant: Fiona's phone number and e-mail address. He opened up the page and gazed at his daughter's picture again. A soft look came over his expression. Claire could see he truly missed her.

"She's a lovely girl. Looks like you," Claire said, stirring the soup.

"You think so? I think she looks like her mother. More and more all the time . . ." He cleared his throat, folded the paper, and put it in his shirt pocket. "Do you need my help serving dinner tonight?"

Nolan only served if there was a full house, as Liza worried about what he might say to the guests. Comments like "What's the matter, didn't you like the fish? Claire worked very hard on that dish. I thought it was excellent." Or "For goodness' sake, what do you have in these suitcases, bowling balls?"

Nolan seemed to have had better control over his blunt speech the last week or so, Claire had noticed. Maybe that book she loaned him had helped.

"An extra pair of hands and feet will make things go much faster," she now told him. She glanced at the clock. "We plan to serve in about half an hour. So come back soon."

"I'll go clean up right now, then. See you shortly." Nolan left, with Edison padding right behind him.

Alone in the kitchen again, Claire sent up a quiet prayer. *Thank You, God, for helping Nolan find that compromise, and for putting a loving thought in his head and heart. I pray that he and*

his daughter are able to forgive each other and make up very soon . . .
And thank You for helping us solve our differences and grow even
closer in our friendship.

The last part of the prayer was important to her, Claire
realized. More important than she would ever admit.

Chapter Eight

THEY had only been apart for two weeks, but to Liza the separation from Daniel had seemed much longer. She was glad, though, that he wouldn't get back to the inn until about eight that night. That gave her plenty of time to do what she had to do—help Claire serve dinner and clean up.

Once the guests had scattered for their evening amusements, she ran upstairs to change. The menu had been steamed lobster, and as much as Daniel loved the dish, she didn't want to smell like one.

She was soon ready and came down to the porch to wait, wearing a new sundress she had bought online. She had been relieved when it was delivered, just in time, that morning. She had fixed her hair long and loose, though it was a nuisance in the humid weather, curling in all directions; but Daniel liked the long, wild curls.

Liza made herself comfortable in a wicker chair with a

magazine and her cell phone. It was a Friday night and you never knew how long the trip from Boston could take with weekend traffic. He could be delayed heading up to the North Shore.

Claire came to the screen door and stepped out on the porch. "I left everything ready for Daniel's dinner. The lobsters are awaiting their dubious fate in the fridge. You just need to pop them in the pot."

"Lob*sters*, as in more than one?"

Claire averted her gaze. "I saved him two. They were very small. But sweet," she added.

"You spoil him beyond belief. But I'm sure they won't go to waste. Daniel will be starving. He might even eat the poor things as sushi."

"There's plenty of chowder to start. That should slow him down."

Sometimes Liza wasn't sure if Claire was being super literal or just had a very dry sense of humor. A little of both, she suspected.

"What a beautiful night," Claire observed, looking out at the darkening sky. "We're lucky to have such clear weather. I hear there are going to be some meteor showers passing by."

"Yes, there are. But they won't pass until much later. We're going to try to watch them from the beach."

"Should be good viewing from down there. No surface lights to distract you. I hope you see some shooting stars. Don't forget to make a wish."

Liza met her gaze and smiled. She certainly had a lot of wishes these days. First of all, for Daniel to pass his tests and find a good position practicing medicine, and second . . . well, just for them to stay together and always be happy. If she had to be perfectly honest about the last few weeks, she had not liked their separation at all. It wasn't just the distance; it was also his attention. Even when they were sitting side by side, Daniel's nose was usually buried in some thick textbook; he might as well have been back in Boston. Or on the moon.

Liza told herself that this was just the exam stage, the studying and cramming for these tests. She reminded herself that she was lucky they hadn't met when he was in medical school; then she might have had years like this. It was only a few weeks. Still, she couldn't help feeling a little worried. She could see that once Daniel was a doctor, their relationship would be very different than it was when he worked as a carpenter, being his own boss and making his own hours. Once he was practicing medicine again, she would have to get used to seeing him less. She was starting to understand that now.

Unless, of course, they got married. But even then, it might not be all that much better. And they'd never even discussed marriage. Liza had been married once, and it hadn't worked out. She knew marriage was a very serious step; one she had taken too lightly the first time. She had always promised herself she would think very carefully before taking that step again. Even with Daniel.

And yet, though she was in no rush to get a ring on her finger, she knew that she loved him with all her heart and wanted to share his life. What she wasn't certain of was whether he felt the same way.

Liza heard the truck coming up the drive before she saw it.

She stood up and walked down the steps. Daniel pulled up next to the inn and jumped out. Then he put his arms around her and hugged her tight, burying his face in her hair and lifting her feet off the ground. "I missed you so much."

Before Liza had a chance to answer, he kissed her, a long, deep kiss that made her feel dizzy. But dizzy in a good way, she decided as he finally set her down. Definitely a good way.

She stroked his hair with her hand and smiled into his eyes.

"You don't look any different. Just a little tired."

"And hungry," he added. He slipped his arm around her waist as they walked back to the inn. "What's for dinner? Did you save me anything?"

"Well, we all had chowder, lobster, corn, coleslaw, and corn bread . . . I saved you a bit of the chowder and some bread. Is that okay?"

"I just had a double cheeseburger and fries on the road. I was just wondering."

Liza stopped and stared at him. "You didn't—"

Daniel laughed. "Had you going there for a minute, didn't I?"

She laughed and shook her head. "If you must know, Claire saved you *two* lobsters. She said they were very small."

"Claire . . ." He sighed. "My ideal woman, second only to you, of course, sweetheart."

Liza smiled. "Sometimes I wonder about that."

In the kitchen, Liza turned the heat back on under the lobster pot. The water was hot already and wouldn't take long to boil. Claire had put a mixture of herbs and special spices that she called her "fish boil" in the water, and the fragrance already wafted into the warm kitchen. Daniel took a beer from the refrigerator and sat at the table while Liza brought out the side dishes.

"I hated staying in the city last weekend, but it was worth it. I aced my practice test . . . Well, it was more of a mid-term, really. It only covered half the course, but it was encouraging."

"That's great, honey. You've hit the halfway point. It's a downhill slide from here, right?"

"Actually, the tougher subjects are in the second half," he reported, though he was still smiling. "So it's more of an uphill slide . . . if that's even possible. Let's just say I'm slogging through it, one multiple choice question at a time."

Liza sat down beside him at the table and watched him devour both lobsters and all the trimmings, including a thick slab of rustic peach tart that Claire had baked earlier in the day. Claire had put the dessert on the menu quite often lately, claiming it was an exceptional summer for peaches. But Liza guessed the frequent choice had to do with Nolan, since the dish was his obvious favorite.

Daniel seemed to like it equally well and asked for seconds.

How did he stay so lean and fit-looking? That was the question. And so annoying.

"That was delicious, every bite. Come here. I want to thank the chef . . ." He pulled Liza down onto his lap and kissed her shoulders and neck.

"I'm not exactly the chef . . . but I don't mind standing in," she admitted, kissing him back.

He held her tight and sighed. "I need a walk or I'll fall

asleep right here. Want to go down to the beach? Or are you too tired?"

"Not tired at all. I was hoping we could watch the meteor shower. It's almost time," she realized, glancing up at the clock.

"Oh, right. I forgot all about that. It's a clear night. We might see something."

Liza grabbed a beach blanket and a flashlight off the porch and they headed outside, where they crossed the road and carefully descended the wooden stairs.

The beach was very dark, but Liza's eyes soon adjusted. A thin crescent moon hung low in the night sky, casting a silvery light on the ink-black water. Just the right amount of moon, Liza thought. A full moon would make it hard to see the shooting stars.

She thought they would see a few people on the beach tonight, waiting for the celestial show. But the best viewing was on the other side of the island.

Nolan, who knew about such things, had told the guests that fact during dinner. He also told them the shooting stars were not really stars, but bits of a passing meteor, which was like a small planet zipping through space very close to the Earth. These chunks of rock had broken off from the meteor, then fell through the Earth's atmosphere and burned up; that was the light of the shooting star. The explanation pretty much drained the magic out of it, Liza thought, but she still loved to watch the amazing sight.

She gazed down along the shoreline but didn't see a soul in either direction, so perhaps the guests had taken Nolan's advice.

She was glad she and Daniel had the entire beach to themselves. It certainly seemed more romantic that way.

They walked hand in hand, in time with the muffled roar of the waves. A short distance from the stairs, Daniel put down the blanket in a spot near a large piece of driftwood, which they used as a backrest.

"Isn't this comfortable? Like sitting in your front parlor. We should have made a bonfire," he said.

"That would have been fun, but you can see the stars better if there's less light, right?"

"That's right." He nodded and slipped his arm around her shoulder. "How was your week?"

"Oh, the usual. Some nice guests, some difficult ones. We're almost full up this weekend, but everything is going smoothly."

"You have it down to a science now, you and Claire. You could run this place with your eyes closed."

"Not exactly, but we're a good team. And you can't forget Nolan." Liza turned to Daniel and grinned. "He's come up with another invention. For sanding his boat. It looks like a huge mitten . . . or a potholder. I think he borrowed one of Claire's hot mitts to make it."

"Can't wait to see that one. Sounds like something I could use when I'm doing carpentry . . ." His voice trailed off with an odd questioning tone.

Liza understood. "Well, you'll probably always do some woodworking. As a hobby, right?"

Daniel took her hand and kissed it. "Our future suddenly looks very different. That's pretty exciting, don't you think?"

She liked the way he'd said "our future"—including her.

She kissed his cheek in answer. "Yes. It's a lot to get my mind around, the fact that by the fall, you'll be a doctor again and not flying around the island in your truck anymore. It's a little . . . disconcerting," she admitted.

"I know what you mean. It's all going to be new. So we don't know what to expect. Just that I won't be flying around the island in my truck anymore. Not unless I set up a practice out here and do house calls," he countered. "Which probably isn't entirely out of the question . . . though I was thinking of spreading my wings a bit more."

Liza wasn't sure what he meant by that, though she hoped he would work close enough to commute every day, so they wouldn't have to deal with long separations.

"I've loved living here," he continued. "And working on these beautiful old houses. The island has changed so much since I first came here. It's come back to life in a way. I'm glad I was a part of that. It will always be a special place for me, and I can never completely leave it. Not as long as you're here," he added.

"I hope not," she said with a small smile. She knew that he loved her, but with his entire life about to be turned upside down, she hoped their bond didn't get lost in the shuffle.

"If all goes well, life is going to be a lot different come September, even if I end up practicing in Essex or Newburyport. But this place was good for me. It taught me a lot. Most of all . . . humility," Daniel admitted. "I think I'm going to be a much better doctor than I was before. I'm glad I'm not able to go back to emergency room medicine, too," he added. "I think

I'm more in tune with being a general practitioner now. Practicing family medicine and helping out in a range of cases. I can specialize again down the road if I want to," he explained. "But it will be better to be a GP while I get my feet wet again. I think I'm going to like it."

Daniel had learned that it was a much longer process to be recertified as a specialist. But he was already qualified to practice general medicine. Working in the island's medical clinic all these years had counted toward his reentry and put him on an easy track for general practice and family medicine.

"You're sure you won't miss the excitement of the ER?" she asked.

"Actually, I am sure," he said, sounding slightly bemused by the admission. "I was a very good ER doc; one of the best on the staff. But I wasn't very . . . warm and cuddly," he confessed. "I think I can do better with my bedside manner this time around."

"Really? I think you're very warm and cuddly," she replied, nuzzling her head into his shoulder. "No complaints here."

"What can I say? You bring out the best in me, Liza. That's why I have to keep you around. One reason, anyway."

He circled her with both arms and Liza leaned her head back against his shoulder. "What are the other reasons? I'm just curious," she said casually, though she was really dying to hear his list.

"Let's see . . . You make me laugh. You argue with me when I'm wrong. Sometimes when I'm right, too . . . but that's not too often."

"You know what Claire says; even a broken clock is right twice a day."

Daniel laughed and squeezed her very tight. "Very funny."

"Go on . . . Is that all?"

"Hardly got started yet . . . You're very smart and kind. And generous to a fault . . . And very pretty. I can't forget that."

"Please don't . . . especially when you have to stay in Boston two weeks at a time. I know there are lots of attractive women in your class. You just won't admit it."

"I already told you, I haven't seen one," he said with a convincing face.

Liza wasn't sure she really believed him. "Well, I like your list. Do you want to hear mine?"

"Absolutely . . . Wait, I need to get a pen and paper. I want to write this down. So I can read it back when I'm studying too much and feeling lonely and blue." Daniel reached into his back pocket, then looked at Liza with surprise. "Hey, what's this?"

He pulled out a small velvet box and held it out to her.

Liza stared at the offering and nearly gasped out loud. She could hardly dare raise her gaze to meet his.

"I think it's a ring." He snapped the box open and showed it to her.

It was a ring—a large, round diamond in a beautiful antique setting. Exactly the style she loved best.

He carefully removed it and held it out to her. "Elizabeth Grace Martin . . . I loved you since the first minute I set eyes on you. I know it's taken me a while to get my act together . . . and it's not quite together yet. But with you by my side, I know I can do anything. I promise to love you and cherish you until the last breath leaves my body. Will you do me the great honor of becoming my wife?"

Liza sat with her mouth hanging open, then flung her arms around his shoulders. "Yes . . . yes . . . absolutely. Yes!"

Then Daniel kissed her and it felt as if all the stars in the sky were spinning around in her head. Or as if they had been lifted up together into the heavens.

When they parted they were both laughing and crying a little, and Daniel slipped the ring on her finger. She held it out in front of her to admire the design of the antique gold setting.

"It was my grandmother's. I went home last weekend to get it," he admitted. "I wasn't really studying. If you don't like the setting, we can have it changed. My feelings won't be hurt. I just want you to love it."

"I do love it, just the way it is. It's perfect. Just what I would have picked out." Liza looked up at him again. "So you had this all planned?"

He nodded. "Are you surprised?"

"Shocked speechless is more like it," she admitted.

He leaned over and kissed her forehead, then smoothed her hair back. The damp sea breeze had whipped it into a mass of dark curls. But Liza didn't mind; she gathered it in one hand and pulled it over her shoulder.

"I was going to wait until I got the test results back—so you'd know what you were getting into. But I couldn't. I want to marry you, come what may. I love you with all my heart, Liza."

"I love you with all my heart, too, Daniel. And all my soul . . . and all my . . . everything." She laughed. "You're my soul mate and my best friend. You're the smartest, handsomest, sweetest man alive. From the minute I met you, you had me hooked. I want to share my life with you. I know I'll always be happy if we're together."

"I do, too," Daniel agreed quietly. He kissed her again and held her close. Just as her eyes opened, she saw a shooting star over his shoulder. "Look, it's starting. The meteor shower . . ."

He sat with his arm around her shoulder and they tipped their heads back, staring at the sky. Moments later, streaks of glowing light arced across the dark blue velvet heavens. Liza could never guess where the next one would appear. Some sped by so quickly, she could only catch the last seconds of their flare.

But there were many stars to watch and they *oohed!* and *ahhed!* out loud, as if watching a fireworks display.

"Don't forget to close your eyes and make a wish," he reminded her.

Liza had forgotten to wish, she'd been so excited. But when she spotted the next star streak across the sky, she did make a wish. And hoped with all her heart it would come true.

"I did it," she said, opening her eyes. "Did you?"

He nodded. "I did . . . What did you wish for?"

"I can't tell you. It won't come true."

He smiled. "That's right. I forgot. But I think I can guess . . ." He leaned closer and kissed her, and Liza forgot all about the meteor shower, lost in the heaven she had found in Daniel's arms.

LATER, when they went back up to the inn, Liza noticed the lights on in the front parlor and heard Claire and Nolan talking. It sounded as if they were playing a game, as they often did in the evenings now.

Daniel heard them, too. "Let's go tell them the news."

Claire and Nolan were playing Scrabble, totally focused on the board between them, which was filled with tiles, Liza noticed. Some of the words were amazingly long, too.

Liza wondered who was winning, then easily guessed from their expressions. Claire looked cheerful, laying down her tiles.

"E-Q-U-I-N-O-X, and on a triple-word-score square," she pointed out.

Nolan looked glum, calculating the score on a pad and mumbling to himself.

They both turned to look at Liza and Daniel as they approached. Claire met Liza's gaze with a curious look.

"How was the meteor shower? Did you see anything?" Nolan asked.

"We did. It was amazing." Liza glanced at Daniel. Then she held out her hand so they could see the ring. "Look what fell out of the sky—and landed on my finger."

Claire looked puzzled at first, then saw the diamond. She jumped up and clapped her hands together, nearly knocking the table over.

"Good heavens! You're engaged! How wonderful! When did that happen?"

"Just now. Out on the beach. Daniel proposed to me right before the shooting stars came."

"How lovely . . . What a beautiful memory you'll always have of this night," Claire said.

"Nice work, Daniel, arranging the celestial entertainment," Nolan teased him.

Daniel laughed. "It wasn't easy, believe me."

Claire jumped up and hugged Liza, and then hugged Daniel, too. "My heart is so full of joy for you both. I had a feeling this happy day was on its way, but I had no idea it would come so soon."

Nolan rose and shook Daniel's hand. Then he gave Liza a hug. "From the minute I met you two, I knew you were meant for each other. It doesn't take a scientist to see that," he quipped. "Though I'm happy to be here and share your good news. All my best wishes for a wonderful future."

"Yes, absolutely. God bless every step of this beautiful journey," Claire added.

Liza and Daniel glowed under the shower of good wishes. Claire suddenly remembered a bottle of champagne in the refrigerator and quickly bustled off to fetch it. Nolan followed, offering his help. Edison was sleeping under the game table, but rose to trot after them. First, though, he stopped to pant happily up at Liza and Daniel and lick Liza's hand.

"Well, they seem happy for us. Even Edison. Our engagement is a national holiday around here," Daniel said with a quiet laugh. "Are you sure that dog didn't lick off your diamond?"

Liza stuck out her hand and showed him the ring, still intact. "Don't worry. It was just his way of saying, 'Congratulations,' and, 'I knew it all along.'"

"Were we that obvious?" Daniel asked.

"I guess so. Everyone seemed to know it was going to happen before me." Liza laughed, gazing down at the sparkling ring again. "I still can't believe it. It feels . . . like a dream."

"Believe it, my love. The best is yet to come." Daniel met her gaze and squeezed her hand. "Let's go out on the porch and see if there are any more stars. I still have a wish or two left."

He led Liza out to the porch, and they settled in their favorite perch—the wooden swing.

Claire soon arrived, carrying a tray with crystal glasses. Nolan had charge of the champagne bucket. He wiggled the cork loose, and it shot out of the bottle with a loud pop. They soon raised their glasses in a joyous toast.

Liza was so happy, she felt as if she were walking on air. It had to be the happiest night of her life, and she knew at least one of her wishes had finally come true.

They sat and sipped the sparkling drink, catching their breath from the excitement.

"Have you given any thought to the wedding?" Claire asked after a few moments. "I suppose not," she added. "It's much too soon for that."

"I have," Daniel announced. "I'd like a small wedding, just our closest friends and family." He glanced at Liza to gauge her reaction.

"Oh, I'd like that, too. Very intimate . . . but nice," she added quickly. "I'd like Reverend Ben to marry us. What do you think, Daniel?"

"I wouldn't ask anyone but Reverend Ben," he seconded. "Unless you want to run down to Cape Light village hall tomorrow and have Mayor Warwick marry us?"

He was teasing, she knew. "I don't think the village hall is open on Saturday. And I'd like to have a little time to plan it. I've planned so many weddings here for so many brides, I've always imagined how my own would be," she confessed. "I'd love to have the reception at the inn."

Daniel smiled indulgently. "That would be perfect. This is where we met, where we fell in love . . . As long as my bride isn't fried to a crisp before she walks down the aisle. I know how you get running those events. But you're the bride this time. Maybe the inn isn't the best idea." He sounded as if he hadn't considered the drawbacks. And now that he did, he was wary.

"I agree," Claire said at once. "Liza is the bride this time, and we can't let her get all stressed and harried. But it would be so fitting to see you married here. I can't imagine the celebration anyplace else. I think if we hire some extra help, a wedding planner, maybe . . . Or Molly Willoughby? She can do everything for you; everything *you* always do for the bride."

"Excellent suggestion, Claire," Daniel said. He turned to Liza. "What do you think? It might be hard to hand over the reins. Do you think you could let Molly do the heavy lifting?"

"Molly has catered a lot of parties here. Once she gets involved, she takes over anyway. So I'll just step back and let her do her thing."

"She does a wonderful job, too. She does excellent parties, and her food is delicious . . . though I'd like to make a few dishes," Claire quickly added. "And perhaps the cake?"

"That would be very meaningful to us, Claire. Thank you," Liza said sincerely.

"Well, this is pretty easy. Why do people complain so much about planning a wedding?" Daniel asked.

Liza rolled her eyes and glanced at Claire. "Men just don't have a clue sometimes, do they? He thinks all we have to do now is rent a tux and order some flowers."

"Exactly," Daniel said. "So how about September? By then I'll know if I passed the test, and we'll be free to figure out our next steps."

Our next steps. Liza liked the sound of that. But September? He was being very unrealistic—in a typical male way, she thought.

She took his hand in hers. "Daniel, I can't plan a nice wedding that quickly. It's much too fast."

"It's more than a month. You already said you've been thinking of what you'd like for a long time," he reminded her. "And Molly is a powerhouse. She could probably put it together in two weeks."

"Whoa . . . two weeks? Let's go back to September . . . late September . . . early October?" Liza negotiated with him. "I still have guests booked after Labor Day," she reminded him. "It's still a busy time for me."

That was true, too. Though summer unofficially ended on Labor Day, many visitors who didn't have to worry about getting their children back to school found September an ideal time to stay on the island. The weather was usually wonderful, too, cooler and drier than the hot, humid days of the summer.

It was a nice time of year for a wedding, too, Liza thought. Though her husband-to-be had proposed a tight deadline.

"All right. Let's look at the calendar tomorrow and at your

reservations," Daniel conceded. "We'll see where we can fit in our wedding," he teased her. "We do want to have some rooms free for family and friends. I'm starting to see a weekend-long party at the Inn at Angel Island."

Claire laughed. "I am, too, truth be told. I can't think of an event more fitting for one, either."

"In many other cultures, weddings are celebrated over several days—India, for instance, and even parts of Eastern Europe," Nolan offered.

"Several days? I'm lucky if I can plan one party," Liza told the others. "But it will be wonderful, I can promise you that."

Daniel leaned over and gave her a quick kiss. "Anytime or anyplace that we get married will be wonderful. That's just a given."

"Yes, it is," she agreed. Her mind went back to the shooting stars streaking across the night sky. Only an hour had passed since they'd seen them, and already so many of her most cherished wishes were coming true.

WHEN Liza woke up the next morning, she could hardly believe that the diamond ring on her left hand really belonged to her. That Daniel had finally asked her to marry him. It still seemed like a dream.

But wedding talk the rest of the weekend convinced her. She somehow managed to take care of her guests in between wedding plans. Daniel was over bright and early, with a stack of books he needed to study and a calendar. While Daniel argued for September, Liza managed to push the date off into

October, pointing out all the reservations she still had booked after Labor Day.

They finally picked Sunday, October sixth, as their wedding day. It wasn't as soon as Daniel had hoped, and not as much time to prepare as she wanted, but Liza found the week clear of reservations, and blocked off all the rooms for her wedding guests from the prior Tuesday on, so they would have enough time to get the inn ready for the wedding.

She would probably hire some cleaning help for that week, so she and Claire could attend to more important matters. She hoped Nolan planned on staying at his job that long. His boat repairs were progressing, but he never mentioned when they would be done or when he expected to leave. Even though the inn would be comparatively quiet after Labor Day, she did need his help. When she thought about it, she had grown so fond of Nolan and Edison the last few weeks that she really wanted to see them at the wedding. And she knew Claire did, too.

On Sunday morning, Claire stayed at the inn to serve breakfast while Liza and Daniel went to church. They needed to speak to Reverend Ben right away about performing their ceremony. Liza hoped he wasn't busy that day with another wedding. It was short notice to ask him.

"I'd be willing to change the date if Reverend Ben can't come," she told Daniel as they drove to Cape Light.

"I would, too. Let's just see what he says and figure it out from there."

They arrived at church a bit early for the service and went into the sanctuary to find a seat. The choir was still rehearsing, and Vera Plante, who was one of the deacons, lit the candles on the altar and rearranged the flowers a bit.

Liza did not attend church as often as Claire, but she had been coming to this church since she was a girl, with her aunt and uncle when she visited them during the summers. Her parents had not belonged to a church, so she always felt most attached and at home in this one.

"Look, there he is," Daniel said. "Let's speak to him now."

Liza turned and saw Reverend Ben standing at the back of the church, talking to Tucker Tully, another deacon. She didn't want to interrupt the reverend if he was busy getting ready for the service, but Daniel had already jumped up and walked over to meet him.

Liza followed, and by the time she reached the two men, she realized Daniel had already delivered their news.

"Congratulations, Liza! What happy news!" Reverend Ben opened his arms and hugged her. Then he stepped back, a wide smile spread across his face. "When did this all come about?"

"Daniel proposed last night."

"Thankfully, she said yes." Daniel gave a mock sigh of relief, and put his arm around her shoulders. "We would be so happy if you would perform the ceremony, Reverend. We're thinking of getting married Sunday, October sixth."

"But we're flexible if you're busy," Liza added quickly.

Reverend Ben thought about it a moment. "I'm totally clear after service that Sunday. I was just looking ahead at my calendar this morning. I'd be honored to marry you . . . but that's very soon to plan a wedding."

"Yes, I know," Liza replied, trying not to sound stressed already.

"It's going to be a small group, just close friends and family," Daniel explained.

"But a nice reception—flowers and music and all that. We'd like to be married at the inn," Liza added. "I love this church, but the inn has special meaning for us."

"I understand completely. It will be a very beautiful wedding, I'm sure." Reverend Ben reached out with a reassuring touch. "Please call my office and make a date for us to meet, to plan the ceremony and rehearsal. We have a little time," he assured them. "How is everything else going? How are your classes, Daniel?"

Daniel met his knowing gaze, remembering their talk on the beach a few weeks ago—and how Reverend Ben had helped him get his worries and doubts in perspective.

"Very well, Reverend. I'm halfway through. The final exams are in August. We should know if I passed by the time we get married."

"Perfect timing. Good luck with the rest of it. Call me if you have any questions."

The seats in the sanctuary were starting to fill, though it rarely got very crowded in the summer. The choir director had come to speak to the reverend, and Daniel and Liza returned to their pew.

The choir was walking in, singing the first hymn, when Liza noticed Molly Willoughby and her husband, Matt, take a seat a few rows behind them. "There's Molly. Let's try to talk to her after the service," Daniel said.

"Good idea. We should invite them back to the inn for brunch," Liza suggested. "If they're free, I mean. Then we can start to make real plans, if Molly will take on the wedding."

"Oh, I'm sure she'll want to cater our wedding. I think she'll be flattered that you're asking her," Daniel whispered.

Daniel was right about that, Liza thought, as Molly gushed with surprise and delight when Liza asked her after the service. "Are you kidding? I'd love to be your wedding planner! My calendar is clear for you two," she promised.

"Well, we were thinking of October sixth. That's a Sunday. Do you have many parties booked already?" Liza knew how popular Willoughby's Fine Foods & Catering was around town. Most people made plans much further ahead.

Molly thought a moment. "I do have a fund-raiser at the historical society around then. But October isn't a real busy season. Besides, you're talking about a small guest list, right? Under a hundred?"

"Under fifty, I'm sure," Liza said.

Molly waved her hand. "No problem. I can do that in my sleep . . . not that I wouldn't be totally focused and make sure that everything was super perfect," she quickly amended.

Liza knew what she meant. Molly did have a way about her that made you feel relaxed and confident. Even if pulling a wedding together this quickly was asking for trouble.

"I'm sure it will be perfect. I've already seen what you can do."

Molly and Matt had been planning to go to a beach on Angel Island straight from church. Their car was packed with bathing suits, chairs, and even fishing gear. They quickly accepted Liza's invitation to stop at the inn for lunch. Molly was even more eager to get started on the wedding than Liza, which was really saying something.

"I just met with a couple yesterday and have all my books in the car. Is that lucky or what?" Molly told her as the two couples left the church and headed for the parking lot.

Daniel glanced at Matt. "I have some fishing gear in my trunk. Is that lucky or what?" he asked, echoing the women.

Matt laughed. "A little fly casting after lunch is fine with me . . . if your fiancée is okay with it." Matt glanced at Liza, who sent Daniel a questioning look. She knew he had his own ideas about the wedding, but it was just a first meeting with Molly. Maybe it was best if he had a little downtime this afternoon—to unwind from all the engagement excitement and from his classes.

Besides, Matt was a doctor with a busy practice in Cape Light, and Daniel might get some good advice from him about finding a position, she realized.

Back at the inn, Claire was very happy to see Molly and Matt arrive. A table was quickly set on the back patio, under the wisteria arbor, where Claire served them lunch.

Liza enjoyed catching up on the news of Molly and Matt's four daughters—Matt's daughter, Amanda, and Molly's two girls, Lauren and Jillian. Betty, their youngest, had arrived about seven years ago and was the only one at home now.

"I can't believe your girls are all grown up and have left the house. Except for Betty, of course," Liza said. "I don't know how you did it."

"Neither do I." Molly rolled her eyes. "In fact, just thinking about it makes me tired. Raising kids is like riding a bicycle. If you think too much about it, you'll fall off. But you just keep pedaling and time just flies. We're really enjoying Betty," she added. "We know she won't be little forever."

"Pretty soon we'll be planning a few weddings of our own." Matt smiled, glancing at his wife. "Amanda and her boyfriend seem very serious. And I'm sure Lauren won't be too far behind. But at least we know someone in the business. She's not that great . . . but we could get a good price." He shrugged and Molly poked him in the ribs with her elbow.

"Thanks a lot, wise guy. Do you want Liza to get worried about her wedding?"

Liza laughed. "Molly, I have no worries with you on the job, believe me."

"Me, either," Daniel agreed. "Which is why it might be good time for me and Matt to head down to the beach, so you and Molly can get down to business?"

"Good idea. Leave the heavy lifting to the ladies. When the going gets tough . . . guys should go fishing." Molly turned to Liza. "This is going to be so much fun. Just let me grab my books. I left them in the foyer. Maybe we should talk in the front parlor? There's more room there to spread stuff out . . . and don't forget your laptop."

Liza was pleased at Molly's all-business attitude. She was ready to jump in the deep end, holding her nose and grabbing Liza's hand. The moment had finally come to really plan her wedding, and Liza was excited . . . and nervous, as well. It was great to have a seasoned guide like Molly. That choice had been an inspiration.

Liza had done this often for so many other brides-to-be. But it was her turn now. She almost had to pinch herself to remember that. Daniel wasn't the only one who had to get used to a new idea of his identity.

LIZA wasn't sure how long she and Molly had been talking. Long enough for Claire to serve them iced tea and cookies, and for them to decide on quite a few important things on the order forms where Molly made notes about the event.

Flowers were discussed and narrowed down, though not totally decided. The size of the wedding party, the way the property would be arranged and decorated, and where the guests would have cocktails and where they would dine . . .

It was a lot to think about all at once. Liza's head was spinning. But Molly was unflagging and still focused when they heard heavy footsteps and deep voices on the porch. Matt and Daniel had returned from fishing, and the heavy *thunk* of a cooler hitting the porch floor hinted that they may have even come back with some fish.

Molly rose and went to the window. "Catch anything, honey?"

"I'll say. Striped bass for dinner tonight," Matt promised. "Daniel is going to find me some more ice."

Liza rose and stretched her legs. She had been sitting a long time. She hadn't realized it.

"Did you catch anything, Daniel?" she asked as she stepped out to the porch.

"He caught a job offer. I'd say that was pretty good for one day," Matt answered, before Daniel could reply.

Liza was surprised and a bit confused.

"Matt has an opening coming up at his office. One of his associates is leaving in October. He was just about to start looking for a replacement," Daniel explained.

"Serena Miller is having her second child. She'll be on a full-time leave of absence for a while, then coming in part-time. We have more patients than we can handle already. I really need another full-time doctor, even after she returns," Matt explained. He turned to Daniel and smiled kindly. "I didn't know Daniel was a licensed physician, but I've seen how he handles cases at the clinic. He's saved a lot of lives on this island. I always wondered how a carpenter could be such a talented, knowledgeable EMT," he added with a sly grin.

Perhaps Matt had already suspected that Daniel had a medical background but had never asked him about it. It sounded as if Daniel had confided in him this afternoon.

"I know you have a lot going on now, with the tests coming up and the wedding plans. But I hope you'll give my offer some thought and come down to the office sometime soon, so we can talk some more."

"I definitely will, Matt. I'm very interested. I appreciate you considering me."

Liza did, too. A position in a practice in Cape Light? How great was that? They couldn't ask for an easier commute or less disruption of their lifestyle. They had already been talking about renovating the third floor of the inn as their living space. Daniel's cottage was charming but very small, and Liza needed to be at the inn so much, it only made sense for them to both live there.

Daniel had already started sketching out some plans for the space, though Liza had been wondering if she would see him there very much—or if he would find a job with some long commute and difficult hours. This news made her practically sigh out loud with happiness. This opening was perfect, especially since Daniel seemed very enthusiastic about the idea.

It was amazing how things were falling into place for them. Once Daniel had decided to take that first step, to return to what he was meant to do, so many doors had opened. A path to the future was unfurling right in front of them, where none had existed before. A path for both of them.

Chapter Nine

"There's nothing like a wedding to lift everyone's spirits," Claire noted. A handful of guests had returned to the inn at noon and had just been served lunch in the dining room. Now Claire was setting sandwiches for herself, Liza, and Nolan on the kitchen table. Nolan helped, bringing a pitcher of iced tea from the refrigerator and setting out three glasses.

"Liza certainly has a spring in her step these last few days," he agreed. "She's walking on air. If I could bottle that, I'd make a million."

"She's only been engaged three days. I think she'll float down to earth sooner or later. In the meantime, she has you and me to pick up the slack."

"Mostly you," he said with a chuckle.

"Come now, Nolan. You have more initiative than anyone we've ever had working around here. With your inventions and the way you spot repairs before they get to be problems . . . We've been very spoiled this summer," she added sincerely.

"That's very kind. I didn't think I'd like this job when you first offered it to me," he said honestly. "But it seemed like a sensible solution to my dilemma. Now, here we are, July is almost over, and frankly, I truly enjoy it."

Claire was glad to hear that. She could see that Nolan took pleasure and pride in his work. Any honest work done well was something to be proud of, she thought.

"Have you ever been married, Claire?" Nolan asked.

Claire was surprised at the question and realized by Nolan's look that her reaction showed. She set down his sandwich, then sat across from him at the table.

"Is that too forward of me to ask you? I'm sorry. I was just wondering."

"It's not too forward. Just not a question many people ask. I was engaged once, when I was quite young. The young man left the island, and I couldn't leave at the time. Family responsibilities held me here. And it just sort of . . . faded out. I had chances after that, I suppose," she said wistfully. "But no, I never decided to marry."

"I'm sorry. I didn't mean to bring up sad memories."

"That's all right. Our sad memories are part of us, too, aren't they? Just like the happy ones."

"Very true. I think I've mentioned before that I'm divorced. When I ran into all those business and financial problems and started pouring all our savings into the lawsuit, my wife lost patience with me. I thought she was being unfair at the time.

But looking back, I can see my part. No one is entirely right or entirely wrong when marriage fails, most of the time."

"That's very true," Claire agreed. "Have you made amends with her?" she asked curiously.

"Not yet, but perhaps we will someday. We had a fairly good relationship for almost thirty years. And we enjoyed raising our daughter together. I'm thankful for that," he added with a small smile.

Nolan had faced so many losses the past few years, it was almost mind-boggling. Perhaps this accounted for his tenacity about the lawsuit, Claire mused. That was one setback he believed he could reverse.

Nolan cleared his throat and gazed at her. "Excuse me for being so forward, Claire. But I must say that any man would have been very lucky to have you as his life partner. Of that I'm quite sure."

Claire was surprised by the compliment. Surprised and touched. But before she could respond, Liza came into the kitchen, a bundle of magazines and envelopes under her arm. More bride research, Claire suspected. Claire had called her a while ago for lunch, but Liza had been busy in her office.

"Oh, great . . . a sandwich. Thanks." Liza picked up the dish and grabbed a paper napkin. "Some mail for you, Nolan." She dropped a letter on the table in front of him. Claire didn't mean to be nosy, but the envelope fell right in front of her, and she recognized the stationery and return address—the lawyers representing Nolan in his lawsuit.

She took a quiet breath and put her sandwich down, watching his expression darken.

"Sorry I can't join you. I'm swamped with work today." Liza swept out of the room as quickly as she'd come in.

Claire didn't turn to glance at her. She was wondering if Nolan was going to open the letter in front of her. He had already picked it up and was staring at it as if holding his fate in his hand.

"It's from my attorney."

"I recognized the stationery," she confessed.

"It's rather thin . . ." He waved the envelope between two fingers. "I'm not sure why that would be."

Claire could barely stand the suspense. But she couldn't tell him to read it if he wasn't ready. She rose and brought her dish to the sink, just for something to do.

While her back was turned to him, she heard the sound of paper tearing. She turned slowly and watched him read the single sheet.

His face turned as pale as the bleached sheets on the clothesline, and his eyes widened.

"This . . . this can't be!" He wasn't shouting, but his tone was even harsher than if he had. He pounded his fist on the wooden table, making the glasses and pitcher jump. "So close . . . so close to the finish line and . . . turned back again." He sighed and shook his head, staring at her.

Claire wiped her hands quickly on a towel. "What's happened, Nolan? What does the letter say?"

"That investor who cheated me, he's hired some new law firm, and they claim I don't have any grounds at all. They say their product is completely different. Well . . . changed just enough so that it's not copyright infringement," he added bitterly. "It's very hard to prove these things in court, very hard. I tell you, Claire, I feel as if this is some sort of giant fish, hooked on my line, and I can't reel it in. No matter how hard and long I fight with it."

Claire stood near him and rested her hand lightly on his shoulder. "Then don't fight anymore, Nolan. Just let it go."

He looked up at her and shook his head, as if he couldn't comprehend what she was suggesting. "But how can I do that? Just walk away, you mean? After all this time? I could never live with the . . . the sheer injustice of it. The best idea I ever had, stolen from me. He may as well have broken into my house and taken everything I own. I trusted that man. I had the idea; he had the funds to invest. He signed an agreement, fifty-fifty. Then he closed down our factory, left the place mired in debt. Wiggled out of that somehow and started up again, with a whole new name. A whole new product, he claimed. Claiming all the profits for himself now. Only it was *my product, my idea, my invention*, with only a few tiny alterations. Don't you see how wrong that is?"

Claire considered this charge a moment. The former partner had, indeed, robbed Nolan. But he hadn't taken everything. Claire already knew that, though Nolan couldn't seem to see it.

"Of course I do," she assured him. "I know what he did was very wrong—"

"Wrong?" Nolan broke in. "I'll say it was wrong. I invested a lot of personal savings in that company and lost it all. I'd taken loans against my house, so I lost that to the bank. I was so distracted and overwhelmed, I couldn't function at all at the university . . . I suppose I lost my temper a few times when this was pointed out to me," he added more quietly. "So there went my job. And my wife—who never had much faith in me, I must say—decided she'd had enough, too." He heaved a sigh, practically out of breath from his recitation.

It was a long, sad story; Claire could never argue with that point. But Nolan had the power to end it. He didn't have to wait for battling lawyers to do that for him.

"You've endured great losses, Nolan. No question. Almost like the book of Job," she conceded. "But you have been left with something—the most valuable thing of all. Your imagination. Your amazing gift to come up with new ideas, new inventions. No one can ever take that from you," she insisted.

Nolan stared at her and let out a frustrated sigh. "You don't understand. This was . . . different. Highly applicable to all kinds of manufacturing. Not just some dime-a-dozen gadget you see advertised on TV."

"Perhaps. But don't you see? The longer you chase him, the more he robs you. This lawsuit saps your precious time and energy. I understand what you're feeling, Nolan. I really do," she insisted. "But if you wanted to walk down a road, is it best to face forward or keep looking back?" she asked, trying to appeal to his logical side. "That's what you're doing. Staring backward at something you can't change, when you should be looking forward, figuring out where you want to go next."

Nolan stopped to consider her words for a moment, his mouth a tight line. "That's well and good to say. But how can I live with myself knowing I allowed this man to cheat me? How can my colleagues ever respect me again?"

Claire was quiet a moment, considering his questions. "And Fiona? Isn't that who you're thinking of?"

Claire quickly realized she'd just blurted out the first thought that popped into her head. Just the way Nolan did at times. She hadn't meant to, but there it was. And now it was too late to take it back.

He stared at her, shocked. "What are you talking about? What in the world does Fiona have to do with this?"

Claire knew she had gone too far. But she had to be honest with him. He would be angry, but maybe it would help him in the long run.

"I'm wondering if it's all tangled up in your head. And your heart. Trying to win this lawsuit and prove to your daughter that she was wrong. That you're not a failure." She paused, wondering if her words made any sense to him. "Are you waiting until you sign a settlement to get in touch with her again?"

"That's ridiculous. Of course not. My relationship with Fiona is totally irrelevant. These two situations are completely separate."

Claire sighed. She could see there was no point in arguing with him about it. And she didn't really want to.

"That's good, then, Nolan. Because you may never get satisfaction from this lawsuit. It would be a pity if all this waiting kept you from time with your daughter. Precious time."

Nolan frowned, his chin raised defiantly. "Easy for you to say. I thought you understood what I'm facing here . . . what I'm going through. But I was mistaken about you, Claire. Very mistaken."

Claire felt his harsh words like a chilly wind blowing right through her. Nolan turned and left the kitchen, calling Edison to follow him.

Claire stood at the sink a moment, then walked to the back window and stared at the garden. Nolan was angry with her, and that made her sad. But she had told him the truth that was in her heart, and she wasn't sorry. She did believe he was wasting his time on this fruitless quest. No one knew the number of their hours on this beautiful earth. Not even a scientist like Nolan. She hoped he didn't end his life with deep regrets. But he was taking a mighty gamble.

DANIEL returned on the weekend, but he was buried in his textbooks and notes, or staring at his computer whenever he was at the inn. Most of the weekend, he stayed at his own cottage, and stopped by just for meals and late-night visits.

Liza missed him almost as much as when he was in Boston. But she knew it was only two more weeks until the exams, and they decided that he should stay in the city until the test was over. He was in the homestretch now, and he thought it best to focus completely on preparing for his tests, and Liza did, too.

She didn't even want to bother him with decisions about the wedding, but couldn't help asking his opinion on items she and Molly had worked on.

"I can't decide between pure white tablecloths or ivory," she told him. "Molly suggested a blush pink. It was pretty but I think that's too . . . girly or something. I think white looks very elegant, especially with the right flowers. But ivory is softer on the eye."

They were sitting in the porch swing on Saturday night.

Daniel had a textbook open in his lap but his head kept drifting toward Liza's shoulder, and she could tell by his breathing he was almost asleep sitting up.

"Daniel, did you hear a word I just said?"

He sat up and blinked. "Of course I did. Tablecloths. I'd like white. You know me, plain vanilla. But I trust your judgment on these things, honey. You know I do."

She gazed at him with a loving smile. "All right. 'Yes, dear' me. I guess it's good practice for when we're married."

She could tell he'd heard that. He turned and grinned. "We'll see about that, Ms. Martin." He took her hand, turning away from his book to look at her. "I know I'm not helping with this wedding stuff, but after August fifteenth, you'll have my undivided attention. For the rest of your life. How does that sound?"

"Sounds good to me. And I'll take care of the 'wedding stuff' too. And don't worry, I'm not going to stick you with pink tablecloths."

He sighed and laughed. "I am relieved to hear that."

Liza was so busy with her wedding plans and running the inn, it took her a while to notice that something was amiss between Claire and Nolan. She thought she might be imagining it at first, then she realized that they really weren't talking to each other. They spoke just enough to get their work done, but not in an easy, warm way, at mealtimes. Or any time, for that matter.

She never saw them together after dinner anymore, not in the parlor playing Scrabble or sitting together on the porch with Edison between them.

Liza thought it was probably none of her business. But Claire did seem distracted the last week or so, and not quite her usual energetic, upbeat self. Liza was concerned about her but wasn't sure what to do.

When Liza came down for breakfast Thursday morning, Nolan was already working in the garden. Claire was in the dining room, checking the breakfast buffet, and soon returned to the kitchen, where Liza had settled in with her coffee and laptop.

"Just a week until Daniel's exams," Claire said, pouring some coffee into the mug Jamie had sent her. "I bet you're counting the days."

"I am. The tests last for two days, next Thursday and Friday. Pretty grueling, right?" Liza asked, making a face. "I'm not sure who wants it to be over sooner, me or Daniel."

"Oh, we all do," Claire assured her. "We should have some sort of celebration for him. It's quite an accomplishment, I think."

"It is," Liza agreed. "But Daniel told me he doesn't want any celebrating until he gets his test scores. Still, he's got to be more relaxed once he gets past them. And his mentor, Dr. Mitchell, and his wife will be visiting the inn as soon as he gets back. So that will be good for him. Daniel is very excited about their reunion."

"Yes, he mentioned that to me. We'll have to work on the menu."

"Daniel says Dr. Mitchell loves shellfish—mussels, clams, oysters. Maybe we should serve bouillabaisse or a seafood paella?"

"Maybe . . . or oyster stew. Any dish with oysters or clams is easy. Once you've shucked them," Claire pointed out.

Liza grinned. "That's always the hardest part of the recipe. Probably because I can barely open a clam. But you—"

Claire nodded, smiling. "It's a knack you get over the years."

"That doesn't mean you should be stuck with all that work, especially at this time of year. Maybe Nolan can help you with that part." Liza paused, noticing how Claire's expression shifted just a tiny bit at the mention of his name. "Claire . . . it's probably none of my business, but did you and Nolan have some sort of disagreement?"

Claire folded a dish towel, her head bowed. "What makes you ask that?"

"Just the way you've been acting toward each other, barely speaking two words in a row."

Claire sighed. "Yes . . . we did have words about something . . . I'd rather not explain it, if you don't mind."

"It's all right, you don't have to tell me." Liza paused, wondering what Claire would say to her if the situation were reversed. "Have you tried to talk things out with him?"

Claire paused, then shook her head. "You probably think it was Nolan who spoke out of turn. I know he doesn't always know the difference between being honest and rude. But it was me. I said a few things to him I probably shouldn't have. With good intentions," she quickly added.

Liza was surprised. That was not like Claire, who was usually the soul of discretion. But Claire's relationship with Nolan was different. When it came to Nolan, Liza suspected that Claire might actually get carried away with her feelings.

"I'm sure you meant well, Claire."

"It's just so hard to watch Nolan spend so much time and energy on this lawsuit," she finally confided, "when he's blessed every day with so many wonderful ideas and such a rich imagination. It just doesn't seem right to me."

Liza heard the frustration in her voice—and her deep feelings for Nolan. Liza didn't know what to say for a moment. Then she rested her hand on Claire's shoulder. "The only advice I can offer is to try and think of what you would tell me if something like this happened between me and Daniel."

Claire seemed amused by the suggestion. "What would I say, do you think?"

"Well, let's see . . . I think you would remind me that the most important thing is forgiveness. To forgive someone if they hurt you, and to ask for their forgiveness." Liza paused. "You don't have to take back what you said, or be insincere, if it's what you really believe. But let him know that you're sorry you hurt his feelings and never meant to do that. How does that sound?"

Claire slowly smiled. "Like very good advice. Thank you, Liza. I couldn't have said it better myself."

"I've learned a few things from being around you all these years." Liza gave Claire a quick hug. "Besides how to crack and separate an egg white and yolk with one hand."

"Well, that's important, too," Claire replied, a familiar sparkle returning to her blue eyes. "Everything has its place in the scheme of things."

How true, Liza thought. She could always learn something from Claire.

CLAIRE was glad that Liza had encouraged her to make amends with Nolan. She had thought about it ever since their disagreement. A week was a long time to converse in monosyllables. Especially for two people who were as talkative as they were, she thought with a smile.

How to do it was the problem. The shoulder he presented was so cold, she felt a frigid blast each time they shared the same room. It was hard to apologize to someone who didn't even make eye contact.

Should she corner him in the barn when he was working on the boat? He might chase her off by turning on some noisy power tool. Or hide in the boat cabin and just ignore her.

She considered writing a note and leaving it near his dinner plate. Then she had a better idea. Something more personal. Just between the two of them.

After dinner, Nolan went out to the barn, as Claire expected.

She went into the parlor and took out the Scrabble set. She wrote her note, then sat knitting until she heard him return to the house and start up the stairs.

Claire came out to the hallway and called him. "Nolan? Could you come into the parlor a moment? I need your opinion."

He glanced at her. She could tell he was curious but still stubbornly clinging to his chilly attitude. "I'm tired, Claire. Can it wait until tomorrow?"

"Probably. But it will only take a minute. Please?"

Claire went back into the parlor, hoping he would follow. *Please, God, please don't let me make a fool of myself. Please put him in a forgiving frame of mind.*

Claire stood by the game table and looked up as Nolan entered the room. Looking annoyed, he frowned at her. "Here I am. What's this all about?"

Claire glanced down at the table. "Do you think that's permitted—spelling out a message on the Scrabble board? I can't find anything about it in the rule book."

Nolan's mouth pulled to the side. She could tell he was trying to hide a smile. He slipped on his glasses and carefully examined the board.

Claire had used up practically all the tiles spelling out a message, the words overlapping, across and down.

I AM SORRY NOLAN PLEASE FORGIVE ME FOR SPEAKING OUT OF TURN I DID NOT MEAN TO HURT YOUR FEELINGS

His gaze lingered on the careful arrangement of tiles. Then he finally looked up. Claire was relieved to see his expression had softened. "So you've been playing Scrabble without me?"

She shrugged. "You left me no other choice."

"Nice work. I see you placed 'speaking' on a triple-word score. But proper names, like 'Nolan,' aren't permitted," he reminded her.

"Oh yes, that's right. I'll have to deduct that one from my score." Now it was her turn to hide a smile.

"And I would have thought you would have figured out

how to fit a Q or a Z in there somewhere," he added, mentioning the letters with the highest points.

Claire shrugged. "Probably could have. But I was in a hurry."

He laughed out loud at that. "It's hard to refuse such a charming apology. Impossible, actually." He paused and took off his glasses. "I shouldn't have carried on so long, either. Let's just put it aside. We don't need to talk about the lawsuit anymore, all right?" Claire wasn't sure that was the best solution, to brush a difficult issue under the rug. But he already knew her opinion on the subject. She didn't need to say more.

"Agreed. Thank you for accepting my apology."

Claire began collecting the tiles and placing them in the storage bag. Nolan reached down and helped her. "It's too late now to start a game . . . But we'll play tomorrow?"

Claire smiled and nodded, feeling their relationship had nearly capsized but was back on course again.

"I'd be happy to . . . and will make good use of the Qs and Zs. Just warning you."

"Thanks. Though I doubt it will help." His smile, which Claire had missed, grew even wider.

Liza and Daniel had agreed that he should stay in Boston and study over the weekend. It was the last week of his courses, his final sprint to the finish line, and he was very anxious about his exams, which were coming up on Thursday and Friday, August fifteenth and sixteenth.

Liza didn't know how she would last through the week, waiting for his exams to be done. But she knew it had to be even worse for him. At least she had plenty of other things to think about. It was mid-August, their busiest time of the season, and the inn was full, with some guests leaving and more expected. She didn't have a moment to spare, and neither did Claire or Nolan. The many distractions and demands had come at a good time, Liza thought, forcing her to focus on each task at hand.

Somehow, the week passed, and it was finally Friday. Daniel sent a quick text to say he was done with the final test and on his way home. While Claire and Nolan served dinner, Liza ran to her room and readied herself to greet him.

She wasn't quite finished when she heard his truck pull up to the inn. She glanced out the window and quickly pulled a comb through her wet hair. Then she ran downstairs in her bare feet to meet him. These days, as long as she had her engagement ring on, she felt completely dressed.

Daniel walked into the foyer and dropped his knapsack near the door. Liza practically skipped down the last few steps and threw herself into his arms. They hugged each other tight.

"Did you miss me?" he whispered.

"What do you think?" She pulled back and looked up at him. She was afraid to ask about the exams, but couldn't help herself. "So . . . how'd it go?"

He winced. "Hard to say. It was tough. A lot harder than the practice tests. I think I passed, but I don't want to jinx it. All I know right now is I could sleep for a week."

"Fine with me. We won't talk about it anymore. I'm just glad it's over and you're back."

And their life together could get back to normal now, too.

Finally. She didn't say that aloud, but had a feeling he was thinking the same thing.

"I'm glad to be back. More than you know." He forced a smile, his eyes soft and loving. He did look tired, as worn out as she'd ever seen him. Liza suddenly felt guilty for pressing him with questions. She slipped her arm around his waist and led him back to the kitchen.

"Want something to eat before you take that long nap?"

"I could eat like a bear—then sleep like one, too," he said with a laugh.

Daniel dropped into a kitchen chair and Liza served him dinner—a pasta dish with grilled shrimp and fresh vegetables from the garden.

"Mmmm . . . this is delicious," Daniel mumbled around a mouthful. "So, what's new around here? How are our wedding plans going? Sorry if I didn't get back to you on all the e-mails. I did love the photos, honey. Everything looks fantastic."

The e-mails and photos were questions for him about choices she had to make. He wasn't supposed to "love" all of them; they *weren't* all fantastic. But Liza couldn't fault him. She had been trying to keep him in the wedding loop, even though she knew he was too busy to help her decide on the centerpieces and appetizers. She now recalled grousing to Molly about Daniel's failure to respond to her notes.

"But it will be different once the big exam is over," she had said. "I'm sure he'll get more involved in the wedding then."

"Ha! Good luck," Molly had replied. "You're marrying a doctor, Liza. Get used to it. Matt comes home so late and tired some nights, he'd hardly notice if my hair was on fire. He's had a wicked tough case this week—a little boy hospitalized with a staph infection. He's been up in Southport night and day. I've hardly seen him."

"Oh, that's too bad. I hope the boy recovers quickly." There was little more Liza could say. She did know Daniel's hours would be demanding at times. Her work schedule was demanding at times, too. She could cope with that.

But it would have to be better than the past few weeks, with her nearest and dearest living in Boston. A new fear began to tug at her. What if Daniel hadn't passed his exams? Did that mean they would have to go through this all over again next year? And how would that affect their brand-new marriage?

"Liza," Daniel said, startling her out of her thoughts. "I was asking you how the wedding plans are going."

"They're going great," she said. "After you rest up, I'll show you everything Molly and I decided so far. I have the invitations all addressed and ready to mail out," she added. A tiny knot of apprehension tightened in her stomach. She tried to ignore it, but it grew.

Daniel had finished eating and pushed his dish away. He looked up at her with a curious expression. "Something wrong, honey? Is it something about the wedding arrangements?"

Liza didn't answer. She looked down at her beautiful engagement ring and twisted it around her finger.

"Hey, I'm free and clear now, totally at your service, m'lady," he teased her. "What's wrong? We shouldn't keep any secrets from each other now," he reminded her.

That was very true. Not that she'd ever kept much from Daniel. She took a deep breath and looked up at him. "Let's just say you don't pass this time, Daniel. I think you definitely will," she quickly added. "But I was just wondering . . . if you don't pass, do you still want to get married?"

A puzzled expression flickered through his eyes. "Of course I do. What made you ask me that?"

Liza felt relieved, but not entirely. "Oh, I don't know. It's just that I've worried lately that you might not feel ready to get married until you're all settled and ready to practice medicine again. Maybe it's too many big life changes at once. I would never want you to feel pressured," she added.

Daniel's expression softened. He rose and came to her side of the table, then crouched down next to her and put his arms around her. "You're a very intelligent, perceptive woman, Liza. But sometimes, you think too much. Did anyone ever tell you that?"

Liza felt herself starting to smile. "Well . . . maybe."

Daniel laughed and kissed her cheek. "I thought you were acting a little funny tonight. But I figured you were just stressed about me finally taking the tests. Of course I still want to get married. I wish we could get married tomorrow. Do you want to drive somewhere tonight and find a justice of the peace? Like people always do in the movies?"

She laughed, but he really did look serious. She held his face in her hands. "We can't do that. For one thing, you're too tired, and for another, my brother and your sister already bought their plane tickets."

"Oh, right, the relatives. Well, we can still give them a party. Even though we might be on our honeymoon."

Honeymoon? They didn't have a clue about that yet. As

long as the wedding was still on, Liza was content to figure that out later.

"Let's stick with the original plan," she suggested. "I'm sorry to be such a silly worrywart."

He smiled at her. "That's okay. I love you anyway. And always will."

He kissed her deeply, reminding her again just how much and how wonderful their life together was going to be. Daniel truly loved her, and they were going forward as one, for better or for worse.

Chapter Ten

Daniel's friend and mentor, Dr. Jim Mitchell, and his wife, Elaine, were expected on Wednesday. They were traveling to Cape Light by train after Dr. Mitchell's conference in Boston. Daniel planned to pick them up at the station at noon and had borrowed Liza's SUV so they would be comfortable. The couple could only stay over one night; their schedule was very tight. But Liza had prepared the inn's best room for them and had worked with Claire on special menus for their meals.

Wednesday was a transition day at the inn; there were many guests checking in and checking out. Liza wanted to spend time with the Mitchells, but didn't think she could manage it until dinner. Daniel probably wanted to spend time alone with Dr. Mitchell anyway, and it was such perfect weather, Liza was sure they would all go down to the beach for the afternoon.

Claire had cut some flowers from the garden—huge, deep blue, luscious-looking hydrangeas, pink scrub roses, and a few orange tiger lilies. Liza was standing at the kitchen sink arranging them in a blue glass vase when she heard their guests arrive.

Claire was working at the kitchen table, putting the finishing touches on lunch. "Sounds like they're here. You go ahead out. I'll finish that," she said calmly.

Liza quickly dried her hands and smoothed down her skirt.

"You look lovely," Claire said, as if reading her mind. "I'm sure they're very nice people if Daniel thinks so highly of them."

Liza knew that must be true, but still felt nervous. After a steadying breath, she headed for the foyer. Daniel was already carrying in the bags, with Nolan's help.

"Here's Liza now," Daniel said, leading the way.

An older couple followed through the front door. Dr. Mitchell was tall and lean with thick gray hair and piercing, dark eyes. Something about him seemed hawklike, but when he smiled, his expression was warm and kind. Mrs. Mitchell was also tall and slim, with short dark hair cut to her chin. Her eyes were blue, matching her turquoise and silver jewelry—large earrings and a necklace with carved animal figures. They lived in the southwest, in northern Arizona, Liza remembered.

"This is Liza," Daniel said, reaching for her hand and pulling her near. "Liza, this is Jim Mitchell and his wife, Elaine."

Jim took her hand with both of his own in a warm handshake. "So good to meet you, Liza. Daniel told us on the ride over that you've just gotten engaged. Congratulations!"

"What happy news!" Elaine Mitchell added. "You must be very excited—and with Daniel returning to medicine at the same time."

"There's been a lot going on here this summer," Liza agreed.

"All good," Daniel added, hugging her close. "But now we can relax and enjoy the rest of the summer, right, honey?"

"Starting today. We've been looking forward so much to having you here," Liza said. "Your visit is perfect timing. Let me show you to your room and you can get settled. Come down for lunch whenever you're ready, and we'll take it from there."

"Sounds like an excellent plan to me," Dr. Mitchell said, politely allowing the women to precede him to the staircase.

"I can't wait to go down to the beach," Elaine added. "It's been so long since we've been near the ocean. Any ocean, East Coast or West," she added with a laugh. "I love living in Arizona, but I do miss the seashore."

Dr. Mitchell nodded. "I do, too. But there are always pluses and minuses in any choices we make, even when we're doing something we love to do."

Daniel, who was walking beside him, nodded. "Absolutely."

He glanced at Liza and smiled. Liza smiled back.

Had Daniel been reminded that he was giving up his carpentry business—and his entirely freewheeling lifestyle—in order to return to medicine and get married? Maybe, she thought. But he didn't seem unhappy about it.

Daniel's friends *oohed* and *ahhed* over the suite of rooms they were staying in, and then again over the lunch of oyster stew and lobster rolls Claire had prepared for them.

Jim helped himself to a second roll. "I might not have room for dinner, but I can't help myself. This is such a treat."

"Absolutely delicious," Elaine agreed. "I hope I can waddle down to the beach and don't take a detour to the room for a nap."

"I've set up everything on the beach for you—chairs, a blanket, and an umbrella," Daniel said. "You can definitely take a nap down there."

"And then a nice long walk along the water's edge," Jim suggested.

"I'm looking forward to that." Elaine glanced at Liza. "I'm sorry you can't join us. But we can see how busy you are."

Liza had been called away from the table a few times by phone calls or questions from guests that Claire couldn't answer.

"I'm sorry, too," Liza said sincerely. "But dinner will be much more peaceful, I promise. We'll have plenty of time tonight to just relax and talk."

Elaine smiled. "I hope so. We've really been looking forward to getting to know you, Liza."

The Mitchells headed down to the beach, and Liza went back to work for the rest of the day. Claire had outdone herself with dinner, cooking magnificent seafood paella that included all of Dr. Mitchell's favorites and then some.

Liza and Daniel ate with the Mitchells at a private table on the patio. As Liza expected, the conversation soon turned to the wedding. Everyone she spoke to lately had so many questions, but she enjoyed answering them and relished her role as bride-to-be.

"So you set a quick date. That was a good idea." Jim nodded with approval. "Some couples get engaged and spend years planning the wedding. It's just a party; one day out of your life. They seem to forget the important thing is the rest of your lives together."

Elaine was far less pragmatic and much more sympathetic to Liza. "But just a few weeks to pull it all together . . . that *is* a rush. You poor thing."

"Oh, she's a pro," Daniel teased Liza. "She thrives on deadlines."

Liza rolled her eyes. "Can't say I had much choice. But we both wanted a small party and wanted to hold it here. So that makes it much easier. Maybe you could come back for the wedding?" she asked. "We would love to have you share our big day."

"Yes, come to the wedding," Daniel said at once. "We can guarantee you more excellent food, and the weather is usually perfect in the fall. And it would mean a lot to us both to have you here."

Jim smiled at them, looking pleased by the heartfelt invitation. "Oh, we'd love that, wouldn't we, Elaine?"

"No question," his wife said.

"But these trips back East are rare," he went on. "We're so busy at the clinic right now. We're down one doc and we can really use two, but I haven't had any luck filling those positions yet."

"Daniel's told me a little about your clinic, Jim. Is it a large staff?" If he was looking for two more doctors, it was larger than Liza had thought. Much larger than the clinic on the island, which only had a registered nurse, and Daniel, flying under the radar as a EMT all these years.

"I've been out there about four years now, and our services

have doubled—maybe tripled—in that time. Though we're still barely keeping up with the patient demand. We started with a very simple, 'patch 'em up and send 'em to a real hospital' operation. But now we're doing much more—prenatal care, family medicine, and regular visits for children and seniors."

"Getting out in front, with more emphasis on wellness and prevention," Elaine added. "The community is really benefitting."

"But there's so much more we could do. There's so much need," Jim Mitchell added.

"More funding, you mean?" Liza asked.

Jim laughed. "We can always use money. But right now, the real need is more medical professionals. We especially need doctors—committed physicians who want to make a difference, who want to work in a community where their intervention really counts. People have such a great choice of doctors in this area, even in relatively rural places like this island. Boston with its huge state-of-the-art hospitals is only an hour or two away, and you probably have big hospitals even closer."

"Southport is about an hour or so," she replied.

"In our village, the clinic is it," Elaine explained. "There's no other medical help for hours by car."

"That must put the pressure on," Daniel said.

"It does," his friend agreed. "But some people thrive on that sort of pressure. We do a lot with a little, believe me."

"It sounds like a challenging but exciting way to practice," Daniel said.

"That it is," Jim replied, "and more."

"I have some pictures on my phone of the clinic and our house," Elaine offered.

"Do you live on the reservation?" Liza asked, curious.

"Well, the Navajo reservation covers twenty-seven thousand square miles. If you practice up there, chances are, you're living on the reservation," Jim explained. "Besides, I need to be close to the clinic."

"He practically lives there," Elaine said, glancing at her husband with a loving smile.

"Oh, come on now, it's not that bad," he said with a laugh. "Well, on second thought, maybe it is."

Elaine had already taken out her phone and brought up the photos. She handed it over to Daniel and Liza to look at together.

Liza peered down at the screen. The first few photos showed the open desert at sunset. The red rock mountains were beautiful and mysterious-looking, the sunset casting brilliant colors in the sky and amazing shadows across the landscape.

"I love that part of the country. The landscape is spectacular," Daniel said. "I've only been to Arizona once, to see the Grand Canyon. I'd love to go back sometime."

"I'd love to go back there, too. It's a perfect spot for painting," Liza said wistfully.

"Are you an artist, Liza?" Jim asked.

"I used to be in graphic arts and did some painting of my own in my spare time. One of the reasons I took over the inn was to have more time for my artwork. But that part hasn't worked out so far," she admitted.

"You're young; you have plenty of time," Elaine assured her. "Life is large, full of possibilities."

"I think so," Liza agreed. She looked back at the photos.

Daniel was scrolling through them. The next few showed a rough, cinder-block building painted a dark ochre color. It had some sort of odd extension, as if a mobile home had been tacked on, but the picture didn't take in the entire structure. A large sign with a red cross on a white background indicated that it was the clinic. Surrounded by sandy dirt and a few scrubby-looking bushes, two little dark-haired girls sat on the cement steps. The girls looked adorable, hugging each other, but Liza noticed one wore a dress that was too small for her, and the other wore a jacket with a rip in the sleeve. A woman holding a baby in her arms stood nearby. She looked poor and careworn and didn't even make an effort to smile at the camera.

Liza didn't know what to say. She felt suddenly tense and quiet. She could feel Elaine and Jim watching them, waiting for their reaction.

"Wow, that looks great. How many exam rooms?" Daniel asked.

"We started with two, and that mobile unit adds one more and a little lab for on-site blood work," Jim explained.

Daniel touched the screen and moved to the next picture.

Liza could see it was the inside of the clinic. Everything looked plain and utilitarian, with only the minimum of what was needed.

"Oh, that's our house," Elaine said happily as Daniel came to another photo. Liza glanced over his shoulder at another squat, square, cinder-block building. This one was painted pale yellow, with dark green shutters on its tiny windows and a dark green frame around the front door. There were two large ceramic pots on either side of the door, painted with a geometric design.

But other than those small embellishments, the house looked to Liza very much like a jailhouse in a movie about the Old West. Two spiky cacti poked through the hard earth in the front yard.

"As you can see, no worries about keeping up the lawn," Jim joked. "That's one job I scratched off my list long ago."

"No real garden, either," Elaine said, "though we do grow a few tomatoes and some other vegetables in a raised bed that Jim built out back."

"How does that work out?" Liza asked curiously. "It has to be hard to grow anything in that climate."

"You'd be surprised. We grow beans, squash, tomatoes, and even some corn. It's a real treat when we can pick our own fresh vegetables. There's really not much at the closest store, which is a good twenty miles away. It's hard to find nutritious food there. I've been advocating for better quality groceries on the shelves, but it's an uphill battle. I think there's a photo of the local grocery store there someplace," she added.

Daniel turned to another photo. This cinder-block building was larger, with several dusty, beat-up trucks and cars parked around it. Signs on the front advertised everything from ammunition to peanut butter to motor oil. Was that where the Mitchells shopped?

"But look at this," Elaine said, showing them a photo of a sand-colored mesa against an endless deep blue sky.

"That's amazing," Daniel said, handing the phone back. "I've heard you talk about the place, but it's been hard to imagine it. I've never been on a reservation. It seems like an entirely different world."

It most definitely is, Liza thought, but she said nothing. She could see why Daniel admired Dr. Mitchell. Compared to her comfortable life on the island—or even working in a Boston hospital—the reservation seemed a harsh place. Only the most dedicated would choose to serve there, she thought.

Liza turned her attention to Elaine. "Are you in the medical field, too?" she asked her.

"No, I'm a teacher at a school on the reservation."

"Was it hard to find a job there?"

"Well, yes and no. I wasn't a teacher back here," Elaine explained. "I did marketing for a publishing company. But when we moved out to Arizona, I realized I wanted to help, too. I started as a teacher's aide and tutor while I worked on my certificate. It's hard work. Many of the kids have very unstable homes—alcohol, drug abuse, divorce, and just plain poverty. But they're terrific kids. Sometimes all they need is a steady support system, and they thrive."

"That must be rewarding, when you see that you're making a difference in a child's life."

"It doesn't happen all the time. But when it does, it's a good thing," Elaine said simply.

Liza couldn't help but be impressed. Running the inn was hard work, but it wasn't a personal sacrifice. And it was filled with so many rewards, chief among them being able to live on this beautiful island in this gracious old inn. It wasn't that Liza thought her life was frivolous. She and Claire provided a wonderful place for others to take a break from their routines, but it was very different from what Jim and Elaine were doing. They were living a life of service to others.

"How long have you been running the inn, Liza?" Elaine's question drew Liza from her rambling thoughts. "Daniel said he worked for your aunt before you, and that's how you met?"

"Yes, my aunt left the inn to me and my brother in her will. My brother wanted to sell it, but I persuaded him to let me fix it up and try to run it. I was in advertising before that . . . I knew nothing about innkeeping at all," she admitted. "But somehow I muddled through, with Claire and Daniel helping me." She glanced at Daniel. "I'm really not sure when Daniel and I first met. We once realized that we both spent summers here growing up, and may have even been building sand castles next to each other on the beach."

"You two seem so in tune, I wouldn't doubt it. It seems to me you were meant for each other," Elaine said with a warm smile.

The two couples soon moved to the porch, where Claire served coffee and tea. Daniel and Jim wanted to take a quick ride around the island. Jim wanted to see some of Daniel's renovations on big, grand old houses, as well as the old fishing colony and the cottage where Daniel lived. But Elaine couldn't get enough of the view and preferred to sit on the porch and watch the sunset. Liza was happy to stay, too. She'd been racing around all day and she did enjoy Elaine's company.

"If I lived here, I would never stop looking at the ocean," Elaine said. "I'd want to be down on the beach all the time. Does it distract you from your work?"

"Sometimes, yes," Liza confessed. "I do love seeing the water and sky the first thing when I get up in the morning, no matter what the weather is. I'm so used to it now, I don't know if I could ever live anyplace else."

Elaine smiled. "I can understand that. It's a wonderful place. I'm so glad we had the time to come here and meet you."

"I am, too," Liza said sincerely. She was sorry the Mitchells couldn't return for the wedding, but she hoped they would stay in touch, and that she and Daniel would see them again soon.

THE next morning, Jim and Elaine had to leave very early to catch a train from Cape Light that would connect in Boston to a train down to New York City, where Dr. Mitchell was going to visit a foundation that might give his clinic a grant. They would stay in New York for two nights and then leave for Arizona on Saturday.

When Daniel drove them to the train station, Liza went along for the ride. There were many fond good-byes and hugs exchanged at the station. Liza felt as if their visit had been too short; she had barely gotten to know them.

"I like your friends," she told Daniel as they drove back to the inn. "I'm sorry they couldn't stay longer."

"They liked you, too. Jim thought you were great, and I think Elaine is already pining for a return visit."

Liza smiled and put her hand on his shoulder. "I hope they will come back. I'm glad you got to spend some time with Jim. Did he like seeing the houses you worked on?"

"He's pretty handy and does some carpentry himself. When he has the time. Turns out, I'm not the only one who put himself through med school renovating houses. Jim and I have more in common than I knew."

"What did he think of you going back to medicine? You never told me," Liza said curiously.

"He thinks it's great, and that it's the right time for me," Daniel added. "He thinks that my living on the island has matured me, made me a deeper person."

"Really? I always thought you were all that, but maybe I met you at the right time, too."

"Maybe," Daniel agreed, with his eyes fixed on the road. He drew in a breath, then said, "He offered me a job at the clinic, Liza. He thinks I have the right stuff—the values and temperament. And I've done a lot of emergency medicine and triage at the clinic here. I know how it goes when you're the only game in town."

Liza felt stunned by Daniel's words. She wasn't really that surprised that Jim had talked to him about a job. That made sense, considering he was looking for new doctors for his clinic. What surprised her was that Daniel sounded as if he was actually considering the idea.

She glanced out the window, collecting herself. She could tell he was waiting for her response. "How did you leave it with him?" she asked carefully. "Are you going to follow up?"

"I told him I'd think about it. It's really a huge jump from any job I expected to land."

"I'll say." Liza didn't mean to sound sarcastic, but the only other opportunity Daniel was considering was a position at Matt Harding's practice right in Cape Light. How opposite could you get?

"I do like the idea of practicing where doctors are needed, using my skills to really change lives," he confessed. "That was part of the reason I liked working at the clinic on the island. It was something that kept the spark alive in me, Liza."

Liza stared out the window, afraid to meet his eyes and let him see the conflicted emotions that were racing through her. His words were heartfelt; she knew he was only being honest. But they were getting married, and it was going to be her life, too. Every decision either of them made now deeply affected the other person. Didn't he realize that?

But before she could find the words to voice her concerns he said, "The problem is, it's so far from this island . . . and from you. I can't expect you to just pick up and leave here. To leave the inn and everything you've worked so hard for."

Liza turned to face him. "I have to be honest with you," she said, choosing her words carefully. "I think Jim and Elaine are amazing people. I admire the work that they're both doing. But for you to take a job with him there . . . that just seems impossible to me. It seems such a harsh and sad-looking place. I know I probably sound spoiled, but I could never imagine living there. I don't know how they do it."

She didn't want to cry. They were having a talk about a serious topic, like married people do. And soon-to-be-married people. But Liza felt tears welling up in her eyes and choking her voice. She took a breath and turned away from him again.

"Liza . . . don't worry. Please. Don't be upset . . ." Daniel took her hand and coaxed her to look at him. "I was just thinking out loud, that's all. Daydreaming a little, I guess. I didn't mean to get you so stressed out. I *am* thinking of you," he promised. "And your obligations here. I could never make a move like that if you weren't one hundred percent on board. Please don't worry about it. Maybe I shouldn't have even told you."

"Don't be sorry. I'm glad you did. It won't do to hide things from each other, Daniel, especially now." She took another breath, and this time got control over her shaky voice. "Maybe once you get settled in a job here, you could go out there for a few weeks sometime, as a volunteer. It sounds like Jim can use all the help he can get."

Daniel's gaze was fixed on the road again. He nodded, taking in her suggestion. And taking her hand in his again. "Yes, maybe I could do that. First things first. We need to focus on our wedding right now; that's the most important thing."

"Yes, it is," Liza agreed, feeling a little better. "And it's coming up really quickly. I know we're trying to keep it simple, but I hope everything will be ready in time."

"It will be perfect, sweetheart. I have no worries. You'll be the most beautiful bride anyone has ever set eyes on, and I'll be the luckiest guy in the world. How can we miss?"

Liza had to smile at his description. When he put it that way, all her worries melted like ocean mist—even the idea of Daniel accepting a job at Jim Mitchell's clinic.

They were going to focus on the wedding now, and everything else would fall into place. Gripping the strong, warm hand that held hers so tightly, Liza felt sure of that once again.

IT seemed to Liza that Daniel had just finished his courses and returned from Boston when the Labor Day weekend rushed up on them like a big wave that welled up on an otherwise calm day and drenched all the unsuspecting bathers.

She was entrenched in wedding preparations and felt overwhelmed by both—the wedding and the last big weekend of the summer season. Daniel's test results were due to come the first week in September, and getting through Labor Day seemed like the last hurdle.

Everyone was working hard—Liza, Claire, Nolan, and Daniel. Guests began to check in early in the week, and by Thursday night the inn was full, right up to a few small rooms on the third floor that were hardly ever used. In fact, until that week, only Claire and Nolan had been using rooms up there.

"I feel guilty taking up saleable space," Nolan said to Liza on Friday morning. "Maybe I should bunk out on my boat a few nights, so you can rent my room, too."

"Nolan, don't be silly. I don't need your room. There are too many guests here as it is," she added in a whisper.

The guests were assembling in the dining room and on the porch and patio, waiting to be served breakfast, while Liza and the others bustled in the kitchen, finishing the last of the breakfast preparations and grabbing quick bites of their own.

"Well, it's the last weekend of the summer. Might as well go out in grand style," Nolan said.

"We always do," Claire assured him as she arranged strips of bacon on a platter.

Daniel gobbled down a muffin, then filled pitchers with iced water. "How's the boat coming, Nolan?" he asked. "I was in the barn the other day. The outside looks great. Did you fix the interior yet?"

"It's coming along," Nolan replied. "I have more sanding and varnishing to do, of course. But any sailor will tell you that."

Liza knew that Nolan had repaired the big hole in the hull and refinished the outside of the boat, so that you couldn't even tell it had been in an accident. But there had been a lot of water damage in the cabin, and he had to throw out all the upholstery and refinish most of the wood interior. Though it seemed like an endless job, she guessed that someday he would be done and then move on.

She had been so distracted with everything going on in her own life, she hadn't given much thought to Nolan's progress. Now she suddenly realized that he might be leaving very soon.

"Nolan, you aren't ready to sail away yet, are you? There's plenty of work to do around here after this weekend, believe me. We really hope that you'll stay through September. At least for the wedding," Liza implored him. She and Daniel had already invited him, but he had never given them a solid answer.

Nolan smiled and cocked his head. He still didn't answer.

Daniel put his coffee mug down on the table with a thud.

"You can't go. Edison is going to be in the wedding party.

He'll be very disappointed . . . and I've already ordered his tuxedo."

Nolan laughed and Claire did, too. She had been standing at the sink with her back to the table, and Liza had not been able to see her reaction to the conversation. She guessed that Claire didn't want to see Nolan leave soon, either. It would be hard for her; she and Nolan had grown very close.

Liza's heart went out to her dear friend. Claire, above all the people she knew, deserved a close and loving companion. She and Nolan seemed like such an unlikely match. And in many ways they were. But when they were together, it just worked. Even their differences seemed suited somehow, like salt is to pepper or a match to a flint. They brought out the best in each other.

Before they could press Nolan further, Claire turned from the open oven, hot mitts on both hands. "This French toast is ready . . . let's get it out to the guests while it's hot," she urged the others, like a general on a battlefield.

It was all hands on deck, and they all hurried to serve breakfast. Just three more days of the long weekend. Liza counted them off in her head: Saturday, Sunday, Monday.

By Tuesday the inn would be relatively empty again. Liza looked forward to that day with a mixture of anticipation and dread. The results from Daniel's exams were going to appear online at midnight. He'd hardly mentioned it, but she could tell it weighed heavily on his mind all weekend. They had already planned to stay up late Tuesday night and wait. They both knew that they wouldn't sleep for a minute, wondering about the outcome.

But every time Liza caught herself worrying, she remembered Daniel's assurances—the results of the exams wouldn't change their plans. They were going to be married and start a new life together, whether Daniel returned to medicine or not. This was just one more milestone they would face together.

Chapter Eleven

"Why is everyone so quiet?" Nolan asked with a laugh. He looked around the table at Liza, Daniel, and Claire.

They were eating dinner together in the kitchen. Labor Day weekend was over, and it was the first Tuesday in September. All of the guests had left but two, a couple from Pennsylvania, who had recently retired and were on a long road trip up the East Coast all the way to Prince Edward Island and Nova Scotia. They would be on their way tomorrow, and had chosen to dine up in Newburyport that evening.

It was a lucky break, Liza thought. She knew Claire felt the same, but perhaps for different reasons.

"Maybe we're all just tired out from the weekend, Nolan," Daniel replied. "But you'll probably go out and work on your boat tonight," he added with a smile.

"I might, after some Scrabble or gin rummy," he said,

glancing at Claire. "Energy is just in your head, young man. So is age."

"I agree . . . but I'm just talked out," Claire said. "I enjoy getting to know the guests, but with a full house like that, it's hard to remember everyone's name, much less learn where they're from and what they do for a living. And admire pictures of their pets and grandchildren," she added.

"You do a good job of it. You both do." Nolan glanced at Liza. "That's one reason people like this place so much. I met more than one family who came here twice this summer. That's saying something."

"Thank you, Nolan." Liza took another bite of the roasted swordfish Claire had made. It tasted wonderful, with a delicious sauce of fresh tomatoes, corn, black beans, and herbs. But she was almost too nervous to eat. She noticed Daniel was not his voracious self tonight, either. "I am relieved the season is winding down. We have other things to focus on."

Daniel smiled and reached over to cover her hand with his. "I'm going to rent out my cottage and start working on a master suite for us to live in here."

"Good idea. I'd love to help you, if I can," Nolan offered.

He picked up his dish and brought it to the sink. "When do you hear back about that test? Isn't it soon?"

Liza was sure Nolan had heard this answer many times, but he could be forgetful about dates and times. The stereotypical absentminded professor.

"Yes, very soon." Daniel glanced at his watch. "About five hours from now."

Nolan's head tilted back and he grinned. "Why didn't you

tell me that before? That's why everyone is so quiet." His tone was very definite and satisfied, as if he had arrived at the solution to some scientific question or math equation.

"Guess it will be a Scrabble tournament tonight," he added, looking over at Claire. "I don't want to retire early and miss this."

"Wouldn't dream of it," Claire replied.

Liza and Daniel took a walk on the beach after dinner, just in time to catch the sunset. Needing some distraction from their long wait when they returned to the inn, they decided to sketch out plans for their new living quarters, which would be on the mostly vacant third floor.

"I've been spoiling myself by keeping a room on the second floor all this time," Liza admitted. "It's one of the nicest rooms in the house, and I can certainly use an extra guest room during the season."

"Our new apartment will be great. I'm sure you won't miss it," Daniel promised as he began to sketch their living quarters on a piece of graph paper. "I may not be able to do all the work myself—if I get a job quickly. But I can probably get it started and leave the finishing work to someone else, like Sam Morgan."

"Of course. If you find a job you like, you might need to start right away." Daniel hadn't mentioned Dr. Mitchell's clinic again, and neither had Liza. She was content with avoiding the topic tonight. Or forever, if she had her choice.

"Have you been in touch with Matt at all about that opening in his office?" she asked.

Daniel nodded, but didn't look up at her as he positioned a straight edge on the paper. "I did speak to Matt. I ran into him in town last week. He went out of town for Labor Day and said he would call when he got back."

"Sounds good," Liza said, trying to keep her tone light. "And you'll know about the exam by then, too."

"Two hours, fifteen minutes, and . . . thirty seconds to go." Daniel glanced at his watch again. He was going to have a sore arm tomorrow from checking the time so often.

She forced a smile and kissed his cheek. "I'm not worried." She looked back at his plans. "I would like a bigger bathroom, though. And can the bathtub have a view of the ocean?"

He laughed. "Bathtub with ocean view." He made a note on a sticky and put it on the corner of the drawing. "I hate these fussy clients," he murmured. "So hard to please."

Liza laughed. "The customer is always right, dear," she reminded him.

He smiled to himself as he continued drawing. "Yes, I know. And so is my future wife. What else should we include? How about some studio space for you? I think this western exposure would be good. You'd get a lot of light during the day." He pointed to a turret room that had been left completely unfinished. Liza had been longing to make some time for her artwork, but was only able to do that during the winter. With her own studio, it would be much easier to paint or draw anytime.

"That would be fantastic!" Liza gave him a quick, appreciative hug. "Ever since I moved in, I've been wanting to find someplace where I could do my artwork." She squinted at him. "But I'm sure I didn't mention it."

Daniel smiled. "I wanted to surprise you. I had a feeling it was something you'd like."

"What about you? You need some space for your work, a home office or something?"

"Got it covered . . . right down here. It's a funky little space with an eave ceiling, but I think it will work out fine. I was also thinking we should have our own kitchen and a room for entertaining. I know we have this entire inn . . . but this will give us some privacy." He pointed out the area he had designated for that. "And we could have a really nice deck off that room, with a fantastic view.

"And," he went on, "if we put a wall here, our suite will be completely private, but we'll still have Claire's room and Nolan's room down this hall. We'll just have to build a storage shed out back for all that old furniture that's been gathering cobwebs in the attic. You don't mind that I'm taking over the attic?"

"Are you kidding? Daniel, this looks beautiful! It's like my dream house. Well, not a house, of course. But a perfect place for us to live together. And even more so, since you're designing it for us."

She leaned over and kissed him. He put his arms around her and kissed her back. "Anyplace I live with you is my dream house, Liza," he said quietly. "I can't wait for us to be married and start our new life together."

Liza couldn't wait, either. And knew that went without saying.

By eleven thirty they had ended up in the porch swing, with Liza's notebook computer balanced on Daniel's lap. Liza tried to stay awake, but even though it wasn't all that late, the porch swing's gentle rocking, the hard work of Labor Day, and the stress of waiting all caught up with her. She realized that she must have drifted off with her head on Daniel's shoulder when his voice suddenly roused her.

"Liza . . . wake up, honey. I got the results from the test."

Her head popped up at those words, and she turned to him.

She couldn't tell a thing from his expression. It was neither happy nor sad. He looked shocked.

"Yes . . . ? So? What is it? Did you pass?"

Finally, he nodded and pointed to the screen. "I did. I just can't believe it," he confessed. "I did a lot better than I expected—top five percent of my class . . . I'm so relieved. It's hard to really take in. I got my certification back, Liza. I'm really a doctor again."

Daniel had put the computer aside, luckily, or she would have knocked it over as she wrapped her arms around him and hugged him tight. She didn't know whether to laugh or cry, and felt as if she was doing a little of both.

They had somehow come to their feet, and Daniel's embrace nearly lifted her off her feet.

"I knew you would do it. I knew it," she said as he hugged her back.

"Then you knew something I didn't," he murmured back. "I said it before—my future wife is always right."

"I wouldn't say *always* . . . but I'm glad I was this time." *When it really counted,* she silently added.

Thank You, God. Thank You for helping Daniel get through this. We are both so very grateful for Your help and love.

Claire and Nolan came out to the porch. They had been waiting, too, and had obviously heard the good news through the open windows of the front parlor.

Claire clapped her hands together. "Congratulations, Daniel! We knew you could do it."

"Good work, young man." Nolan patted his shoulder. "You prevailed with flying colors. And you'll make a fine doctor, too. I've no doubt about it."

"Thank you, Claire. Thank you, Nolan." Daniel stood with his arm around Liza, looking breathless and elated, as if he had just run a marathon. His eyes were bright and his expression was so much lighter than it had been the last few weeks. Liza had thought he had just been tired from all his studying and stress. But now he looked as if a heavy load had been lifted. Something vital had been restored to him, she understood. Something that had been broken in him was finally whole.

"Now I can really dig in with the job search," Daniel said, taking Liza's hand. "Maybe I'll even have something by the time we get married."

Before Liza could respond, Claire did. "Oh, don't you worry, Daniel. God has a plan for you. Put your trust in Him and it will come together for you."

Daniel smiled at her and nodded. Liza smiled, too. Though she didn't always share Claire's all-abiding faith, she knew that was true. God had a plan for Daniel. For both of them. And she was so grateful for the many blessings He had showered on them so far.

CAPE Light Founder's Day, a holiday unique to the village, fell on a Saturday, September fourteenth, about two weeks after Labor Day. Claire noticed on Monday that the upcoming holiday, combined with a forecast for summerlike weather, had inspired a few last-minute reservations. The inn was expecting another wave of guests on Thursday night and into the weekend.

Nolan had just come inside with a bushel of vegetables he'd picked in the garden when she told him about it. Tomatoes, green beans, squash, and kale were ripening fast and furiously. Claire could hardly keep up with the bounty and had started to freeze and preserve some of the extras.

"Founder's Day? Who found what and what are they celebrating?" he asked in his typical style.

"The founding of Cape Light village," she explained. "There are a few enactments in period costume. Colonists arrive by boat and land near the green. Members of the Wampanoag tribe, I believe it is, come out to meet them. That's followed by a big parade down Main Street, which is closed for the day with lots of vendors and food stalls. The first and second houses built in the town are open for tours, and there are demonstrations of traditional local crafts—pottery and glassblowing, shearing and spinning. We have a lot of history around here," she noted. "And the town does love a celebration."

"Sounds interesting. I'd like to go to town and observe for a while, if you can spare me from my duties?" he asked with a smile.

"I'm sure you can take some time. There won't be all that many guests. And most will be down in town all day. I probably won't have to worry about serving them lunch or dinner."

"Most likely," Nolan agreed. "What happens after that? I

mean the rest of September. It seems pretty quiet around here already. I don't want to overstay my welcome."

Claire was not surprised at his question. She knew that the repairs on Nolan's boat were almost complete. She had peeked in the barn yesterday to check his progress. The *Ariadne* looked better than ever, with a glossy white hull and gleaming wood within. Nolan even had a new set of sails and had ordered new cushions for the cabin, which would soon arrive.

Was he that eager to leave them? From his question, she guessed he was too proud and independent to take a "handout," and as he had said, he didn't want to take advantage of Liza's generosity.

The question was really Liza's to answer. But Claire couldn't help offering her thoughts.

"We still have guests into October. Just on the weekends, but we get the leaf-peepers roaming around New England."

"Is that so? There aren't many trees turning out here to see," he observed in his practical way.

Claire shrugged, lifting a handful of green beans into a colander. "I guess they like the ocean and the leaves." She glanced at him. "Are you eager to leave? Is that why you're asking? I thought you would stay for the wedding. It's only three weeks from now." Claire tried to keep her tone light. The truth was, she knew he had never really said one way or the other.

She *hoped* he would stay. She couldn't imagine the celebration now without him. He had been witness to the happy steps leading up to the big day, and all the wedding plans.

Being totally honest with herself, when she imagined the

day, she automatically saw herself celebrating with Nolan. She had become so accustomed to his company, she would feel very lonely there without him.

"I'd like to, but . . . guess I'll just see how it goes," he answered vaguely. He was quiet a moment. "I can't stay here forever," he said finally, "though it would be very pleasant."

Claire nodded. She knew that. The inn had been a good place for him to rest and get his bearings, but they all knew he had to move on sooner or later. A part of her did want him to stay. A selfish part, she knew.

But another part wanted to see him go forward with his life and find some peace and satisfaction in his work again.

"Where will you go?" Claire asked, glancing over her shoulder. "Have you made any plans yet?"

"Not really. I might try to get another teaching position somewhere, even part-time. Or a job as an engineer. I still have some contacts in that world. I might find some part-time work as a troubleshooter, consultant type."

"I think you have a real gift for that," she said quickly. "And you seem to enjoy it—figuring out a better way to do something."

"Pays pretty well, too," he added with a laugh. "If you solve the problem. A job like that would give me time to work on my own ideas. I wouldn't be pinned down to a nine-to-five schedule."

Claire was pleased to see that he was looking to the future, figuring out how to get back to work, back to doing what he loved best. She wondered what he thought of the lawsuit now. They had agreed not to talk about it, but she was curious.

She brought a bowl of beans over to the table and started to snap the ends off. Nolan reached over and began helping her, without a word passing between them.

"I know we agreed not to talk about a certain subject," she began quietly. "But I was wondering how things sit now with . . . with a certain matter," she said cautiously.

Nolan glanced at her. His expression was serious, but in his eyes, she saw a glimmer of amusement.

"Still on it, Claire, if that's what you're asking. I've filed another complaint with the patent office, to counter what those new attorneys claim. I'm waiting to hear back. If the patent people still back up my complaint, it will help the negotiation."

"And if they don't?" she dared to ask.

Nolan frowned, his jaw jutting out in that expression she had come to know too well by now. "Then they don't. It won't persuade me to throw in the towel," he insisted. "It shouldn't, anyway. Though I will admit, if I find a new job somewhere, I'll have to put this on a back burner."

Claire nodded and turned her attention back to the green beans. While Nolan's passion for justice hadn't dampened, she did detect a tiny crack in his stone wall of determination.

Maybe a few words of reason from their argument had gotten through to him? Maybe a few of her prayers, too? Even though she had promised Nolan not to talk about the lawsuit with him, she had continued to talk about it with God, asking Him to help Nolan with this quest, and help her dear friend see the right path out of this stalemate, so that he wouldn't end up wasting any more of his days and valuable energy—and so he might one day reconnect with his daughter.

Perhaps a few of those prayers had been answered, Claire thought. If the cost of that was Nolan leaving the inn and the island, well then . . . she could live with that. She could even be thankful for it.

"So . . . what do you think? Did it go well?" Liza didn't mean to pounce on Daniel as soon as he came through the door. But it was hard not to. His visit to talk with Matt Harding about the opening at Matt's practice had been canceled once, but had finally taken place on Friday, the day before Founder's Day.

Liza was glad that all of the guests had gone to town and she and Daniel had some privacy. She was watering the planters on the porch, and Daniel sat down on a wicker chair, quickly loosening his tie.

"It went very well. I haven't been in that office since Dr. Elliot practiced there. Everything's been remodeled and updated. I didn't even recognize the place."

"Nor does Dr. Elliot, whenever he goes there." Liza laughed.

"My aunt always took me to Dr. Elliot if I got sick while visiting over the summer. Even back then, I felt as if I were stepping into a Dickens novel. And Dr. Elliot looked like a perfect character for one of those stories."

Matt had taken the practice over from Dr. Ezra Elliot, who had been the reigning physician in Cape Light for decades. Dr. Elliot was still alive and lived with his wife, Lillian Warwick Elliot, in town. The senior physician had become very good friends with Dr. Harding, whom he thoroughly approved of as his successor.

There was a pitcher of iced tea on the end table, and Daniel poured himself a glass. "It's all changed now. Matt's got state-of-the-art exam rooms, an X-ray machine, and a lab right there. And everything is computerized."

Liza rarely got sick, and when she did, she visited a doctor in Newburyport. But she truly felt Daniel would be happy there, at least for a start.

"It sounds great, honey. I've only heard good things about Matt's practice. Everyone in town seems to love him."

"Yes, he has a lot of patients—a lot of family medicine and preventive medicine for children. Which I'm very interested in now," Daniel said. "He offered me the job, and we even talked salary."

"Well . . . that's fast. But good, right?"

Daniel took another sip of tea. "It's all good," he agreed. "I can start after the wedding. The doctor I would be replacing isn't leaving until late October, so we'd even have time for a honeymoon trip."

"You do realize we haven't even discussed a honeymoon?" Liza reminded him with a grin. "And I'm not sure I'm ready to. It's hard enough pulling the wedding together. Still, Matt's job offer sounds like perfect timing for us." Liza set down the watering can and pulled a few yellow leaves off the geraniums.

"Matt didn't press me for an answer, which is fine. I guess it would be good to think about it a little."

Liza glanced at him. She didn't see that there was much more to consider. It sounded like the perfect spot for Daniel to get his feet wet again. Busy enough, but not a caseload of life-or-death emergencies. And a boss who was already a good friend. But this was Daniel's decision, and she didn't want to start off their marriage sounding like a know-it-all, bossy wife.

"You should think about it," she agreed finally. "Have you sent your résumé anywhere else yet?"

"Two other places. There's a job up in Newburyport, and one in Salem. I haven't heard back from either yet. It would be nice to know before the wedding," he added. "So that's another count in Matt's favor."

"Did Matt say he wanted an answer by any special date?"

"Not really. I think the job is mine if I want it. But I don't want to hold him up if he needs to look for someone else."

Liza certainly hoped that was not the case. She couldn't understand why Daniel didn't sound happy to find a great job so easily. Maybe once Daniel explored these other possibilities, he would see the job at Matt's office in a different light. She just hoped Matt didn't get tired of waiting and find someone else in the meanwhile.

But Matt wouldn't do that, she reminded herself. For one thing, Molly wouldn't let him, Liza realized with a secret smile.

Daniel's concerns were just a little blip on the screen, par for the course for someone who was reentering the medical profession. Everything was working out for them, she reminded herself. Their ship was sailing in over smooth seas, and she couldn't be happier.

DANIEL did receive positive replies from his inquiries at the practices in Salem and Newburyport. The week after meeting with Matt, Daniel was very busy with more interviews. He had also started renovating the third floor of the inn, and Liza never knew if she'd see him at breakfast dressed in a suit and tie or in his work clothes—though he looked remarkably handsome to her either way.

On Thursday night, they decided to take a walk on the beach after dinner. Even though Liza was no longer busy taking care of guests, the last-minute details of the wedding had been demanding. It was exactly seventeen days until they were married. How could there still be so many little details to work out?

". . . so we decided to skip the roses altogether and go with plain white hydrangeas for the centerpieces. Molly offered to send someone in to Boston to get roses, but I don't think it's worth the bother. I don't think it will look too plain though. There are going to be some greens and ribbon." Liza knew she had been rambling about wedding plans, and Daniel had probably not followed half of it. But it did feel good to vent.

"It sounds very . . . elegant," he said finally. "But I thought once we brought Molly in on the plans, you'd have less stress. Sounds to me like you have more."

"Molly has been terrific, but it is my own wedding. *Our* wedding," she corrected herself. "So maybe I have been a bit over-involved."

"Maybe a bit," he conceded. He squeezed her hand and smiled. Their pace matched, step for step, along the smooth, damp sand. Liza felt the seafoam lap at her feet and ankles. The water was cool but refreshing.

"I know I've complained a lot, but I have enjoyed making

all these decisions. Even the silly, trivial ones, like how the napkins should be folded."

"That's not silly and trivial at all," Daniel said very seriously. "By the way, what did we go with—the swans or the bishops' caps?"

Liza was amazed he even remembered that conversation. "Just a sort of fold over fold." She gestured with her hands, sure that he couldn't picture it.

"Perfect choice," he agreed.

They walked a bit more without talking. Liza didn't want to be one of those crazy brides who couldn't stop talking about their wedding, though she could suddenly understand how it happened. She knew it was time to talk about something else, to turn the conversation back to Daniel. He hadn't said much lately about his job hunt, and Liza was curious. Did Matt's offer look good now, compared to his latest interviews? Or was some other practice luring him? Never mind the way the napkins were folded at their wedding reception—this choice was anything but trivial.

"So what did you think about the practice in Rockport? You didn't say much after your meeting. Did it go well?"

"It was fine. I liked the head physician there, an older woman, Esther Oakely. She's thinking of retiring and wants to bring in a successor."

"That's interesting. Do any of these other practices seem better to you than working with Matt?"

Daniel didn't answer right away. "They each have their pluses and minuses, I guess. I haven't had any offers yet from the others. Only Matt's so far."

"I was just wondering," Liza replied. She had an intuition he was holding something back from her. Something he didn't want to say.

"Is something wrong, Daniel? Is something about the wedding bothering you? Do you think I'm getting too carried away?"

Daniel glanced at her and shook his head. "Not at all. You're happy and excited, just as it should be."

Liza was relieved to hear that. At least they weren't fighting about the wedding, like so many couples she had met. But there was something bothering him. She had known him too long and too well to deny it.

"Well, what is it, then? Is the job hunt getting to you? You don't have to pick one by the time we get married. Maybe none of these jobs is the right fit. You'll be moving into the inn and will have free room and board for as long as you need it," she teased him. "I'm happy to take care of you, honey. Honestly."

He slung his arm around her shoulder and pulled her tight against his side. "You guessed it . . . my secret plan to freeload. And here I thought I'd been so good at hiding it from you."

Liza laughed as a big wave fell nearby, spraying them with foam. "I just don't want you to feel pressured," she went on, wanting to be clear. "I think all these jobs sound like good opportunities, but I know it's your call."

A smile flickered for a moment on his lips and then changed to a more serious expression. "Thanks for saying that, Liza. It is my call . . . though it's also our future, together. Wherever I decide to work will impact our life. There's no getting around that."

Liza wasn't sure what he was driving at. Was he worried about the long hours he would spend in his office? The visits to Southport Hospital? A long commute?

"Yes, we'll have to be flexible and see what the job you choose asks of you . . . of us. Being a doctor isn't like working nine to five in an office. I understand that," she assured him.

He kept looking at her, and she could see her reply hadn't answered his concern. Finally, he said, "I heard from Jim Mitchell the other day. He was wondering if I'd considered his offer."

Daniel's admission hit Liza like a blow. She tried not to show her shock, but it was impossible. She turned to face him. "Really? You never told me that. When was this?"

"Oh, I don't know . . . earlier this week. I'd sent him an e-mail a few weeks ago and let him know I passed the exams. He was very happy for me," he added. "Does it matter when he wrote me?"

She could tell from his tone he felt annoyed at her question. And he was right; it didn't matter. He didn't have to tell her about every single e-mail he received.

"No, it doesn't matter. But I'm glad you're telling me now. Did you answer him yet?"

Daniel took a breath. She felt her stomach knot, waiting for his answer. "I told him I'd had some interviews in this area. And I was waiting to hear back on them. And . . ."

"Yes?" she asked eagerly.

"He didn't answer me yet. That's all I said."

"Oh . . ." Liza felt so relieved. She felt like a balloon that was suddenly deflating. "So you've turned him down. I mean, in a nice way."

"More or less," Daniel conceded. He paused and picked up a pale white shell in a delicate fan shape, which had somehow survived the rough waves and tides whole and unbroken. He handed it to Liza. "Something for your collection," he said quietly.

"Thanks." She dropped it in her pocket, still feeling uneasy about his answer. She sighed and looked over at him. "I'm sorry, Daniel. Maybe I've just let the wedding plans get to me. My nerves are a little jangled right now . . . But what does 'more or less' mean? Are you still interested in that job? Are you still taking it seriously?"

Could he possibly think they would just pick up from this beautiful place and move out to a reservation in the middle of nowhere? Did he think she could just drop everything and leave the inn, a business she had worked so hard to build for the last three years . . . and follow him to a rough, impoverished place? Where she would have absolutely nothing to do but stare at the barren landscape and cacti?

Had he been thinking of her at all? She looked over at him, feeling her temper rising.

He turned to her and took her hand again. "I . . . I guess I do think about it," he admitted. "It's a different kind of medicine, Liza. I can't deny that it attracts me. But I also know that it's not possible for me to take a job with Jim when you're still here, thousands of miles away. And it wouldn't be fair of me to ask you to give up the inn and everything you love. I know that marriage means making compromises," he assured her. "It's not like being single, and able to do anything I want."

Liza felt a little stunned by his answer. She knew that he'd been trying to reassure her and yet . . . his words had been anything but reassuring.

She suddenly felt as if she were seeing this situation clearly for the first time. She had been so focused on their wedding and running the inn, she had turned a blind eye to the truth. And Daniel had hidden it from her, too, trying to spare her feelings.

But the idea of working with Dr. Mitchell on the reservation had never lost its attraction for him. If anything, going on these nearby job interviews had only made that distant opportunity seem more attractive. More challenging. More rewarding.

Even the job at Matt's practice, which she thought was tailor-made for him, paled in comparison. And that changed everything in her mind. Everything . . .

"Liza? Could you please just say something?" Daniel was staring at her with a curious expression. She had been so upset and lost in her own thoughts that she hadn't realized he was waiting for a response.

"I'm sorry . . . What did you say?"

"I said, I know what my responsibilities are now to you—and our relationship. To our marriage."

Liza stared back at him. "Well, that's great. But I don't want you to decide this out of some sense of duty to me, Daniel. Do you think I could be happy like that? Watching you go off to a job every day and knowing you think it's boring and soul-numbing? Thinking that you gave up what you really wanted for me? And knowing that you weren't giving your best to the world, after all you went through to get back to medicine?"

"Liza, I never said that. I never said the jobs around here would be soul-numbing. Or boring."

"Not in so many words," she replied. "But I know you. Even if you don't think that now, I'm sure in time you will . . . and, in time, you might blame me. Or resent that our marriage has limited you, prevented you from doing what you really want to do." She felt her voice shaking as she said, "I don't think I could live with that."

"Liza, please. I don't feel that way at all. How could I resent you? That's crazy. If it wasn't for you, I wouldn't even be able to think about these choices. I'd still be lining up carpentry jobs right now."

"That's the irony of it all, I guess. I encouraged you to get back to what you love, and . . . well, 'watch out what you wish for' is the lesson here for me. Taking a job with Jim Mitchell— that's what you'd really love. In your heart, I feel you've already made the choice . . . But where does that leave me, Daniel? I feel as if you've already chosen between staying here with me and going out there to do the work you . . . you're *meant* to do," she finished. She felt heartsick as she looked out at the end- less stretch of waves. She knew that if she met his gaze, she would cry.

"Listen . . . let's just slow down and talk this out calmly.

There are always possibilities. It doesn't have to be so . . . so black-and-white," Daniel pleaded.

Liza took a deep breath and glanced up at him. "All right. I can talk calmly. What do you think the possibilities are?"

She was honestly interested. She couldn't think of any.

"Well . . . I know moving out there is a lot to ask. I really do. I was thinking that maybe I could go out and come back, say, once a month or so? And you could come out there to visit. We could try that for a while, see how it goes. Six months, maybe?" he asked her.

Liza felt her jaw drop. She couldn't help it. How could he possibly think that was a solution? "Start off our marriage with a long-distance relationship? Is that what you mean? I wasn't very happy with you living in Boston all summer and coming back just about every weekend. I thought that you didn't like it, either . . ."

"I didn't," Daniel insisted. "I didn't like it one bit. But—"

"But now you want to move even farther away? And be apart for a month at a stretch, or longer? That's what you just told me," she pointed out.

"I know. But it would be for a good reason. An important reason," he insisted. "It's not that I want to be away from you."

Liza stared at him. She wanted to believe him, but actions spoke louder than words. That's what Claire would say, and Liza knew it was true. At the end of her troubled first marriage, another wise friend had advised, *Shut the sound off and just watch what's on the screen. That's what's really going on.*

Liza didn't like what she saw going on here. It hurt her deeply. She felt as if a giant rug had just been yanked out from under her.

"Okay, bad idea. I knew you wouldn't want to do that." Daniel waved his hand, backtracking.

"What about what we talked about before," Liza said. "You could accept a job around here, as we'd planned, and you use any time you have off during the year to volunteer out there? Matt's such a great guy. He might give you three or even four weeks off at a time if you could line up a substitute."

Now it was Daniel's turn to look surprised. He frowned at her. "Go there as a volunteer, once a year? Like going to . . . to summer camp or something? That's what you think I should do?"

She felt hurt by his tone and the way he had twisted her words. "It's just a suggestion. A possibility. You offered yours, and I'm offering mine." He didn't answer, just kept scowling, his arms crossed over his chest. "You've only been to Arizona once in your entire life, on a vacation," she reminded him. "You might not even like living out there, on a reservation."

Daniel shook his head, as if trying to shake out distracting thoughts. "You're right. The place looks pretty bleak," he admitted. "But in fact, that's part of the reason it draws me. It's the type of place that needs the type of medicine I really want to practice. It's the perfect combination of what I've been trained to do as an ER doctor and the areas I want to go into—family practice and children's health—in a severely underserved community. It's a place to be really and truly needed. Not just one doctor's office among hundreds." He sighed. "I thought that you got that at least."

Liza felt stung by his last words. "I do get it. I get it loud and clear. But while you're feeling so fulfilled and satisfied and just where you need to be, what about me? What am I supposed to do out there—or all alone here, without you? Do you think I worked so hard building up this inn to just walk out on it like that? Did you design our beautiful new apartment so I can live there alone? I wouldn't even want to," she insisted.

"Liza, come on." He reached for her but she pulled away. "Don't get so angry at me. I'm trying to be honest with you."

Liza felt tears well up again, and this time she didn't try to stop them. "I know you're being honest. I just wish you had been honest about this sooner." She wiped her hands over her eyes so she could see him clearly. "I need to be honest with you now. I don't think we should get married. I don't think I can," she said finally.

Daniel stared at her in shock. He gripped her shoulders with his hands, forcing her to look up at him. "How could you even say that? Of course I want to get married. I love you more than anything. I want to spend our lives together. Please don't say you won't, Liza—"

"How can we? I can't walk down the aisle knowing that you feel so torn. Knowing you're not really happy . . . or might be moving a thousand miles away. Or really wish you could. Maybe someone else could do that," she added quietly, "but not me. I'm just not that woman."

Daniel's expression was bleak. He stared down at her and didn't answer.

Liza felt tears spilling down her cheeks. She felt so confused and turned around. Moments ago, it seemed her whole future was set, like a shooting star streaking across the sky.

Now everything was shattered, all the pieces at her feet. She didn't know how to fix it. Or even if she should try.

Chapter Twelve

"I know it seems awful, but please don't cry." Molly sat with Liza on the porch, the binder of wedding plans on her lap.

It was Friday morning. Liza could barely believe that she and Daniel had ended it all the night before. She had woken up too heartsick and dazed to remember that Molly was coming over, and that she needed to cancel their meeting. Molly had arrived right on time, and Liza had told her the bad news— and had quickly melted into a puddle of tears.

"You know what I think? I think it's going to be fine," Molly insisted, answering her own question. "Then you're going to say, 'Why did I cry so much? My nose is all chapped and my eyes are so bloodshot, they look like a road map.'"

The comment made Liza laugh a tiny bit, through her tears. She knew Molly was trying to be positive. But she knew it could never be "fine" again between her and Daniel. Not when he was so willing to move thousands of miles away from her.

"I don't have to worry about my nose or my bloodshot eyes," she mumbled. She knew Molly had dealt with a lot of couples who got cold feet. But this was different. Very different.

Molly seemed about to offer more comforting words, then sat back in her seat. "Listen," she said finally, "here's my advice . . . You already put down hefty deposits on all these party orders—chairs, tables, flowers, china, flatware, napkins . . . whatever."

The mere mention of the napkins made Liza feel all weepy again, remembering her conversation with Daniel about how they would be folded. *I was walking on a cloud and I didn't even realize it.*

Why did this happen, God? Did I do something wrong? Did I take it all for granted and not feel thankful enough? Liza covered her face with her hands.

Molly paused and gave her a moment to collect herself. "I'm listening," Liza assured her.

"Of course you are," Molly said in a gentler tone. "The thing is, it doesn't make sense to cancel anything now. Let's just wait and see how it goes. There is a moment when it will make sense to pull the plug. But we have a little elbow room. I've seen this happen before, and nine times out of ten, the couple gets all lovey-dovey again, right on schedule."

Liza glanced at her wistfully. It was a nice thought. But that wasn't going to happen for her and Daniel. They couldn't be all lovey-dovey if he was on the Navajo reservation, a zillion miles away.

But she was too worn out to argue with Molly. And she had a feeling that even if she did tell the intrepid wedding planner to cancel everything, Molly wouldn't do it anyway.

"All right. Whatever you say. But please be mindful of that pull-the-plug moment?"

"I hear you," Molly promised, gathering up her things. She stood up, then leaned over and gave Liza a huge hug. Which was a formidable experience. "Chin up, pal . . . and please use the tissues with lotion? You'll see. You're going to end up thanking me."

Liza nodded. It was hard to resist being mothered by Molly. And hard to resist offering a small smile as they said good-bye.

Liza stayed on the porch, with her computer in her lap, staring at the reservations screen that showed the weeks to come, which was mostly blank, since she had blocked off two weeks for her wedding.

She pondered sending a message to her e-mail list with a special rate for the end of September and early October. She could probably fill many of the rooms with regulars.

Before she could consider the idea further, Claire came out to the porch and placed two dishes with thick sandwiches and some mixed greens down on the table nearest Liza.

"Is Molly gone already? I thought she might like lunch."

"Yes, she had to go . . . other clients." *Brides who are actually getting married,* Liza thought.

Liza had told her the news that morning, and Claire had tried to console Liza as best she could. But there was so little that anyone could say. Even Claire, with all her wisdom and faith, seemed to realize that.

Claire sat and gazed at her. Finally Liza looked up. "I know you're hurting, Liza. I also know that you and Daniel truly love each other. And love is the most powerful force in the entire universe. Just don't give up on it. Don't let it go. You might have to follow it blindly, like a compass in a storm," she suggested. "But if you both fix your faith on it with all your heart . . . it will show you the right way to go, I promise you. God doesn't create a problem without creating a solution."

Liza wanted so badly to believe Claire's comforting advice. She did love Daniel. She knew she always would. But she didn't see how they would ever find their way back to each other now.

"Thank you. I will try to remember that . . . But Daniel left me a note this morning. He's leaving for northern Arizona tonight. He's not even going to stop here to say good-bye."

Claire looked surprised to hear that. She sat back in her seat and sighed. "Did he really?"

Liza nodded bleakly.

"What did he say?"

Liza reached into the pocket of her sweatshirt and took out a crumpled piece of paper. "Not too much. Here, you can read it," she said, handing the note Claire.

Liza knew if she read it out loud, she would just start crying again. She was already blinking back tears, just recalling the words, as Claire slipped on her reading glasses and read it to herself.

Liza,

It's hard to express all I'm feeling right now. Shock, mostly, that you so quickly decided you don't want to marry me. I guess you don't understand what this opportunity in Arizona means to

*me. Even so, I would have thought you'd be a little more willing
to compromise. Seems nothing is left for either of us to say.*

*I've decided to leave for Arizona today and find out if this
really is the work I want to do. I believe that it is and that I
won't be disappointed. Not by this choice, at least.*

*This isn't what I wanted, Liza. I hope you can remember
that. But maybe it's the right thing, after all. You seem to
think so.*

Daniel

"I see . . . Well, that is serious." Claire paused, collecting
her thoughts and saying a silent prayer for God to give her the
wisdom and words to soothe Liza's soul, even if just a little.
"The sooner he goes out there, the sooner he'll figure out what
he really wants," she said finally. "A person can't fly over a river
like this. They have to swim through it. Would you be happier
if he didn't go and he just . . . pushed this down and didn't try
to get to the bottom of it?"

"That's just what I told him I didn't want him to do. I told
him that I didn't want him to stay here and take some job,
knowing he wasn't happy or feeling fulfilled. I couldn't be
happy knowing he felt that way."

"You said the right thing. It was the only thing you could say
if you really love him. And I know that you really do," Claire
assured her.

Liza sighed. "He said I wasn't willing to compromise, but
what are the choices here, Claire? It seems to me that it's either
I give up the inn to go with him, or we try to have some sort of

long-distance marriage." Liza shook her head in frustration. "That's not what I want, either—to see my new husband once a month, or maybe less?"

Claire nodded. There was no clear answer here. "I don't know what to say, Liza. I don't know what the answer is," she said honestly. "I do know that sometimes, compromise is not a fifty-fifty thing. Sometimes one person gets ninety percent of what they want, and the other person gets ten. But they're willing to accept that arrangement because the happiness and welfare of the person they love is more important to them, and it more than compensates for what they've missed out on."

Liza nodded. "Do you think I ought to give up the inn . . . or leave you here to run it?"

Claire shook her head. "I'm not making any suggestions at all. But I do know there's an answer. It just hasn't come to you or Daniel yet. I'm going to pray, my dear, that it does."

"Thank you, Claire. I know I'm a horrible mess right now, but I appreciate you listening to me." Liza leaned over and patted Claire's hand. Claire took her hand and held it.

"You be just as horrible as you like if it makes you feel any better. And don't worry about a thing around here. Nolan and I will take care of everything."

"Thank you, Claire." Liza was about to say more when she heard the phone ring at the reception desk in the foyer. Claire jumped up to answer it. "I'll get that. You relax."

Liza was soon alone again on the porch. She sat back and stared out at the sea. Claire seemed to think she had done the right thing. But to her mind, there had not been any other choice—or a compromise she could live with. She had done what she had to do. Even though it had cost her dearly.

WHEN Claire returned to the kitchen a few minutes later, she found Nolan at the table reading the newspaper. He looked up curiously as she walked in.

"Is the wedding really off?" he asked. Claire set down the dishes she had carried in. Liza had barely eaten a bite of her sandwich. Claire had to watch her. She didn't want the poor girl to get sick now, on top of everything.

"Seems so. Daniel has gone out West, to the Navajo reservation. He left today," she added sadly.

"Sounds very serious. Not just a lover's spat. I feel sorry for them. They seemed so perfectly in sync . . . and here I was, thinking I might stay for the party, after all."

Claire smiled. "Don't hoist anchor yet, Nolan. It's not over till the game ends . . . or something like that." She suddenly couldn't recall the exact words of the adage. Not like her, but the news was upsetting. She hated to see poor Liza so heartbroken. Especially after these last few weeks of pure bliss.

"'It ain't over till it's over.' Yogi Berra," Nolan reminded her. "I think you feel a little blue over the lovebirds. It's only natural. I think I do, too," he admitted.

Claire smiled wistfully. Nolan acted as if he were just about the facts, but he wasn't any more immune to emotions than anybody else.

"Yes, only natural. Maybe a walk on the beach will clear my head. It's a very fair day." She glanced at Nolan as she took her apron off. She wondered if she should ask him to take a walk with her. Even this far along in their relationship, Claire still felt shy—as if such a simple question would be very bold and forward. But Nolan would probably be leaving soon. She wouldn't have too many chances to share his company.

She took a breath and squared her shoulders, preparing to invite him, when he looked up and put his newspaper aside.

"It is a lovely day. Despite the abandoned wedding plans. The sea is as calm as glass, though there's a nice enough breeze out there, as well. Would you like to take a sail on the *Ariadne*? Test her out with me?"

Claire was so surprised by the invitation, she couldn't answer for a moment. "You mean, on the water?"

Nolan laughed. "I realize you don't know much about sailing, Claire. But surely you know a boat floats on the water?"

Claire laughed and blushed. How silly that had sounded. "I didn't realize the boat was ready to sail, Nolan. You didn't say a word."

"With all this hoopla going on, it didn't seem that important. Daniel left his trailer here. I hooked it up to your Jeep this morning and took the boat down to the dock. She's definitely watertight. I just checked about an hour ago. I think she's ready for a little test drive. See how the new sails fill and if all the lines are strung up right."

Claire squinted at him a moment. "You mean you haven't actually sailed it yet . . . to make sure the holes are fixed?"

He laughed again and patted her arm. "I've still got the life jackets. And you can swim, can't you? I promise not to go that far out from shore."

Claire had to smile at his negotiations. "I'm a strong swimmer. And if anything happens, Edison will save us. Won't you, pal?"

The dog sat right beside Nolan, as usual, and stared up at them, seeming to understand the conversation. Claire heard his big tail thumping on the floor and had her answer.

"All right, I'm game. I'll just go up and change my shoes." She stared down at her sandals a moment. "I do know rubber soles are best for boating. So I won't slip off the ship."

Nolan patted her arm. "That's my girl. I'll make a sailor out of you yet. Meet you out back by the Jeep in five minutes."

THE sun had peaked at noon and was already slipping toward the sea, but was still strong enough to make Claire glad she had brought her dark glasses. She stared out at the waves as the sunshine sprinkled the crests with starlike bursts of light.

Nolan had tied his boat to the end of the wooden dock that was down the road from the inn, the same place the injured *Ariadne* had been beached so many weeks ago.

Claire couldn't help remembering that dark moment when he had surveyed the damaged vessel and nearly cried. Now he was returning with the same boat, seaworthy after his own careful efforts and repairs. *Time has a way of healing most wounds*, she thought. In this case, it was happily true.

As they walked up beside the boat, Nolan began loosening the tie lines. Edison jumped off the dock and landed on the deck with a thump. He certainly had not forgotten what to do. Claire wondered if the dog had missed sailing. His tail was wagging wildly as he stared up at the humans, beckoning them to join him.

"Hold your horses, Edison. And don't sail off without us," Nolan told him.

Claire laughed as Nolan held her hand and helped her down to the deck. Moments later, she sat on the bench near the steering wheel and, with his instruction, helped him pull in the tie lines. Then she sat back as he motored away from the dock. Once they were out on open water, he shut down the engine and raised the mainsail.

"Nice steady breeze, perfect for taking her through her paces. She's riding the water very smoothly," he observed, peering over the rail. He looked over at Claire and smiled.

"Oh yes, it's a very smooth ride. It's such a pretty boat, Nolan. You've done a wonderful job repairing it. I would have never known what it looked like before."

He smiled, and she could tell her compliments had pleased him.

But before he could answer, the canvas began to snap, and he jumped up to tighten the sail. It seemed to Claire that Nolan was transformed into another person on his boat. He was so agile and adept, hopping from one side of the deck to the other, practically anticipating the boat's needs before they happened.

Not that he wasn't energetic and very able around the inn, but he was somehow different out here, on the sea. He was clearly in his element—totally focused, confident, and in command. Yet very relaxed, as though he didn't know the meaning of the word "failure," and had certainly never had its painful arrow aimed at his own heart.

As the boat sailed along, changing its tack just a bit, Claire felt suddenly peaceful and light, as if the gentle breeze had lifted away the turmoil at the inn, at least for a little while. It wasn't as if she had forgotten about Liza and Daniel. How could she? But she did feel a bit distant from the drama and was able to focus instead on the beautiful view of the water and the deep blue sky that simply enveloped them.

"Thank you for taking me out here, Nolan. I'm thoroughly enjoying it."

Nolan smiled. "I thought so. I'm glad you are . . . I'm glad you're here, Claire. For this first sail."

Once the sails were adjusted, he returned to the stern and took the wheel again. "It turns out, I had a very productive summer out here on this tiny dot of an island. Very interesting . . . and memorable, too," he added, looking at her.

Claire wondered what he meant. Was he talking about her, about their relationship? She felt the color rise in her cheeks and was glad for her sunglasses—and the fact he would think it was just the effect of the wind and sun.

"I had a memorable summer, too," she told him. "It was wonderful getting to know you, Nolan. You kept the summer full of surprises," she confessed. "I never knew what new invention would greet me when I glanced out the window."

Nolan laughed. "You made my time here very special, too. You gave me a reason to smile when I got up in the morning."

Claire felt very flattered by his compliment. And touched.

But she still felt inclined to tease him. "I think you were just anticipating breakfast," she replied.

"That, too," he laughed. "And your good conversation.

Talking things over with you," he added in a more humble tone. "Even though I didn't always act very appreciative of your wise words while you were dispensing them."

Claire smiled at his confession. At least he'd given her well-intentioned words some thought. That was all one could ask.

"We had a lot of fun, the most I've had in a long time, so I thank you for that . . . And I'll be sorry to see you go," she said honestly. "I'll miss you."

Nolan turned and smiled wistfully at her. Then he looped a cord through the wheel and sat beside her. He put his arm around her shoulder and smiled into her eyes.

"I'll miss you, too, Claire North. I can't begin to say how much. Not quantifiable," he added, with a shake of his head. "It's very tempting to stay here longer. Mainly because of you. But that would make it even harder to go. If I had something to offer a woman like yourself . . . well, maybe I'd recalculate and things would have a different outcome. Sadly, I don't."

Claire rested her hand on his. "I know what you're trying to say, Nolan. I understand . . . I accept your decision to go. But you've always had something to offer me: your wonderful friendship. You're a once-in-a-lifetime person. I'm very blessed to have met you." He started to answer, but she hushed him and continued. "And you have so much to offer the world." She swept her free hand across their view of the open sea and the wide open sky. "You don't need to be a famous inventor or a millionaire. You have it all right now—your amazing imagination and all your amazing ideas."

"Claire, you're a once-in-a-lifetime person, too. Once in a hundred lifetimes would more likely be the probability," he said, "if you do the math." He smiled very softly and gazed into her eyes. Then he pulled her close and their lips met in a sweet, gentle kiss.

Claire savored the moment, the wind lifting her hair as the sailboat skimmed along, Nolan's embrace warming her.

She knew he would be gone soon. That was the way it had to be. But she and Nolan had touched each other's hearts, changed each other. For the better, she believed. Very much so.

Like watching a butterfly settle on a flower, one was helpless to do anything but simply appreciate the moment. It did no good to try to grasp at it. That would only make it melt away.

For better or worse, change was the only thing one could depend on in life. She had already learned that lesson by heart.

Liza heard from Daniel once, a brief e-mail, letting her know he had arrived safely. After that, nothing. At first she checked her phone constantly for e-mails and texts. Then she purposely kept the phone in her desk drawer so she wouldn't torture herself.

When she had first received his farewell note, she had been upset that he hadn't called or come to the inn to say good-bye in person. But she knew it would have been too hard for both of them. He had sounded hurt and angry in his brief note, and the truth was, she still felt hurt and angry, too. In between missing him terribly. Wasn't he the one who was leaving? What right did he have to be mad at her?

Still, she couldn't forget the last lines of his note and sometimes read them over, alone in her room at night.

This isn't what I wanted, Liza. I hope you can remember that.
But maybe it's the right thing, after all.

Liza wasn't sure about that now. She wasn't sure of anything. But she didn't want to admit that to him. Right or wrong, he had left her two weeks before their wedding. Didn't that say it all?

Liza cried herself to sleep each night and woke up with a headache each morning. Despite the tissues with lotion, she looked like a wreck, and felt that way, too. She felt lucky there were no guests coming to the inn. She had never followed through on her idea to drum up last-minute business and was glad now for all the vacancies. As for the wedding invites, family members who had made plans to fly East were able to get refunds or credits on their airfare. She was relieved to hear that.

Her brother, Peter, had been very concerned and offered to come anyway, to console her and keep her company. She would have enjoyed a visit with Peter, showing him all the improvements she had made lately on the inn. He was still half-owner—a very silent half who mostly let her do whatever she liked. And he visited at least once a year with his son, Will, to check on her and his investment. But she knew she wasn't up to seeing him and preferred to be alone right now.

Alone with her confusion and broken heart—and the wedding dress that hung on the back of her bedroom door in a long plastic bag. She felt as if the dress were taunting her. And so was the mess up on their third floor, the torn-up space that was supposed to be their new living quarters—hers and Daniel's.

Something would have to be done about that. Maybe she would complete some version of it and rent it as an apartment for families. She certainly didn't want to finish it for just herself. It would break her heart to live there alone now, in the space Daniel had designed for the two of them. She could never do that.

It exhausted Liza just to think about it. The night she had called off the wedding, she had taken off her engagement ring and put it back in the velvet box. Her hand had felt strangely light ever since. She wondered if it would ever feel normal again; never mind her heart.

When Daniel had been gone about a week, Molly came by to visit, unexpectedly. Liza had been taking a nap in the middle of the day and felt a bit embarrassed when Claire roused her. She came down to the parlor in her T-shirt and sweatpants, trying to act alert and awake. But Molly quickly saw through her.

"Liza, you look terrible," she said in her blunt way. "Are you okay? . . . Of course you're not. Look at you. I love Daniel, but this makes me so mad at that guy. This whole entire mess . . . Have you heard anything from him? Does he really like it out there?"

Liza sighed and smiled. She appreciated Molly's angst on her behalf more than she could say. "Not a word. I guess he's pretty busy."

"I'll say—pretty busy messing up everyone's life." Molly pressed her lips together as if suddenly remembering her tendency to speak too boldly. "That's all I'm going to say, honestly. You guys will get back together, and I'll have to apologize for trashing him."

Liza doubted there was any chance of that. But she didn't want to hear Daniel trashed by anyone. Underneath her own anger at him, she knew he had a right to pursue his dream. She would never fault him for that.

"The reason I'm here is . . . well, it's September twenty-seventh. That's nine days to the wedding, so this is sort of the ten-second warning. We need to cancel the rentals and all that by the weekend . . . if the wedding is really off."

Liza sighed. She really didn't want to think about this anymore and wished now that Molly had just done as she had asked last week and canceled everything then.

"Yes, cancel it. Cancel all of it," Liza insisted. "I don't see any reason to wait another day. Give me the receipts; I'll make the calls," she added, putting out her hand for the thick folder that held her wedding arrangements.

Molly deftly moved it out of her reach. "I'll handle everything. I couldn't let you make those calls. It wouldn't be right."

Liza understood what Molly meant. If she had been planning a wedding for someone with this problem, Liza would have said the same thing.

Liza drew a deep breath and calmed herself. "Thanks, Molly . . . I'm sorry if I lost it there for a minute."

Molly leaned over and patted her knee. "I'll give you a pass under the circumstances. And if you call that losing it, you have no idea what losing it really sounds like," she said with a laugh. "Let's not even go there."

Liza had to smile, just a little.

"What are you going to do this fall? I think you should go on a trip," Molly added, answering her own question. "Go out to visit your brother! Doesn't he live in Texas or something?"

"Arizona," Liza replied quietly. She glanced at Molly but didn't say more.

"*Right* . . . I knew it was someplace hot and dry. Well, guess you don't really want to go *there*." Molly bit down on her lip and made a face. "Hey, how about New York? A weekend with some girlfriends? Shopping, eating out . . . getting expensive haircuts? That would be fun. I'll go with you. I can stick Matt with driving Betty to her soccer games and sleepovers. He'll definitely pitch in for such a worthy cause."

Liza's smile grew even wider. A weekend in New York with Molly would certainly be diverting. She could barely imagine it.

"Great idea . . . I'll definitely give it some thought," Liza said, grateful for Molly's efforts to cheer her.

Molly rose and patted Liza's shoulder. "Hang in there, kid. Love finds a way," she promised.

True love does, they say, Liza wanted to counter. Maybe what she and Daniel had just wasn't true enough? All she could do was nod her head.

Liza knew that it wasn't Molly's fault, but that evening, one by one, e-mails confirming the many cancellations boomeranged into her inbox. She had been keeping an eye on the computer night and day—despite her vow not to look at it—in the slim hope a note from Daniel would appear.

Instead, she had to suffer through the torturous reminders that their wedding—their entire future—was now officially canceled.

She went to bed early and cried into her pillow, so Claire and Nolan wouldn't hear her.

She couldn't sleep and there was no use trying. Her head was pounding, and she felt as if she might have a fever. But she knew it was just the stress and all the tears. Again.

Liza sat up and took Daniel's farewell note out of the night table drawer, where she had stashed it. She read the brief lines over again, the last few words still giving her some small hope.

This isn't what I wanted, Liza. I hope you can remember that.

She did remember. She wished she could forget. But she had prayed and prayed for some solution, some answer. For their love to "find a way," as Molly and Claire promised it would. But she felt time was passing. And without a single word more from Daniel.

She got out of bed and walked to the window. She pulled back the curtains and looked out at the clear night sky and shimmering blue-black sea below. The sky was full of stars, reminding her of the night Daniel had proposed on the beach.

How could something so beautiful and fine end this way? she asked herself bleakly. *If God put this love in my heart for Daniel— and in his heart for me—how could it be destroyed so easily?*

Liza sighed. She would have cried, but there were no more tears left. She closed her eyes and her mind went blank . . . with only Daniel's face rising up before her.

The answer to her question was simple. Their love for each

other was not destroyed. She still loved him. She felt it deeply, in every fiber of her body and soul. That's what made this all so horribly painful.

She had to believe Daniel felt the same way, too.

She decided to write him a letter. Her head felt like a pressure cooker about to explode. If she couldn't talk to him for real, at least she could get it down on paper. Maybe she would feel a little better after that, she reasoned, even if she never sent it.

She picked up her laptop and got back into bed. With the computer balanced on her lap, she started to write:

Daniel—

It's been a week since you left Angel Island. Since you won't get in touch with me, I decided to get in touch with you.

She paused, wondering what to say next. Her fingers wrote automatically.

Of course, I wonder if you like the clinic and practicing medicine there. And if it's all that you hoped it would be. I hope it is.

She stopped and stared at the words. She knew that was her honest feeling. She did not want him to be disappointed, even if that meant he might not come back.

You see, I still love you. I want you to be happy. That was my whole point, the reason I broke off our engagement. But I've realized now, I can't truly be happy without you.

Liza knew the truth of that down to the bottom of her soul.

The inn is important to me, I'd never deny that. And it's hard for me to picture myself living on the reservation, from what I saw of it. But . . .

She stopped, wondering if she dare write out the thought that had come to her. *Well,* she reasoned, *I probably won't ever send this e-mail, so what's the harm? I'll just write what I'm thinking. What I'm truly feeling.* She started typing again.

. . . I could have tried harder to figure this out. I think you were right when you said maybe I don't completely understand what it means to you. But I would like to. And maybe I needed time apart to understand what was most important to me.

I see now that the thing I want most is just to be with you. Not to run the inn, or even to stay on this island. As much as I love those things, I can see now I love you more. Way more. There's just no comparison. And this place just isn't the same without you. It never will be.

I want you to know that if you've found what you were looking for out there, I'd like to visit you, and see the clinic and understand what it all means to you.

If you want me to, of course.

That's all I have to say for now. Except that I still love you and I always will.

Love, Liza

Liza read the note over, then stared down at it a moment. The clock on the computer read half past two. She wondered what time it was in Arizona. Earlier—but she could never get those time zones straight.

She wondered if she should send the note or wait until tomorrow. Perhaps this was just some emotional vent she had needed and she would have second thoughts—and even third thoughts—about it in the cold light of day.

But from some calm, still place inside, a feeling of certainty emerged. She knew this was the right thing to do. If she really loved Daniel and wanted to be with him again, she had to let him know. There was no reason to be coy about it or play some stupid game.

What had Claire told her? Sometimes compromise means one person gets ninety percent of what they want and the other gets ten? Liza understood now that she would be more than making up for her missing share by being with Daniel again and knowing he was expressing his gifts in the finest way possible.

I never expected to take over this inn. Making that choice felt like jumping off a cliff. But I got my mind around it, and it turned out to be the biggest adventure of my life, she realized. *This is the same sort of choice. And I have even more reason to jump this time.* Liza took a brief breath, then she moved her cursor and hit the SEND button. A window popped up. MESSAGE SENT, it read.

Liza's eyes widened. *Well, I've done it. Let's see if he even answers me.* She suddenly felt exhausted, as if she couldn't keep her eyes open. She put the computer aside and shut off her light, then fell instantly asleep.

Liza slept fitfully, tossing and turning, disturbed by vivid dreams. It was almost dawn when she dragged herself out of bed so she could head downstairs for some headache pills. She couldn't find her robe and felt so chilled from the early morning air flowing through the open windows that she wrapped herself in her quilt and padded downstairs in the darkness.

She entered the kitchen and walked over to the sink, then took a glass from the drain board and turned on the water.

She heard a sound. Someone clearing their throat. She dropped the glass in the sink and spun around quickly to see who it was. Her heart thudded and she froze with fear. A man sat at the far end of the kitchen table. He stood up and came toward her, and Liza screamed.

"Liza, it's me. I didn't mean to scare you."

Daniel reached out, and she felt his strong grip through the thick quilt. She stared up at him in shock. She thought she must be dreaming . . . sleepwalking, definitely. She didn't dare move. Didn't dare breathe . . . afraid to dispel this marvelous vision. He looked so real. So true. She reached out and touched his cheek, scratchy with a day's growth of stubble.

"Daniel . . . is it really you?"

His serious expression melted, and he laughed. "Of course it's me. Who else would it be?"

"You scared me . . ." She let out a long breath. "What are you doing here?"

She felt so confused. And so tired. Nothing made sense. Had he read her e-mail already? That was impossible. Even if he had read it, he could have never gotten back East so quickly. He looked exhausted, as if he had been traveling for days.

"I had to come back," he said simply.

"You didn't like the work?"

He shook his head. "I liked the work fine. It was wonderful, more than I ever imagined . . . But I couldn't stay there. I missed you too much. I was utterly miserable. What joy could I find in my work without you near me—to share my thoughts and my worries? To share my life? I thought I knew that already, but I guess I had to learn it deep inside." He touched his chest. "You and me, forever. That's the center, and everything spins around that."

Liza was so happy, she could barely believe it. Daniel had come back to her. He really loved her the way that she loved him. She had been a fool to ever doubt that.

"Oh, Daniel . . . I wrote you a long e-mail. I just sent it tonight. I said the same things to you. I've been miserable here without you. I don't care about running the inn or living on the island anymore if you're not here. I wanted you to know that I should have been more willing to talk things out. To compromise with you. If you want to stay on the reservation, I'll go there. I'll try it. I just want us to be together again."

Liza knew she was rambling, and crying a little, too. But out of pure joy; her heart felt so full, exploding with love for him. Her prayers had been answered. Love had found a way after all.

There was so much she wanted to say. So much she needed to tell him. But she didn't have to say anything. He took her in his arms, quilt and all, and kissed her as if he had been away twenty years instead of two weeks.

A short time later, they sat curled together on the porch swing, watching the sun come up.

"So what now?" she asked quietly.

If he wanted to go back to Arizona after they were married, she was fully prepared to do that. But maybe he would look for a job in some underserved area closer to Angel Island? That might be some compromise for them, she thought, even if he needed to be away a few nights a week. Compared to the alternative, it didn't look that awful anymore.

Daniel leaned his head to one side. "Well, I have a suggestion for you; a proposition, actually. I found another doc who wants to be on the staff out there, too—but doesn't want to stay year-round. So I talked Mitchell into considering a job shared between the two of us. You and I could go out there from October to March, and the rest of the year we could live here and run the inn for the busy season. The other doctor would have April through September. He's very eager to seal the deal. But I said I had to talk it over with my wife. My *future* wife," he added softly. "What do you think? Could you leave the island for half the year and go out there with me?"

Liza sat up and slung her arms around his shoulder. "What a brilliant solution . . . Are you sure Nolan didn't figure this out for you?"

Daniel laughed. "This was all my own idea. But I have to admit, I nearly called him to help me think of something. You don't have to give an answer right now. But does that mean you'll think it over?"

"Yes . . . and yes . . . I thought it over. It's perfect. I've been thinking, too. Claire can run the inn with some help in the slow season, or I could close it entirely. And maybe I can find something to do out there, like teaching children art or working at an after-school program? I'm sure Elaine would help me figure it out. And the inn would always be our home base. Our special place," she added.

Daniel's expression lit up at her reply. "You would really do that for me, sweetheart?"

"I'm willing to try. I can see that, no matter what you say, you would love to be a doctor out there. And I'm willing to try something new, to join in on the adventure . . . as long I have you."

"Oh, you've got me," he promised, hugging her tight. "You'll never get rid of me. Even if you try."

"I wouldn't dare," Liza whispered back. Holding Daniel tight at that moment, she felt as if she would never let him go.

WHEN Claire came down to the kitchen to start the coffee, she had the shock of her life. Liza and Daniel, at the stove, cooking breakfast together, smiling and laughing. They turned to her and cheerfully called out to her, "Good morning!"

Claire clutched her heart, thinking she might faint.

A short time later, she was sitting in a kitchen chair, sipping coffee while Liza explained everything, all the happy news—that they were back together again and had figured out the perfect compromise.

". . . and the wedding is still on. We might have to push the date back a week or two. But our out-of-town guests can probably book their flights again and come," Liza said, thinking out loud. She turned to Daniel. "I'm going to call Molly in a little while. She'll probably run right over. You'd better make yourself scarce."

Daniel laughed. "You mean Molly is mad at me for leaving?"

"Oh, you could say that. And you know how she gets. But I think she'll get over it once she hears we're going forward again."

"Good. I'd rather not wear a disguise to my own wedding." He turned and flipped a perfect pancake.

Claire watched, amazed. "Daniel, all these years you've made such a fuss over my pancakes. I didn't know you could cook them just as well . . . even better."

Daniel glanced at her, looking suddenly embarrassed. "Just a lucky batch. The pan is the perfect temperature. And I'm the luckiest guy in the world this morning. It only makes sense they'd come out right."

Claire decided to accept that explanation and just laughed.

Chapter Thirteen

CLAIRE could not recall a happier day at the inn. Not even the day Liza had decided to stay on and had so graciously asked for her help in starting up the inn again. Or even the day Jamie had found her in the garden, appearing out of the clear blue.

This day was even more joyous than either of those. Even though Claire had prayed for God to guide Liza and Daniel to some resolution, the answer to this question had come in a way no one expected. Surely the hand of heaven had moved the confounding pieces of this puzzle to fit together, and Claire's prayers today were full of thanks and praise.

She felt so lighthearted to see her most cherished friends re-united, she wondered if Liza could be feeling any happier. Well, of course she was, and for much different reasons. And Claire had to admit there was still a small shadow lingering over her own heart.

"So the wedding is on again," Nolan had said, after Liza and Daniel had left the kitchen. "Glad to hear it. Those two belong together. It just didn't seem logical for them to be parted. So when's the big day? Have they set a new date?"

Claire felt pleased to hear the question. Did that mean he might be considering staying on for the celebration? "They're not sure. Molly just canceled everything yesterday. She's coming over in a little while to try and sort it out with Liza."

Nolan nodded. "Well, if anyone can put Humpty Dumpty back together on short notice, my money is on that Molly."

Claire laughed at his analogy. "Mine as well," she agreed.

Nolan soon disappeared out the back door to do his chores, and Claire never got to ask if he would stay for the wedding— if they managed to reschedule it in the next few weeks. She didn't want to press him, but she did want to know.

A few hours later, Nolan came back into the kitchen and found her folding the linens. When he walked in, she looked up, and finished matching the corners of a fluffy white towel and folding it into a neat square with no edges showing.

"All done outside. Not much left in the garden, except for some cabbage and squash . . . oh, and a few pumpkins sprouting up. Now there's a sign of autumn for you."

Claire nodded. She balked at the idea of the summer ending, even though it had officially ended on September twenty-first. "It's been so warm and sunny, and everything still looks so green. But I know what you mean . . . Would you like some lunch?" she asked, changing the subject. "There's some cold chicken for sandwiches."

Claire knew by now she didn't need to wait on Nolan, and

if he fixed himself some lunch, he would happily make hers, too. That was another thing she would miss about him: his thoughtful consideration. She was so used to taking care of everyone else, and she had been very spoiled these last weeks by Nolan's small but meaningful gestures, taking care of her.

"I'm okay right now. I was wondering if I could borrow the Jeep. I need to run over to that marine supply store, near Harry Reilly's yard. Restock the *Ariadne*. She's getting restless now," he added cheerfully.

Claire forced a smile, though that was a hard thing for her to hear. "Of course. The keys are in the mudroom, on those hooks near the door."

Nolan headed to retrieve them just as they both heard the heavy knocker on the front door. He paused and looked at Claire. "Should I get that? You look busy."

"It's all right. I'll go." Claire put a hand towel back in the basket. "It must be Molly Willoughby, swooping in to save the wedding."

Nolan laughed. "You make her sound like a superhero."

Claire nodded. "You've never seen Molly at her best. She is."

As Claire walked quickly through the foyer, the knock sounded again. "Be right there," she called out.

She soon pulled open the door and smiled, fully expecting Molly's excited expression, all prepared to talk over the happy news.

Instead she found a stranger on the other side of the door.

A young woman with long, dark hair and bright, dark eyes who didn't smile back. In fact, she looked quite serious . . . and a little nervous as well. There was something familiar about her, but Claire couldn't quite place it. Did she know her from a shop in town, or maybe the church?

"Yes . . . may I help you?" Claire asked politely.

"This is a little awkward," the young woman began. "But I've come here looking for someone . . ."

Claire's eyes widened. Suddenly she knew. She remembered the photo from the newspaper, though the blurry image had hardly done Fiona Porter justice.

"Nolan Porter, your father," Claire said simply, opening the door wider. "He's here, back in the kitchen. I'll take you to him."

Fiona Porter looked shocked, but quickly stepped inside. "I'm Claire North, the housekeeper and cook here," Claire explained. "I saw your picture in the newspaper . . . Oh, it's a long story. Your father will have to explain it to you," she added.

"I hope so," Fiona replied. "As long as he's okay—physically, I mean," she added with a questioning glance.

"Oh, he's in perfect health, God bless him," Claire said cheerfully.

She entered the kitchen, fully expecting to find Nolan there. But the room was empty. Had Nolan heard Fiona's voice and slipped out the back door—and jumped into her Jeep for a hasty escape?

He wouldn't be that desperate to avoid facing his daughter . . . would he?

Fiona had followed her, and looked around as well. "He was in here a moment ago," Claire murmured. She walked into the mudroom. No sign of Nolan; and the keys were gone, too.

She came back out, wondering if she should run out and try to catch him. Then she saw him at the back door. He opened it and blithely came through, Edison at his heels. He was carrying a metal tape measure and some note cards and a pencil. He must have gone out to his boat to measure something, Claire realized.

Lost in his own thoughts, and talking to himself quietly, as so often happened, he didn't notice anyone in the kitchen until he was almost face-to-face with his daughter.

"Dad, thank God you're all right." Fiona spoke quietly, her voice ragged with relief, on the very edge of tears. Claire felt as if she might cry, just hearing the simple greeting.

Nolan stood frozen in place. He stared at his daughter in shock. Edison was not nearly as surprised. He barked happily and ran to Fiona, his tail beating wildly. She bent down to pet him and let him lick her face, then glanced back up at her father.

"Fiona . . ." Nolan said finally. "Did Fowler tell you where to find me?" Claire knew that Frank Fowler was Nolan's attorney, the one who had passed on Nolan's letter to his daughter. "He wasn't supposed to. He—"

Fiona shook her head. "No, Dad. Mr. Fowler has been very discreet. He kept your confidence, even when I asked him a few times. I know you said in your letters that you weren't ready yet to see me. But I had to see you. To make sure you were all right."

Letters? Did that mean there had been more than the one letter that Claire knew about? It sounded as if Nolan had been corresponding with his daughter, through his attorney—a revelation Claire found very touching and encouraging. He had truly missed Fiona, more than he wanted anyone to know.

"So how did you find me?" Nolan asked, still clearly astounded. "Did someone finally reply to that newspaper article?" Nolan glanced at Claire, and her eyes widened.

"Oh, it wasn't me," she said quickly. She looked at Nolan and then back to Fiona. "And I should be making myself scarce. You two need some privacy."

Claire grabbed the linen basket and headed off to the dining room. Out of their way, but not so far that she couldn't still hear them, she soon realized. She thought she might retreat even farther, to the front parlor, but heard Liza and Daniel in there, waiting for Molly.

Well . . . I won't eavesdrop on purpose. That wouldn't be right. But I can't very well stuff my ears with cotton, she decided.

". . . private investigator?" she soon heard Nolan saying. "You went to all that trouble and expense to find me?"

"Of course I did. You're my father. I'd been going crazy, thinking you might be lost at sea, and then when I got that first letter from you . . . I'm so sorry for what I said. I tried to explain in my letter. I thought you would at least answer me. Didn't you read that part?"

"Yes . . . Yes, I did. But I . . . I couldn't answer. I didn't know what else to say. I suppose I didn't really believe you, dear. Not in my heart," he confessed. "I thought you were just saying what you thought I wanted to hear. Understandably," he added softly.

"But I love you, Dad. I'm so, so sorry. I didn't mean any of those terrible things I said to you. We were having a fight, and I just . . . lost it. I felt frustrated about a lot of things. I was so happy when I got your letter and I knew you were alive. I couldn't stand the idea that I might have lost you and I never got the chance to tell you how sorry I am. And that I'm so proud of you. Wherever you go, or whatever you do, Dad. Whether you live on your boat for the rest of your life or camp out in a lab somewhere, I'll always be proud to say I'm your daughter. No matter what."

"Oh, Fiona . . . I love you so much. I've been a stupid old fool, hiding away from you. Maybe I knew in my heart that you did forgive me, but I couldn't forgive myself for disappointing you," he confessed. "You are the greatest creation of my entire life, my dear. And the one I am most proud of," he added with a laugh. "Can you forgive me for making you worry so much?"

Claire had to imagine that Fiona's answer was in the affirmative. She could tell that they were hugging each other, just from the sounds and lack of conversation. And the way Fiona sounded as if she was now laughing through her tears.

Claire felt herself crying quietly, too, and reached into the laundry basket to find one of her embroidered hankies.

Thank You, dear Lord, for making this right again. Love finds a way, doesn't it? With Your help, she added.

A few moments later, Nolan poked his head into the dining room and beckoned to her. "Claire? Come meet my daughter. I want to introduce you."

Claire nodded and smiled. She tucked her hanky in her pocket and smoothed back her hair. Although she had already met Fiona in a way, it would be much different having Nolan introduce them.

"Fiona, this is Claire North. My supervisor," he added with a grin. "She's the best boss I've ever had, not to mention a dear friend. She makes this place hum, and her cooking is divine . . . and her advice, even better," he added.

Claire felt herself blushing after his flowery commendations. She stepped forward to shake Fiona's hand. "It's been an absolute pleasure to get to know your father these past weeks. He's the best helper the inn's ever had," she quipped back, "and certainly, the most ingenious one."

Fiona smiled, her expression now relaxed and radiant. "I can almost imagine."

"Would you like some lunch?" Claire asked her. "Please, make yourself comfortable. I'll fix something for us."

Claire had nearly retied her apron when Nolan took it from her hand. "You sit down with Fiona. I'll fix us lunch," he insisted. "And something special for Edison, too."

Fiona was already seated at the table with Edison's head in her lap. His tag wagged happily as she petted his silky head. She spoke to him quietly.

"I missed you, Edison," Fiona said. "But you look like you've had a good summer here, too."

"Oh, he has," Claire assured her. "I've pretty much spoiled him," she admitted.

"You've spoiled everybody," Nolan replied. He was standing at the counter, setting slices of bread on the wooden cutting board. "It will be very hard to leave this place," he added. "But my boat is fully repaired," he told his daughter. "I want to bring you down later to the dock and show you. Maybe we can take a little sail if you don't have to rush back to Portland." He hesitated a moment, then asked almost shyly, "Any chance you might stay overnight?"

"Do you mean here, at the inn? Are there any vacancies?" Fiona turned to Claire. "Can you tell me the rates?"

"Oh, dear, don't even mention it," Claire said with a smile. "I'm sure you can stay a night or even two. The place is absolutely empty. Liza won't mind. In fact, she won't hear of you leaving, once she learns what's happened."

"Liza owns the inn," Nolan explained to Fiona. "She's the most generous soul. And she's about to be married after some . . . mayhem and confusion," he explained briefly. "She's floating on a cloud right now and may not even notice you're here." He turned back to his sandwiches with a laugh.

"Oh, she'll notice. Liza's not quite as single-minded as some people around here might be," Claire said in a telling tone. "But she'll love to have you stay as our guest. I'm sure of that."

Fiona seemed very pleased at the invitation and the chance to spend more time with her father. Claire enjoyed getting to know her over lunch and hearing all about her life. She was almost finished with her studies to be an architect, working part-time at an architectural firm and finishing her degree. She had obviously inherited Nolan's creativity, as well as his mechanical and mathematical talents.

"I'd love to see what you've been working on lately, honey," Nolan said to his daughter. "You should see some of the buildings she's helped design already. She's so talented," he said proudly.

"Oh, I'd love to see them. Do you have any photographs with you?" Claire asked Fiona.

Fiona looked embarrassed at her father's praise, but pleased as well. "They're just models at this stage. But I have some photos on my phone, I think. Let me take a look."

Her big leather bag was hanging on the kitchen chair. She put it in her lap and started searching for her cell phone, but suddenly pulled out a letter instead.

"Oh, I nearly forgot, Dad. This was delivered to your old office at the university, and they sent it to me a few weeks ago. I thought it might be important."

Nolan looked curious. Claire felt her heartbeat quicken and her stomach tighten in a knot of dread. She so hoped it was not a message of more bad news about the lawsuit, marring this beautiful afternoon.

Nolan glanced at the return address. An official-looking letterhead. A company name, Claire noticed, but not the law firm that had been arguing his case. *Thank goodness for that*, she thought.

Nolan zipped his finger under the seal and took out the letter. He put his reading glasses on and read it quickly. Claire noticed his thick eyebrows draw together. He looked quite confused for a moment and seemed to read it a second time before glancing up at the two women, who were watching him, waiting to know what it said.

"What is it, Nolan?" Claire asked quietly. "Some news about your lawsuit?"

He swallowed hard and shook his head. "No . . . nothing to do with that at all. It's about an old patent I'd put aside, a solar energy cell I designed years ago. This company says they want to buy the rights and are making . . . making quite an impressive offer in black-and-white." His voice was hoarse. He had to stop and clear his throat.

Claire sat in utter shock. Good news . . . finally. Good news for Nolan! One door had closed but another had opened— one that seemed to lead to a great opportunity.

Just as she had hoped and prayed it would.

"That's fantastic news, Dad! I remember that invention. It was one of your best, I thought. I always knew it would work out for you." Fiona reached over and grabbed her father's hand.

He smiled at her, his eyes glassy. "Well, at least one of us did." He laughed and looked at Claire. "I'd submitted this idea to these folks before. They liked it, but it was too expensive at the time to produce. But seems some new money-saving technology has come into play, and they never forgot about it. Imagine that." He shook his head in astonishment.

"I'm so happy for you, Nolan. This is such wonderful news, and you so deserve it. So many of your ideas are amazing. I'm really not surprised at all," Claire said honestly.

"When you put it that way, I'm not, either," Fiona said, gazing fondly at her father. "My dad has worked so hard and for so long. He's just like Thomas Edison, never giving up on his inspirations."

Claire agreed. Nolan was one of the most persistent people she had ever met. Talent and persistence were an unbeatable combination, she'd often heard. Nolan was living proof of that.

"Thank you, ladies. I have to say, I really can't take too much credit. *Someone* just designed me this way." He smiled happily and shrugged, then glanced at Claire with a teasing light in his eye.

She smiled back and laughed. She knew who that *someone* was, too, and had just been thinking the same thing.

Nolan suddenly turned to his daughter, holding out the letter she had brought him. "Though I must say, while it feels good to be acknowledged for my inventions with a letter like this, it pales in comparison to the feeling of finding you here today, sweetheart. That's the true joy that fills my heart to overflowing." He stopped speaking for a moment, because his voice had become shaky. He took a breath, and when he spoke again, his voice was firm and confident. "Knowing you're back in my life, Fiona, that's what makes me a truly happy man."

"Oh, Dad, I love you, too." Fiona looked as if she might cry as she leaned over and shared a heartfelt embrace with Nolan.

When they parted, Nolan looked a little teary-eyed but was laughing, too, Claire was glad to see. "We all have a lot to celebrate today," she said happily. "I'm going to make a special dinner . . . and dessert. Any requests?"

Nolan leaned back and grinned. "My, my . . . what a question. I really have to think carefully about that." He turned to Fiona. "Claire is the most wonderful cook in the world. Wait until you taste her cooking. You won't believe it."

"Oh, now, Nolan . . . I thought scientists never overstate the situation. You're losing your objectivity," she teased him.

"Maybe. But it's hard to be objective when I feel so happy," he said honestly. "Why, it seems a sign that I must stay for the wedding now and join in all that celebration."

"Oh, a sign? I thought you didn't believe in such things." Claire couldn't resist teasing him.

Nolan laughed at her again. "I only meant it as a figure of speech. Like saying 'I'm so happy I could dance a jig.'" He suddenly stood up and took her hand, pulling her out of her chair, as he hummed a familiar, lighthearted tune. "Like this, you see. Because I am that happy now," he stated between his music-making.

"Nolan . . . what are you doing?" Claire protested a bit, but really had no choice but to follow his steps, dancing around the kitchen. She felt a bit silly and self-conscious at first, holding on tight as Nolan swept her around the room, his hand at her waist and his other hand holding her own. Edison jumped up and followed them, barking and dancing along in his own way.

Nolan was a good dancer, easy to follow, his feet moving smoothly and lightly across the shiny pine plank floors. Just as she was getting used to their little jig, she felt herself flung out and spun around. Then Nolan was pulling her back again with flair, like a dance team on a TV show.

"Oh . . . my . . . You should have warned me about that," she said, feeling both thrilled and a little shocked.

Fiona laughed, cheering them on. "You two make a good pair. It's wonderful to see you dancing again, Dad."

"It's nice to be dancing. It's good to be alive." He smiled into Claire's eyes and suddenly stopped. "I've learned something here. Come what may, every day, good or bad, every hour . . . is a great gift. Just as you told me, Claire."

She smiled up at him, feeling breathless from the dancing and joyful from the fullness in her heart. She felt peaceful, too, thinking back to the morning Nolan had been rescued and how he had confessed that, at one point, he'd been resigned to going down and wasn't even sure that would have been such a bad thing.

But now he knew how wrong that had been. He was a new man, finally able to look forward and live his life to the fullest, and with joy.

Epilogue

Liza and Daniel could have reserved the best suite at the inn for their honeymoon night. Instead, they decided to leave that room for their relatives or friends who had traveled from a distance. "I think on that very special night, we should go camping," Daniel had suggested a few days before the wedding.

Liza had just looked at him, wondering if he was totally serious. Did he really want to pitch a tent out on the beach on such a momentous night in their lives? Besides, it was getting cold out in the evenings.

But before she could gently present the reasons why camping might not be the best idea, Daniel added, "Up in our new apartment, I mean. I know it's not the most comfortable spot in the world right now. But it would have lots of meaning, starting off our life together in our new home."

Liza smiled instantly. "What a great idea . . . that's perfect. Perfect for us," she added, hugging him tight.

Their wedding ceremony, presided over by Reverend Ben, and their celebration, which had filled every room of the inn and lasted for hours, had all been perfect, too. The most beautiful and joyous day of her life, Liza was sure.

Liza didn't know how she would have gotten through the final days and hours building up to the wedding without Claire, who had so calmly managed all the last-minute details of the wedding, helped her dress, and even walked her down the aisle as a surrogate mother, with Liza's brother, Peter, on the other side.

Much to everyone's delight, Edison had led the way as the official flower dog. Nolan had fastened a red satin bow tie to his collar and trained him to carry a basket of miniature roses.

Liza had been glad to see Claire and Nolan enjoying the evening together. Nolan was leaving bright and early tomorrow. He was heading back to Portland by train and coming back in a few weeks to pick up the *Ariadne*. The unexpected sale of his invention had changed his life dramatically; he was going back to tie up loose ends, as he put it. Liza was sure that he and Claire would keep in touch, and that this was hardly the last they would see of the eccentric inventor and his dog.

It had been a perfect day in every way. A day of pure, overwhelming happiness—and Liza knew its glow would last in her heart forever.

It wasn't quite midnight when she found herself alone with Daniel—and very thankful for that fact—as he led her up to the construction-in-progress space that would soon be their new bedroom.

Daniel had carefully set up everything, telling Liza not to peek. Some walls had been torn down, and more would be soon, so there wasn't any electricity in that part of the house. But when he allowed her to open her eyes again, Liza found a cozy, inviting space lit by camping lanterns and candles and decorated with vases full of flowers swiped from their wedding reception, and even a midnight snack on a silver tray. There was a large, soft mattress on the floor, covered by a beautiful quilt and piles of pillows that he must have found in storage somewhere. With Claire's help, no doubt.

Liza stood in the doorway and took it all in. "Oh my goodness . . . you've thought of everything, haven't you?" She turned to him with a surprised laugh.

He smiled at her lovingly. "I got a kit from the camping store. The package said, 'Just add bride.' And here you are," he added. Before Liza could protest, he swept her up and carried her over the threshold.

When he put her down again, they kissed and held each other tight. Liza pressed her cheek to Daniel's chest and gazed out the new glass door, which would soon lead to a private deck. The moon was bright and the night sky was sprinkled with a thousand stars, the blue-black sea shimmering and mysterious. The light in their room was so low, she could see it all quite clearly.

"I'm so happy tonight, it feels like a dream to me," she confessed.

"I feel the same. At least I did when I watched you walking

down the aisle toward me. You were the most beautiful bride I've ever seen. And celebrating with everyone we love, it was the most wonderful day of my life, too. By far." He was quiet a moment, softly stroking her hair. "But I know that tomorrow is going to be even better. Because it's not a dream, Liza. Tomorrow is the first day of our new life together. After all this time . . . after all we've been through together, it's finally here. I feel as if we've run some marathon but . . . we made it," he added with a small, deep laugh.

Liza smiled. "It got a little scary there," she admitted. "But love pulled us through. Our prayers were answered . . . in a way I'd never imagined, with the most perfect solution. I'm still so amazed and thankful, I can't believe it's true."

"So am I, sweetheart. So am I," Daniel said quietly. "I know there will be other challenges for us somewhere down the road. But I know now that we both learned something— how to stick together no matter what life throws at us."

He leaned his head down and kissed her, and she knew it was true. They had both learned an important lesson the last few weeks; one she would never forget.

No matter where they went, or what obstacles rose up in their path, they would always find some solution, some new direction that would lead them out of their dilemma, even where there didn't seem to be any. As long as they remembered to believe in their deep love for each other . . . and in help from heaven above.

Claire North's Rustic Peach Tart

Claire loves to make this tart at the height of the summer, when peaches are ripe and sweet. When the mood strikes, she tosses in ½ cup blueberries or raspberries to make the tart more colorful. But pure peach filling is perfect on its own. Served with vanilla ice cream, the dessert makes a memorable treat on a warm summer night.

You can use any recipe for pie dough. Claire's own is below. Or use premade pie dough or puff pastry sheets.

Ingredients

Claire's Dependable Pie Dough (recipe follows)
    Or: 1½ sheets premade pie dough or puff pastry
4–6 ripe peaches (about 3 or 4 cups, sliced)
1 tablespoon fresh lemon juice
½ teaspoon lemon zest

½ cup brown sugar

½ tablespoon cinnamon

¼ teaspoon ginger

¼ teaspoon nutmeg

1 tablespoon flour, plus extra for rolling dough

4 tablespoons butter

1 beaten egg

1 tablespoon water

1 teaspoon white sugar

Equipment

Rolling pin

Pizza wheel

Parchment paper

Cookie sheet—rimless is best

Pastry brush

Directions

Preheat oven to 375 degrees. Line cookie sheet with parchment paper.

Prepare Claire North's pie crust recipe as directed on the next page. (Or use 1½ sheets premade pie dough or puff pastry. Flatten sheets and lay side by side, slightly overlapping in order to stick together to make one large sheet.)

Roll out dough, large, flat, and square. Using a large pot cover (10–12 inches wide) as your guide, cut out the largest disc possible with a pizza wheel. Loosely roll it up on the floured rolling pin and unroll onto the center of parchment-lined cookie sheet. Chill in refrigerator while you make the filling.

Peel and slice peaches ¼-inch thin into a large bowl. Add lemon juice, zest, sugar, cinnamon, ginger, nutmeg, and one tablespoon of flour. Mix thoroughly but gently, so that the peach slices don't break.

Pile peaches in the center of dough circle, leaving a 3-inch border. Pull up edges of dough toward the center of the circle, draping and folding. The center of the tart will be open.

Dot uncovered peaches at center of tart with bits of butter.

If desired, cover dough with egg wash: In a small bowl, beat together egg and water. Brush mixture on dough with pastry brush and sprinkle lightly with a teaspoon of white sugar.

Bake for 25–35 minutes, until the peaches are tender and the crust is golden.

Claire's Dependable Pie Crust

Ingredients

2½ cups flour
1 tablespoon sugar
1 teaspoon salt
1½ sticks (¾ cup) unsalted butter, very cold
2 tablespoons shortening, chilled
⅓ cup ice water

Directions

Combine dry ingredients in a large bowl or a food processor. Mix through by hand with a fork or wire whisk. (Or pulse to mix.) Add butter and shortening.

Mix by hand with pastry tool, or fork, until butter is in small bits—you should still see pieces about raisin-size. (Or pulse to mix.) Do not overmix. Better to be lumpy and under-mixed.

Add water and continue to mix until dough just begins to make a ball. Pour out on floured board and shape into a ball. Chill for one hour in refrigerator.